THE 26TH PROTOCOL

TIM HEATH

I wrote this first draft in eight days at the end of the first month of lockdown in Estonia.
With a full-house, two daughters who were distance learning and a teacher wife live-streaming lessons.
And I thought I could only write at home, alone, in silence?
March 2020.
This is for us all
Those who remember the old-normal...

ALSO AVAILABLE BY TIM HEATH

Novels:

Cherry Picking

The Last Prophet

The Tablet

The Shadow Man

The Prey (The Hunt #1)

The Pride (The Hunt #2)

The Poison (The Hunt #3)

The Machine (The Hunt #4)

The Menace (The Hunt #5)

The Meltdown (The Hunt #6)

The Song Birds

The Acting President (The Hunt #7)

The Black Dolphin (The Hunt #8)

The Last Tsar (The Hunt #9)

The 26th Protocol

Short Story Collection:

Those Geese, They Lied; He's Dead

1

The light poured in through the tall, ornate windows, the immaculate school lawns on show beyond. The sun caught the edges of the glass cabinets, causing several students to need to squint, though their attention didn't waver. It didn't falter. They had been trained better than that.

Their teacher glanced once more at the clock above the door—he might have been looking for someone in the corridor, save for the fact the corridor was empty. It had been empty each of the four times he'd glanced that way, the slow hands of the clock finally confirming the lesson was finished.

"Assignment pads open," the teacher called. Herbert Bradley had taught in that school for thirty years. A good teacher, popular with the students, solid and reliable among his peers. A flurry of activity told him his instruction was being followed, though that never surprised him. These kids were good; and hardly kids for much longer. In a little over five months, most would wrap up their student days as they hung up their student clothing too; the real world called them inevitably into their future. A bright future was always the promise.

Herbert wasn't so sure about that vision now.

"You have exams coming up on Protocols Twenty through to Twenty-five," he confirmed; nobody present was surprised by that. The school had been clear not to take things beyond there, though the reality of the final protocol, firmly established by law, sat squarely on the teacher's mind that day. "I want a full summation with external links taking you over everything we've covered these last six months," he said. He wouldn't be handling the revision, nor the examination. Others would step in for that, he knew. Today was his last day as a working man. Not that anyone present knew this yet. "Mark my words, the final exam will demand everything you have, squeezing you for all that you know. Make sure your minds are fresh and your brains heavy with the good juice of education."

The *good juice*. He'd always called education that, juice for the mind, food for the soul. His comment brought smiles from most, though they remained silent, diligently copying down their assignment, unwittingly seeing out the last moments under the tutorage of their favourite teacher, and favourite by a long shot. The man was a legend around the building and a little way beyond those walls too. Several members of the Council had come through Herbert's classes.

The bell rang, on cue, as reliable as anything: sunshine, rain and even death. Death sat heavy in Herbert's thoughts that morning, had done for a while; except he'd never felt better. And the good times were just about to begin.

Soon the last of the students had packed their bags, the group rarely in a hurry to rush from his classroom. One or two of them had a passing farewell to their teacher; several students down the years carrying a passing fancy for the man, though as far as that went, his best days were behind him.

He watched the last one leave the room, closing the door behind them. They were not children any more. To Herbert, surrounded by students all day, they seemed to get younger every year, though perhaps it was just him getting older. This last group were all nearly eighteen. Unprepared for the world outside, though as prepared as any on the planet, he knew. What were they really teaching these young souls?

Herbert watched the last students disappear into the throng of the corridor, a motorway of people, each with a specific place to be.

He unplugged his computer and dropped it into his bag. The docking point could stay. It would be needed by whoever came after him; not his concern at that moment. He packed away the few items he had, the school not keen on too many belongings, though for Herbert, these rules seemed to be less enforced than with others. He didn't have much. A photo of a woman with three children: his sister, her three sons. The only family he knew. Herbert assumed most of the students would have thought the picture was that of his wife and boys; a few students down the years had asked and been told the truth. Perhaps they all knew now, though gossip was forbidden. He didn't mind what they thought. The picture made him smile, told him he wasn't alone.

The tinge of sadness filled him once more. He'd not even told his sister the day had come.

"You going somewhere?" a voice from the doorway asked, Herbert looking up in obvious surprise. He'd not heard the door open, despite the babble of noise the action had allowed into his quiet space. It was the Director, a man Herbert spent relatively little time with, though he had been intending to see him straight after the lesson. It seems the gods had saved him a trip.

"It's time," Herb said, always called that by his friends; nobody had called him Herbert in a very long while.

"Time?" the Director asked, taking in the box, the empty room, the lack of personal items. A blank canvas, ready for somebody else to come in and make it their home. Herb nodded slowly, understanding sinking in on the face of the man in front of him. "Herb, you said nothing."

"Didn't know what to say," Herb admitted. The Director pursed his lips for a moment; the school would lose an excellent teacher, that much was clear. But the day needed to be a celebration; this was what they were there for. They'd not had someone leave in seven years.

"Congratulations!" the Director beamed, his facial expression transformed from that of seconds before, the eyes ablaze with pride, his hand thrust out in resolute determination. "You've truly earned all that is coming."

That felt somewhat double-sided, this reward. This retirement package that fell to them all eventually. Nobody shared when theirs was. Not at their age. The students might, each one showing the date as if it were a battle scar. Decades away in nearly every case. Yet the closer you got, the more guarded you became. For Herb, it had become his secret.

The two men shook hands for longer than was comfortable, the Director finishing with a hearty pat on Herb's back. His visit there now redundant; Herb would not be working another day in the school.

They parted once more, two gladiators retiring after what might have been an epic duel. Herb spotted a glimpse of emotion in the eyes of the man in front of him, though neither would want to draw attention to that.

"I'll make sure the department knows," the Director said.

"Really?" Herb protested, though he was cut off immediately.

"Herb, you've been a valuable part of this community for three decades. You've taught an entire generation: men and women who now control some of the most important positions in the world. Few teachers have made the impact in this place that you have, my friend." Herb was sure they were far from friends, but the sentiment went deep. "You aren't to leave the building until I let you, okay?"

Herb nodded his agreement, the Director hurrying away soon after. He never had told Herbert what he'd come there for in the first place; it didn't matter anymore.

"How are you doing?" a female teacher asked. Someone close to Herb, someone as shocked as the rest were to hear the news, though her tone suggested she knew more about Herb's inner thinking than anyone else. She'd seen it in his face.

Herb glanced around, the staffroom crowded, the festivities

generous. He stepped a few more paces into the corner, pulling his colleague with him.

"You think you are ready; but you're not," he said. "I've known all my life, naturally. Most of those years it didn't matter. The right thing to do. But now..."

She held his hands in hers, allowing him time to stand there, say nothing, let the emotion fade. She didn't want a scene, not there. Not in front of them all, not on a day chiseled into human existence as the most celebrated day on Earth. A day they were born to reach, a day for pride and jubilation.

"You should have mentioned it to me," she pleaded. Most people shared their coming retirement with others, their coming windfall.

"And say what, exactly?" His eyes stung with a flash of something: rage, anger, passion?

"You've worked all your life for this!" she stated. She had twelve more years. She couldn't have been five years younger than Herb. Retirement ages differed significantly.

"I'm fit," he said. That was the point. They were always meant to be fit.

"Then live the best year of your life!"

That was the promise, the giant carrot to draw them all silently to their *Jubilee Year*. It was the same hope he'd instilled in his students down the years, school the breeding ground for this belief. He'd told boys and girls for decades that they were doing the honourable thing. *Don't be a strain. Don't cause the System harm.* Did he even believe it now? Had he ever?

"It doesn't feel right!" he snapped, fear immediately visible in her eyes. She took in the room, scanning for anyone who might have overheard, relief flooding her mind like water on a dry riverbed at the confirmation that nobody had.

"Keep your bloody voice down!" she warned.

"It doesn't," he repeated, somewhat more steady now, though he hardly cared. What could they do to him, anyway? Kill him? Kill him at the beginning of his Jubilee Year?

"It's how it has to be," she said. She'd had this conversation only a few times over the years, almost always with students, themselves trying to grapple with the idea; they would come around eventually, accept it as their part of the human chain. Doing their bit for society. By the time they started work, they would have accepted it. Unquestioning, unwilling to step out of line; fearful of being a voice against the masses. Just one of the crowd: a good citizen, a loyal part of humanity.

"Is it?" he said.

She'd never seen Herb acting like this before, though now both knew the pretence didn't matter. It was his last day there. She'd heard of others reacting similarly to Herb on their last day. She'd never been around someone who had, but there were always stories. She'd never believed them herself. How could anybody be so selfish? Now she wasn't so convinced about her own assumption.

A raised voice from the front of the room drew their secret conversation to an abrupt close, the Director now addressing the staff, calling all to order, inviting Herb to stand alongside him. Without another glance at his female colleague, Herb continued to play the part of the diligent man, doing his bit. He stood next to the Director, glancing at the faces of those before him, all younger, most with decades left. Some of them perhaps with forty or fifty years. Nobody really knew.

"It's my honour to raise a toast to this great man beside me," the Director boomed, his right hand in the air, the champagne flute dancing in the sunlight. His left went around Herb's shoulders, another hearty pat of affection drawing Herb a half pace forward. "If you'll do the honour, Herb," he said. These were words that the Director had not spoken in seven years, though everyone knew they were coming. An employer had to know for certain. They wrote it in the laws as much as anything else.

Herb lifted the hair on the side of his head, thick and lush. Only a few grey streaks showed, though most would assume he dyed it. Three inches above where his hair hung down to, in the same place everyone had it, were six numbers. Numbers that defined everybody on the planet and had done for sixty years. Each number separated by a black dot, nothing but a pin-prick really, though as clear as the day it had been put there.

Zero one. One zero. Ninety-six.

A date that was one year from tomorrow. A roar went around the room.

"To a wonderful Jubilee Year, my friend," the Director said, his salute complete. The room echoed the phrase, Herb taking in the faces, each beaming at him. Some even seemed jealous as he embarked on the best year of his life. Money to spend, time to spend it, places to go. He could go anywhere, do anything, see anyone. Real wealth, a real difference. It was what they were all looking forward to, why the Jubilee business was such a huge focus. Magazines were written on how to spend that year: what you had to do, where you must go. All designed to ignore the blindingly obvious, all there to overlook the one huge elephant in every room across the planet.

At the end of that year, you would be dead.

THIRTY MINUTES later Herb had extracted himself from the staffroom, his final handshakes made. He would likely not see any of them again, this really was goodbye. With box in hand, his sole personal items there along with a few hastily arranged leaving gifts, Herb strode across the carpark towards his car, though a huddle of bodies told him there were students waiting for him.

They parted as he approached, all silent, the crowd dividing as if he were Moses, they the Red Sea.

"You said nothing," one girl said, there in his last lesson that morning. She'd been crying, that much was clear.

"I didn't know what to say," he lied. There was plenty he might have said, though it would have gone against everything he'd believed for years, everything he'd taught his pupils. It would have got him arrested.

"You are the best teacher I've ever had," the same girl said. She flung herself forward and embraced him, her words cheered by many in the crowd, though they resisted the physical demonstration.

"You pass those exams," he said, already spent of emotional energy, not able to put into words what he now wanted to communicate. He looked at their faces, each filled with pride, each with the blinding ignorance of youth. A free generation, as they would describe themselves. An enlightened people, in a time like no other. It was all they'd known, all anybody had known. Few were now still alive from when things were different. Herb had not known a different world. His entire life had been heading for this moment; now it was here, he didn't feel ready. He wasn't ready.

They cleared a path to his car, which they had affectionately decorated. Shaving foam covered his rear window, the words *Have a great Jubilee* plain to see. That would cause many people to cheer him as he drove home, random strangers, all with the same belief. That he was a hero, that good awaited him, that this was the right thing to do.

As Herb pulled out of that carpark, the student group around him silent as they watched him leave for that last time, these thoughts were far from his mind.

He wasn't sure if he believed it all anymore. He wasn't ready to die.

2

The boys chased around the house, each aged between ten and twelve. The middle boy lived there, the other two were friends from school. His mother was preparing food in the kitchen, father due home within the hour.

The latest game was laser tag, the boys jumping in and out of various rooms, their VR goggles transforming the house into a wild forest. A wake of debris littered the house, chairs on their sides, shoes kicked all over the place, as the boys continued their quest.

The mother had given up trying to clean up after them. She would put food in front of them and tidy up before her husband got home.

The fathers of the two friends were both in the military. Naturally all three fancied their chances in that field, one that promised better pay, better conditions. The home they lived in was a fine example of what was possible in a culture that prized wealth, that rewarded those who knew how to keep it.

Another crash from upstairs was the last straw.

"Boys, outside!" the mother ordered. The garden, lush and spacious, had everything a lively group of boys could need.

She heard her son put up some protest. Apparently the house made a far *better arena than the open garden, where little existed to hide behind, the VR making the garden into nothing but a desert, easy shooting.*

"I'll get the football," the son said, the three taking off their headsets, putting the guns back on charge. It was possible his dad might join in later when he got home, the three of them against him. He remembered the ball was in his father's cupboard. He'd had it taken from him the other week for kicking it against the garage door. He went to get it, stopping at the clothes drying on a rack. His friends came looking for him.

"Wow!" one friend said. "Is that your father's?"

"Yep," the son answered, smugly. His friends might have had Black-Collars for fathers, but his father was a Red. The shirt lay ironed and pressed, the collar as vibrant as ever.

"You ever try it on?"

The son smirked. "Sometimes." His father had assured him that one day he would get one of his very own. Red-Collars ran in the family; they usually did. Few outsiders ever got ushered into the elite, and if they were, there needed to be a special reason for it. Something that benefited the rest of them.

"Go on then, show us," his mate egged him on. Inside, this was no issue. The son pulled off his own shirt and grabbed his father's. It was far too big for him, naturally, but the collar sat well around his neck.

"Mint," the two friends said in unison. They'd never been that close to a Red-Collar themselves.

"Do your folks let you try their uniforms on?"

Both boys nodded. Their mothers only had White-Collars; those were boring. Ninety-six percent of the adult population had one of those. They too would start adult life with one. Everyone leaving school traded their Blue-Collar uniform for a White-Collar one. Only a select few might then move on to a Black or, rarer still, a Red-Collar.

All got the Gold-Collar in their last year. Something that they said united everyone. A Gold-Collar opened almost every door.

The son threw the football to his mate, who dropped it down the stairs. It bounced several times, gaining speed, before knocking a vase to the floor in the downstairs hallway. A scream from his mother told them all that she'd heard it smash, and they raced after the ball, dodging the broken pieces and escaped out into the garden. They hid at the end of the garden for five minutes, and once she didn't emerge from the back door, they went onto the lawn, kicking the ball around.

It was their last shot that finally launched the ball high over the fence. The football bounced clean over the front lawn and out onto the road. The three friends raced down the driveway, checking for cars as they skipped across the road.

A screech of tyres from the end of the road caused them to freeze on the spot. No sooner had one car rounded the corner, than another two did. They braked to a halt in front of the house, between the three terrified boys and the lawn they'd been playing on seconds earlier.

The boy's father came running from the other direction, sheer panic on his face. In their haste to get out of the house half an hour earlier, none of them had realised that the son still wore his father's Red-Collar.

"What are you doing?" his father demanded, stepping into the scene, his voice shaking.

"Stand back, sir," the military man warned, not taking in the Red-Collar of the visitor, his eyes fixed firmly on the group of boys in front of him.

"That's my son, and you'll address me properly!" the father demanded, the officer turning and taking in the collar. He spoke quickly into his earpiece.

"What were you thinking?" his father asked, now approaching his son. The military personnel did nothing to stop him getting close.

"I'm sorry," the boy wept, beside himself in despair now, knowing what he had done was something his father had warned must never happen.

His father drew his phone from his pocket, handing it to one of his son's friends. "Call your father. I need him aware of this immediately!"

The father turned to the officers, who were now closing in.

"I need to test this boy," the military man informed.

"He's my son!" the father demanded.

"He's wearing a Red-Collar. You know the rules."

"Don't you tell me about rules!" the father snapped. He knew them all right. At that moment he didn't care if he had broken them all. The other two men stepped forward, one even placing a hand on the father's shoulder.

"Don't you dare lay a hand on me!" the father snapped, shoving the hand to one side. This caused both Black-Collars to jump on him, pinning him to the ground. The boys screamed, the one on the phone to his father passing the handset back, before running away. The other did the same too until it was only the son left; his father lay face-down on the pavement, two men holding him.

"Step forward," the Black-Collared leader said, the boy trembling with fear, though doing as commanded.

"I was only playing," the son said.

"Hand!" the officer demanded. The boy raised his finger. A blood sample was taken instantly, the man looking at the device as if in no doubt what the outcome might be. Its warning tone confirmed that this boy was not in fact a Red-Collar.

A female screaming from behind soon told them the boy's mother had now spotted the commotion, running onto the scene, seeing her husband manhandled on the ground, her son standing not two feet from the officer.

"No!" she bellowed, making to get closer, though two other personnel stepped across her path. Her husband looked up at her, his eyes piercing, searching for an explanation. How could you let this happen? How could you let him leave the house like this?

"Do you have a name, boy?" the officer asked, addressing only the eleven-year-old in front of him.

"Jake," he confirmed, eyes streaming.

"And you know that wearing a Red-Collar which doesn't belong to you is a serious offence?" the officer asked, the boy unable to answer for the crying. "Well?"

Jake nodded.

"We'll make sure he learns his lesson!" his father shouted, still pressed to the ground, his cheek stinging from the stones pressing into his skin.

"It's gone beyond that, I'm afraid," the officer sneered.

"Don't you dare!" screamed the mother, neighbours now appearing and taking in the scene, called to their windows by the commotion, though once spotting the Black-Collars, they soon vanished again.

The officer drew his weapon. This caused the boy to cry all the harder, as he tried to take off the shirt.

"Under section twelve of the third amendment to protocol fourteen, I find you guilty without trial of imitating a Red-Collar," the officer spoke, his parents now screaming in desperation, the officers struggling to restrain them both, the noise so great that the boy could barely make out the words being spoken to him, not that he understood what he could hear, anyway. "This crime is a capital offence, punishable on the spot by a bullet to the head," he finished, firing his weapon at point blank range, the sound of the gunshot sending birds from nearby trees into the air in a great cloud. Nothing but silence enveloped the scene, the parents in utter despair, their boy lying dead on the road, the military personnel releasing their grips on them both as they tentatively left.

"I'll have your head for this!" the father demanded, staring the leader in the face.

"No, you won't!" he said back defiantly. The order had cleared from Control, the man performing his duty to the letter of the law. He knew the System had his back. "A van is on its way to clean up this scene."

They wouldn't even get to bury their son. Criminals could not be remembered.

3

As Herb pulled into the restaurant that evening, he could already see them waiting for him. They'd insisted on a proper celebration that night, just those closest to him. The five teachers had worked together in the same department for twenty years.

He still felt a little bad about not mentioning anything to them in the buildup to this day. They spotted him get out of the car, each head turning his way. He lost no time in entering the building, weaving his way through the crowds and taking the seat that remained vacant at the head of the table. A few bottles of wine had evidently been ordered, the white wines in two buckets of ice.

"You took your time," someone joked. He was barely three minutes past their agreed time. "Thought you might have started the year already." Fat chance of that. The money would only arrive the next day, or at some point soon after. Herb still didn't know the formal details, these kept from the general population, relevant only to those entering their Jubilee Year. The next batch of people would do that the following morning, Herb amongst them.

"You know me, I like to make a scene." They knew him, or

thought they did. Herb never made a scene. Perhaps that was the joke?

An hour later, the mood had softened. Three empty bottles stood at the end of the table, Herb enjoying the evening more than he had thought he would when it was first mentioned during the gathering in the staffroom. Herb had been the first colleague any of them had worked closely with to reach this milestone.

"So what time are you due there?" one man asked. They all knew he meant the Colosseum, an almost sacred venue everyone got to visit at least once in their life. There had been a school trip arranged for a select group of students a few years back, a very rare event. None of those present had been on the staff team who eagerly assisted on that excursion.

"Ten," Herb said.

"It'll be amazing, I'm sure." All smiles, all eyes on the day in front of Herb and not on the end of the year that would follow. Nobody really talked much about that, not this close to someone's Jubilee. That was all dealt with at school, in the earliest years. The first three years of school firmly settled this issue. Now the state controlled it. No longer would old age be a drain on the planet; a strain on hard-working families, a challenge for the individuals themselves. The world had sanitised death, and all its associated problems.

Now they controlled it. The twenty-sixth protocol had seen to that.

Herb grinned at the comment. It was well meaning and sincere. He couldn't believe the day had come, that was all.

"They say you never feel ready," a woman, now a former colleague, said, as if reading his thoughts at that moment. She was perhaps the person who knew him most in the world, save for his sister.

"Damn right," he smiled.

"You ever met a Red-Collar?"

Herb fell silent at that question for a moment. He hadn't, not really, though he would see plenty the following morning during his date with destiny. He would even hand over his own shirt, its White-Collar having served him well for his entire working life. White-Collars filled the restaurant; students with their Blue-Collars could not come in there that late. They might see the occasional Black-Collar—the military wore these. He'd seen plenty of them over the years. Yet, despite teaching a few students who would become Red-Collars, he'd never met one in person. Not sporting the actual Red that signified their place in the elite. What made them elite, he still didn't know. Tomorrow they would surround him: them and the masses of Black-Collared military. The Colosseum stood at the epicentre of the System, the home in that part of Europe for the World Council.

"I don't move in those circles," Herb answered. Who did?

"You taught a few though, didn't you?"

"Yes," he said. It was a special honour to see a student rise from Blue to White to Red. Most assumed it might earn the teacher special privileges, Herb by far the teacher with the most Red-Collars in his ranks of former students. His seemingly unaltered course now shattered that illusion. Their influence had done little to change things, though what these changes might have been they didn't know. It was their duty to obey; nobody argued about this, nobody escaped. Death remained the one common destiny shared by all, regardless of race, colour, wealth or anything else. "I'm not sure if I'll see them tomorrow or not?"

"I hear they make a special mention for teachers," another said, something Herb had been told. He wasn't sure he believed it; wasn't sure he wanted it, even if it was true.

"I'll find out tomorrow, I guess."

They drank a little more, the silence enough for them all for the time being, the surrounding tables noisy. Life happened, perhaps other parties were celebrating somebody else moving into their last year. The start of each month always brought a new intake of people, all heading into a year they had dreamed about since school. Lavish wealth, endless entertainment. A new colour to their collar, one that would open doors before they'd even made it up the stairs, give them access to places they would otherwise never get to see. The year ahead was special. It offered Herb all the chances he'd never managed before, the space to explore, the freedom to travel. He still had his health––that was important. It was why the dates always seemed to land so early, catching the individual off-guard, the unanimous thought each time that they weren't ready. Nobody ever felt ready. That's why the teaching was so important, the message carried from a young age. This was the responsible thing to do. The honourable thing. They had saved the economy billions in health care, only those with critical conditions or unexpected accidents now needing a hospital bed. Retirement homes and hospices were only a thing read about in books. They didn't exist anymore. They had sanitised frailty too.

With no need for a pension plan and no cost for looking after the elderly, people could reach their Jubilee Year and expect a million unit payout, easily enough to see them live the most extravagant year of their life. That was how the system worked. They had cured most diseases, criminality appeared to be finished. The more recent protocols had cracked down heavily, the punishments for anyone committing a crime severe and beyond a balanced response. They were punitive. With a growing surveillance system, and the compulsory identity chip, there was no longer any escape for those breaking the law. Crime didn't pay.

The ultimate enemy had been death itself, the final protocol ushered in amid great fanfare as if the welcome of a returning king. Sixty years later it was, for the vast majority, all they ever knew. Nobody alive on the planet was older than the age of eighty. They had restored dignity, the System heralded. The days of parents losing their minds, of relatives living long past their best days, were history. The era of the Red-Collars had come, the New World Council sweeping to power globally almost overnight, though the process wasn't complete for five years. Military action was only required in a few nations, something never reported. Soon the System controlled all media: everyone on the same page, with the same currency and slowly moving towards the same language. *We are one people*, they would say. *We should destroy all barriers that separate us.* Those that disagreed soon started vanishing. Then the dissident voices went away altogether.

Now nobody spoke against the System: generations of teaching at schools, of sharing this new insight, and people embraced the truth. Embraced the reality. *We control death; it doesn't scare us anymore.*

As the evening came to a close––the place open for another couple of hours, though for those with Herb, they at least had work in the morning––their words turned to wishing him all the best for the following day.

He stood, swaying a little though he could soon steady himself. He shook them by the hand as they each told him to go wild, travel the world, see everything. That was always the promise, always the dream. Some people ignored that, using the money and privileges on their families, helping lift them out of poverty and giving them a better future. The money didn't go too far but usually enabled a better school, perhaps a home in a better area. Things that would have a positive impact on the next generation.

Herb didn't have a family to leave anything to, though he had thought about his sister. She was alone now; her husband, his brother-in-law, had died in a plane crash twelve years earlier. There still seemed some things the System couldn't control. Herb's sister had never remarried: she still mourned her husband's passing. A payout from the airline company had at least set them up for a while.

Herb walked to his car, the others filing out with him, each giving him a last goodbye, his female colleague another embrace. She held this one longer, their bodies close. She seemed unable or perhaps unwilling to let go this time. Herb had always wondered if she had feelings for him. He'd wondered that about himself too, in regard to her. It all seemed too late now: perhaps twenty years too late.

"What you told me earlier," she whispered. Just the two of them now, standing only a foot apart. The others had driven off. "Have you had time to bury those thoughts?" She had the following day in mind; if Herb were to shout about the injustice of it all at the Colosseum in the morning, she didn't know what they might do.

He smiled. Even now, in what might be their last moments, she was looking out for him. Perhaps he'd been wrong about her intentions for him all those years? Perhaps she really had been interested?

"Are you worried I'll get myself arrested and have my glorious *death prize* taken from me?" That phrase had been outlawed a decade ago, as they both knew it had. Her eyes had gone wide at the mention of it, telling her all she needed to know. All she now feared.

"Herb, you can't!"

"Relax," he said. "I'll play along with their little game," his speech somewhat slurred. Before he set off, she would make sure his car was correctly programmed to deliver him home.

"This isn't a game!" she pleaded. "What you are doing is heroic!"

"Look at me!" he said. "Do you think I feel old?"

"It isn't about whether or not we are old," she said, well aware he knew all the reasoning, all the teaching. He'd delivered countless classes on the subject, as they both had.

He reached his hand forward, as if to embrace her, his fingers touching the side of her cheek for the moment, the woman rooted to the spot. She let him stroke her face, but his hand moved up to her hairline, and he took in her date.

She took a step back.

"That wasn't fair!" she said.

"Fair?" He laughed at that thought. "How old are you?"

"What?"

"You heard me."

"I'm fifty-five, Herb." She knew what was coming. He repeated the age, swearing under his breath.

"I'm just five years older than you, and already I'm here," he said. Her date showed she had another fifteen years before reaching her Jubilee Year.

"You know how these things work." He did. She added, "And do you think it's fair that I've got to work ten years longer than you to reach retirement?"

He would beg to differ. He would take another ten years of work rather than start his last year the following morning.

He swore again.

"It doesn't seem fair, does it?" he said at last, though she didn't answer. She wasn't sure to which of them he was really referring.

Sat in the front seat of his car two minutes later, she watched him select *home* from the list of destinations and then the engine started. She stood back as the door closed, one last glance at the man she'd loved for more years than she would admit. A tear ran down her face as she watched him pull away. She shielded this from him as he passed, waving at him from a distance as he made it to the main road. Before long the car took him out of sight. Probably out of her life forever.

4

Hospitals still had their place in the new world order, as sickness, while mostly treatable, was far from eradicated. While cancer now no longer aroused the fear it once did—heredity cancer still limited the years given to future generations, the System's way of fighting back against the disease—people still fell ill.

The staff at the George Tyler Memorial Hospital did their best to keep their patients informed. They were Council controlled, as all hospitals were. They connected their computer terminals to the mainframe, the data flowing both ways. George Tyler had been the first Supreme Commander to chair the World Council. He brokered the peace and put the first six protocols into place. They had named the hospital in his honour; the ceremony taking place at the newly rebuilt facility months before the man himself entered his Jubilee Year at the ripe old age of eighty-two.

Now it stood as the largest hospital in the region, covering a population of thirty-million people, easily able to cope. With most conditions now controlled with over-the-counter medication, only the extreme cases needed hospitalisation. Their Serious Conditions ward was one of the leading establishments anywhere on the planet.

Medical coverage was universal and available to all. There were no exceptions, something those early protocols set into place. Wealth might *afford a patient a better hospital, perhaps a more comfortable room and the best doctors available, but everybody had access. What people did with that access was up to them.*

The System did its best to stop anybody dying before their time. Accidents happened. While driving had become incredibly safe thanks to the automated cars, construction accidents were still common. People still tripped over things if they didn't look where they were going. Planes still crashed. As much as the System wanted people to believe they had controlled death now, they couldn't say that. It wasn't true. They had significantly limited the numbers. They only spoke of a choice now, death no longer the great mystery. They could control it, talk about it. Anything discussed became less fearful. They had attempted to take the sting from death, making it a less taboo subject. They could now look it in the face and say screw you. *And they did. Every month. That's exactly what they did.*

However, the beds at the George Tyler Memorial Hospital were seldom empty for long. When a person in their forties fell ill with cancer, they made sure the patient got the very best treatment that modern medicine could offer. They spared no expense, the person perhaps with twenty or thirty years still to go. Any premature death spoke of a failing in the System, showed them up as unable to protect their people. It would rob the patient of their Jubilee.

The waiting room was usually busy. Those who were sick always accompanied by worried relatives, the numbers suggesting more were ill than was the case. However, the fact anyone was there told its own story.

For many families, treatment was the only option. In former centuries, these people would not have survived. The medical breakthroughs were not there then, nor could they have afforded it, anyway. That had all changed now. These families would wish their loved one well as they went from consultation to testing and from there to treatment once it became clear what the problem was. Doctors would guide the family through each stage, offering their expertise as to the best course of action. Machines nearly always did the actual surgery now, every time guided by a human mind, though these super machines' ability to home in on the area and eradicate all diseased cells far surpassed even the most gifted surgeon.

Any treatment offered its own caveat. While the patient would live to see out their years—assuming they didn't become sick again—the legacy and need for the treatment in the first place would remain on the permanent record. It was why so often entire family groups came. When the children were adults and accompanying one of their parents to the hospital, they too had a vested interest in the decision. The patient was rarely the only one considering the best way forward, though with treatment, it was solely their right to choose. If a patient with years left to live said they wanted the treatment to make them recover fully, then the hospital would oblige. They were duty bound to adhere to such a request, regardless of what the often screaming families might do.

Cancer treatment would go on the record. The unborn generations in that family line yet to arrive would count the cost, this disease in the genes, even while treatable, something that the System would factor into the equation when dating all future descendants. The effects were therefore generational. Under an amendment to one protocol, only three clear generations with no sign of a returning cancer would see the removal of the note from the family line. Given the infancy of the System, there were no examples yet of such a black mark ever being removed.

Some conditions were still a challenge to treat. In these cases, while the disease went on record—anyone visiting a hospital with any confirmed diagnosis meant this went on the record—the patient might opt for no treatment. Schools taught their students to praise such brave decisions, holding these people up as selfless. The money that would otherwise get spent on treatment would be given to the remaining family, an often very handsome figure, perhaps as much as one hundred thousand units. That was often enough to set families up for some time. When this situation arose near to a Jubilee Year—perhaps a year before they were about to retire— then the money on offer increased. They would pay the full million units early if the patient chose to forgo the treatment, sparing the cost to the System for what would only be an extra year or two of life. They highly esteemed such actions, the families gently pushed towards this option which was praised as better for all.

The extra money went some way to undo the damage that the disease might do to future generations.

Two family groups sat in the main consultation room waiting area that day, at opposite ends of the spectrum. The first group was for a woman in her early sixties, diagnosed with a brain tumour six weeks previously, her thirty-six-year-old daughter and son-in-law both sitting with her. The daughter had never had children, the couple deciding they wanted to enjoy what they had together.

For the three of them, with treatment prospects good—brain tumours were highly treatable now—an operation was the only thing they would consider. The daughter couldn't face losing her mother, and without children of their own, the impact the illness would have on their future was negligible. Her mother would recover, able to get back to work within a month, and continue until she reached retirement, when she could take her payment and live the good life along with her peers. She had a close group of ladies who she had got to know. They would all enter their Jubilee Year the same month. It wasn't uncommon for such groups to meet, plenty of online forums existing that matched people by the month and year that they would enter their retirement. This way it enabled friendships to form and bonds to be made down the years so that, come Jubilee, they would merely move into that phase together. Adverts the world over broadcast and praised this form of connection.

The other group in the waiting area, formed of ten people across three generations, wasn't as easy. The grandfather had lung cancer, the man's three grandchildren colouring quietly in one corner, his daughter present, baby number four on the way and four months to go until her due date. Her father's condition would impact this latest child. Its older siblings would undoubtedly live for a long time after this unborn brother or sister entered their own Jubilee Year. Money was also tight. Her younger brother, also married and with his wife present, hadn't yet started a family. His younger sister was unmarried. The news that their father had contracted this disease had hit them all hard. The patient had three years until retirement, his working life not helping his lungs. He had been a heavy smoker for some time.

Both groups sat pretending they couldn't see each other, though it was the larger of the two groups, naturally, that had the more eager discussions. They seemed there to talk the patient out of taking any treatment and instead to take the money option. The family had mentioned the figure of one million units more than once.

"I won't do it!" the patient said, adamantly. "I've worked over forty years in that bloody factory making those ruddy things, the least I'll do is enjoy one of them in my retirement." He had evidently worked in the booming industry of leisure items, the fastest growing market in the world. With every person on the planet given such a sum and with so little time to spend it, the market had blossomed, offering everything imaginable. Only those firms controlled by the Council were afforded a booth at the monthly Celebration Day events, where they could explain what they offered directly to that prime audience. The other million firms out there had to settle on advertising.

This statement from the old man seemed to set his relatives off again, the adults in the group bickering frantically amongst themselves, the children at least knowing enough to leave them to it.

The other party, when called through, merely stood, grateful their situation was altogether different. They didn't even offer a passing greeting to the miserable bunch, who seemed more desperate for the money the longer their argument went on.

However, nearly all those who ventured into that room were White-Collar families. Had somebody been there to observe, they might have wondered why so few Red-Collars grew ill, perhaps putting it down to good genes, which they often had. The Red-Collars had money and privilege, for sure, but they were just as likely to get ill as anybody else on the planet. And they did. Except, for them, alerting the System to the fact would only threaten their fortunes, and those with wealth would do anything to protect and keep what they hadn't earned. Wealth stayed within the families, passed on from generation to generation, and had done for centuries. Those who now formed the elite class—known only by their Red-Collars—were the CEOs and millionaires of the twentieth century, the oligarchs and celebrities of that generation. Royalty across the centuries no longer had those titles but still maintained the same distance from other working people. The same separation that vast inherited family wealth enabled. The same lavish homes too spacious to justify. The same freedom never to work, to have others do that for them. To pay others. To control others.

The System was no different from any other time in human history. Those with all the wealth still held power over everybody else, and they would do everything possible to keep it exactly like that. They let very few people from outside into their exclusive network, and when they did, it was only to better the collective. If somebody showed a level of expertise or ability, they were in. Becoming a Red-Collar was the highest achievement available in a System that didn't do celebrity. They talked about the collective, talked about the greater good, the duty of all citizens.

Yet it was a rotten system, like any system of control.

For those who defied the System and took their own life, the System fought back. A suicide might cover up something they needed to know. If they didn't know why a person had died, they couldn't factor that in to future generations that might yet follow in that family line. Bad genes needed exposing. They made suicide illegal in one of the first amendments to the crime protocol. Anything that took control away from the System caused a threat to all. People could pass diseases along without the Council's knowledge. Now every student knew the dire consequences a suicide in the family would have for all. Every citizen on planet Earth stood to gain one million units for playing by the rules but there were no Jubilee payments when someone died by suicide. Payments to the rest of the family were threatened too. Several high-profile examples had already happened where the relatives were penalised. Payments were either reduced, or in a few extreme examples where the System deemed that the surviving relatives had encouraged the behaviour of the deceased, the million units were refused altogether.

In a later amendment, they made suicide a mental condition, also harming the length-of-life prospects for the next three generations. A family had to do everything in their power to stop this from ever happening.

Still, and unreported mostly, every year thousands chose that way out. For different reasons, they felt trapped, trapped in a world supposedly open to them, supposedly advanced in its treatment of all known threats to life.

For the wealthy, however, the stigma of a suicide was too much to bear. So what happened when someone grew ill in their latter years but didn't want to draw their family line into trouble? What then? While the System did nothing centrally—to have done so would have threatened the very morals they claimed to be built on—they weren't unaware. There was a way, something they turned a blind eye to. The terminally ill person would even get a payout as part of the process. The world none the wiser to the disease in question, the family able to keep their reputation and wealth intact, and after mourning the tragic loss of their dear relative, they could move on as they had done before, life very much unchecked. Unchallenged.

And for another batch of three hundred Red-Collars, that was exactly what they were about to do.

5

Vivian stirred as a nurse entered the room carrying a vase which she had gone to collect for her. Flowers adorned most surfaces, Vivian not taking them all in.

Babies cried in the distance; other children, other mothers. Vivian's own child lay sleeping in the glass box next to her bed, barely hours old. The evidence of so many flowers told her that word had got out.

"How are you feeling?" the nurse asked, placing the vase down, dropping another bunch of flowers into the half-filled container as she spoke.

"What time is it?" The lighting made it impossible to tell what time of day it was; she'd felt like she'd been there for ages, though this wasn't the room in which she'd given birth. That much was clear. Vivian glanced at her little miracle sleeping contentedly next to her.

"It's nine in the morning," the nurse confirmed, glancing up at the clock above Vivian's head, the rhythmic ticking on the second hand now connecting with Vivian's tired brain. She glanced up at it herself, seeing the clock upside down. Vivian had arrived in a hurry yesterday lunchtime, all signs showing the baby would be out any moment. As the hours dragged by, it became a battle of wills. Her son was born shortly before six that morning.

Vivian glanced at the flowers, the latest vase joining the other dozen.

"Can I hold my son?" she asked, the nurse looking down at her, as if appraising if she were up to the task.

"You need to rest," she said. It had been quite an ordeal. They'd been minutes from rushing her to surgery when the baby turned and the last moments proceeded as God had intended.

"Please," Vivian said. She might not get the peace to hold her son for a while when they found out she was awake.

"Your son is sleeping," the nurse informed her, though as if listening to their conversation and wanting connection to his mother, the baby stirred on cue, his tiny wrinkly pink hands reaching up as he stretched, the beginnings of a cry then leaving the boy's mouth. "Oh, okay then," the nurse relented, seeing their conversation had evidently woken the child. She went alongside the baby and reached in, cradling his little head carefully before handing the baby to his mother.

"Thank you," Vivian said, taking the child, her eyes enraptured with the wriggling human being in her arms.

"I'll leave you two alone for a moment," she said. "I'll let your husband know that you are awake." She left the room.

Vivian glanced at the boy; he was the most beautiful thing she'd ever seen, her love for him more than she knew. She'd feared there would be no connection. She'd never felt maternal, never particularly liked holding other babies, though her friends seemed to think she needed the practice. That behaviour only got worse when they discovered she was pregnant. She and her husband had not planned on having children. They'd thought that remaining childless was the right thing to do, yet she fell pregnant anyway. Lying there in that bed that morning, baby in arms––her baby, her son––she couldn't have been more happy.

She held his little fingers, the grip strong as he clamped around her finger. She'd read about the mother-bond, read all about feeding from the breast, though only now, seeing her little boy suckling, did she get that connection. It was fundamental, something inbuilt, designed.

She'd always wondered what type of mother she would be, even before getting pregnant, even when she had told herself it wasn't for her. She'd seen those women who openly breast fed, getting their boobs out whenever they wanted, it seemed, anything for the hungry child. She'd also seen women resolutely bottle feeding, vocal against those who did otherwise.

As her boy reached up for the nipple, she let him drink—the connection was immediate. She didn't care what anyone said; this was what she was made to do.

She held him there for as long as he wanted, this little body, this life still untouched, unblemished. That thought instinctively caused her to stroke his head, that soft, misshapen egg-head yet to form a solid skull. Little wisps of hair stood on end. He had her husband's colouring, even if also his thinning hairline. It would grow, she knew that. Most children had longer hair.

She stroked the point where the markings would go, the boy's one eye looking up at her from above her breast, the pair connecting. His skin seemed so soft, almost too soft. Soon they would date the boy, his permanent marker, the end of one stage and start of the final. It seemed all too early for that. He had only been born that day, and yet the entire length of his life would be dictated before they even left the building.

For the moment his skin remained untouched, unspoiled by human machine. Her son pulled off the breast as the nurse came back into the room, Vivian covering up quickly.

"Oh, very good, you've fed him already," she said, taking the boy from Vivian, putting the baby on her own shoulder, patting the baby's back gently. The mother said nothing; she'd not wanted to give up the child, not yet. Never. "Your husband is on his way." The boy cried, the nurse handing him back to Vivian as a man appeared in the doorway. He bounded over, embracing his wife, taking in his son for the first time.

"Viv, he's stunning," he said, taken aback by how his wife looked holding their child, their son.

"He's got your hair," she mocked.

"Poor git," he laughed.

"Do you want to hold him?"

He looked a little hesitant for a second. "Sure," he said, eventually.

"I'll give you both a moment with your son," the nurse said. "But we need to take him through soon."

"Already?" Vivian asked.

"He'll be back in no time, I assure you." The imprinting only took a moment; its effect would last a lifetime.

Soon it was just the three of them––mother and father with this baby boy.

"I've never seen a person without a date on before," her husband confirmed.

"Me neither. I kind of assumed he would be born with it," she said, which was silly. They all knew: the System decided. Blood records were checked, with the family history also taken into account. Rumours would say other factors came into play––wealth, the unvoiced assumption––but these were rubbished. The System was impartial. The science precise. The results didn't lie. Nearly everybody now lived a healthy life right up to death.

"And they know about the cure that's on the way?"

That had been the one concern during birth, the confirmation that their baby carried one of the half-dozen newer diseases which had sprung up in recent years. No cure existed yet. That could have had a significant impact, but for the fact that under an amendment to Protocol Twenty-Six, whenever a scientific breakthrough was rumoured to be close––by that they meant within the lifetime of those born with the condition––then it would be taken into consideration. There had been twelve births the previous year with this same condition. They had given none of them more than forty-something years. Within the last twelve months, research had progressed significantly. Vivian had made sure that she made this information widely known. It was the only hope for their son.

"They know," she confirmed. It'd not made a difference to those twelve families the previous year. At least two of them had been as vocal as she had; perhaps more so. Vivian had only heard about them because of their many conversations with the press about it. When Vivian's own unborn child was given the same diagnosis, she'd taken the fight on from where they had left off.

"You said one institute thinks they will find a cure within twenty years?" her husband asked.

"Yes," Vivian said. The institute in question wasn't one of the top ones, where only the brightest scientists went as deemed by the System. White-Collars, like them, ran this one. General folk and not the Red-Collars of the official medical research centres battling to find a cure for all known and future diseases.

"Well, twenty years is terrific," he said. Forty years was the statutory time within which a cure needed to be found if it was to be considered in the dating of any baby.

"If they listen," Vivian said. She had a sense of confidence that she'd got the message to the right people.

"They have to," he said, passing their son back to his wife. She'd heard the same thing when talking with those families the year before, each coming to terms with the shorter life deemed the only acceptable outcome for their latest child.

Moments later the nurse swept back into the room, this time with two others joining her.

"We'll take your son for his marking now," she informed the parents, something done for all children born in any hospital in the world. She reached down and took the boy before Vivian could protest.

"I wrote to your bosses," Vivian called after them, the three turning at the door, the baby now crying in the arms of the nurse holding him. "They've got documented evidence that they will cure his condition within a matter of years," making twenty years sound as if it might be only a matter of three or four. It didn't matter. Twenty was a lot less than forty, the number needed for it to count as a within-lifetime-cure.

"We have no say on any of that," the man at the door said.

"But they will consider it?" she called back, none of them answering as they walked down the corridor with their crying child. "You will look into it, right?" she shouted all the louder.

"They're just doing their job," her husband said, sitting on the side of the bed, his wife close to tears. She wanted nothing more than to hold her baby boy, to do nothing but embrace him. And they'd taken him away from her, the child merely hours old, so that they could signify how long he would live.

They remained silent for a while, neither able to look the other in the face; the emotion flowed too readily in each of them.

THE TWO MEN who had followed the nurse from the new parents remained in the room, the nurse lowering the baby carefully into the waiting cot before taking her leave.

The room was immaculate and white, almost otherworldly, a stark contrast to the cosy and colourful maternity wing. It was System run and looking more like an upmarket tattoo parlour than an ancillary room in the main birthing hospital in the region. The team got to work processing the latest arrival.

"Names?" a woman called from behind the mainframe computer.

"Mother is Vivian Bryant, father is Stuart Bryant."

"Code?" the same woman asked, going over the repeated process she must have done ten-thousand times and counting.

The man read off the twelve digit code strapped to the baby's foot, his personal code that would link him for life to his parents and his date.

"The mother mentioned filing a report," the man said confidently, though soon that confidence faded. The woman at the computer looked up at the man, before glancing over his shoulder to another door, through which emerged a stranger seconds later.

The vibrant Red on his collar struck them the most, the two men who'd accompanied the nurse with the latest baby now silent.

"We have taken it into consideration," the Red-Collar informed the woman at the computer, who tapped away at the screen, completing the formalities. She set the date into the system that would forever ink a mark onto the skin, before entering the same date against the unique twelve digit code. She barely seemed to show any regard for the numbers: just another six digits for a job she would have for the next twenty-two years.

"Well?" the Red-Collar called, his presence there he knew unsettling to the two men; very few people ever encountered one of the elite, these occurrences designed to be rare. It was what kept everyone in a state of shock should they happen to meet someone from the other side. One of the two men stepped towards the baby who had gone quiet, the mild sedative administered in the cot in which he now lay enough to keep him calm for the duration of the procedure. The man picked up the child, careful to move him onto the main machine, laying the baby on his side, one hand keeping the head in place.

The other man positioned the laser to the skin, on the same spot they marked everyone; two centimetres above and to the left of the right ear.

"Ready," he called, a firm hand holding the baby who seemed to be asleep by this point already. The woman at the machine pressed *Enter*, the laser getting to work in no time, imprinting the six digits that would remain forever. Removing them was a capital offence, and as the adults who had tried it had found out, the skin didn't heal well. Alterations were always obvious.

Sixty seconds later, and it was done. The ink needed time to dry, the skin noticeably red and vulnerable for a few days, sometimes up to two weeks. They stuck a plaster in place, there to protect the area and hide the number. Most families did an unveiling at home; the System had taught that this was a date to celebrate.

For many, it was still a day to mourn.

K ate busied herself with the last items, putting things back in place at the end of every day as she always did. Cleaned, dried and germ free, everything she'd used now slid or dropped or placed back to where it started the day, many hours ago. She'd worked late once more.

Kate called out as she switched off the lights—a courtesy really, nobody else was there anymore—the room she shared with several others plunged into darkness.

She refused the panic that darkness still caused her body to fight; just one of many phobias she'd yet to grow out of, and time was running out.

She hung her work gear on its usual peg, the item now swinging freely next to the other four, those of her colleagues—three men, one other woman—who were most likely well into their evening routines by now.

She cursed as she spotted the time, the hour already ten minutes after eight.

Grabbing her bag, she hurried more quickly—she wasn't a runner, not even a jogger. Slender and petite, she still didn't go in for the cardio stuff. Didn't see the point. Walking with purpose, she reached the corridor, the lighting low; security at least still on site.

"Evening, Miss," the man called, as Kate reached the entrance hall.

"Night, George," Kate obliged, the same security guard who always seemed to work that shift, the same one who always seemed to greet Kate last as she so often was the final one to leave.

"Late one again, Miss," he observed, always willing to make conversation. She winced at the truth of his comment. She couldn't imagine him talking to the others in the same way as they left the office, passing comment on someone's appearance or at what time they were leaving. *Gained a little weight, have you, sir? You're not pregnant, are you Ma'am? Leaving early again, sir?*

"You know me," Kate called. He didn't. She didn't even know if he knew her name; she'd only taken in his because he always seemed to make a point of greeting her whenever he saw her. Plus, he wore a name badge. She figured sitting on the desk all night, with little danger that someone would try anything untoward, it was what kept him going.

"Back in early, are you?"

"As always," she called, now at the door, their usual routine. She'd not stopped her determined pace across the floor towards the exit during their exchange.

"Well, have a good night and I'll see you tomorrow night then," he called, Kate waving a hand––she assumed he would understand she had caught his meaning––as she left the building.

There were two vehicles in the carpark which when full had space for forty. Her car was shiny and relatively new. She'd got it eighteen months before directly from the factory and was paying it off monthly. The other car––which had to belong to George––must have been twenty years old. She wondered if he had to drive it the old-fashioned way. Perhaps that was the point? She'd even heard of a new factory launching a retro range, where a driver actually had to drive the thing. Insane. She wouldn't have a clue.

Kate jumped into the front seat, the car switching on given her proximity. She confirmed home as her destination; the vehicle moved moments later as it began the ten-mile trip. Home to work and back again seemed the only trip she ever used the thing for. She suspected if she lived a little nearer, she might not even need a car. Though the area around work didn't have enough trees for her, nor places to walk. She needed air to breathe, loved being on the edge of the city. She sat back as the car pulled onto the main road, a route that would take her most of the way save for the last twist of smaller streets before arriving home.

She switched on some music, spotting a text from her mother as she looked at her phone––she kept the phone in the car; she didn't like being disturbed at work and if anyone needed her, they could call the people there. The text read: *Call me when you get this, it's Joe.*

Her kid brother, Joe, was four years younger than Kate and about a metre taller. An enormous man in both stature and personality, though his black moods had been equally huge lately. At some points, the life of the party, always popular, able to make others laugh without hardly saying a word. Then the depression would set in; he would spend days in bed, unable or unwilling to move.

A text from her mother suggested, yet again, that the latter condition was once more plaguing her brother.

Kate pressed option one on the speed dial––she only had two numbers stored, the only two she ever called, one being her mother. Joe lived at home still, so it covered both relatives. The other number was work, where she spent most of her life when not sleeping.

"Kate, thank goodness," her mother said, answering almost immediately. She must have been expecting the call any second, the longer the evening went on.

"What is it?" Kate had picked up the anxiety in her mother, who seemed to worry about everything now, though this seemed different.

"It's bad this time."

"How bad?"

There was a pause, Kate edging forward on her seat a little as the car continued to drive her along the mainly empty road.

"Says he's had enough," came the reply.

"He's said that before," Kate confirmed. Joe's lows always seemed like the bottom was falling out of his world, though he soon pulled through.

"He said he would kill himself," her mother replied, now in tears.

"He actually said that?" Kate asked, alarmed now herself. Joe had never gone that far in his threats before; he had been on a downer before but not crossed the line. Suicide was both illegal and hugely damaging to the remaining relatives. The System didn't tolerate it, couldn't allow people to decide when they died. That was what the date did. It settled the issue, made it all clear. Took the worry out of it. Or it was supposed to, anyway. Education supported how the System removed concerns to allow you to live without worry over employment and secure on the knowledge that your final year would be one of happiness and not a lingering decline towards death. Anybody taking death into their own hands brought shame on the System and those surviving relatives. It would taint all future generations, as if suicide itself were a disease. *If one of them killed themselves, then perhaps later generations would too?* It took years off their life, from future babies yet to get dated. Not that Kate saw a family of her own as an option. If this happened, if her brother really carried through with it––she couldn't really stop him if he truly meant it––then that decided it. She would never have children. She would have to live with the shame of having a suicide in the family. Society could be so cruel. She doubted she would lose her job, though she had heard that happen too. It was the System's way of making sure family members stepped in and controlled the risk.

Still, suicides happened. They always had and probably always would. It was humanity's way of raising the finger, telling the System it couldn't control them. These situations were soon buried, soon went away. People and life moved on. They never celebrated those who challenged the System.

"He said he would kill himself?" Kate repeated, her mother silent since her last question, though Kate could hear her weeping.

"Yes," she confirmed.

"Is he there now?" Kate asked.

"No," came the response. Joe had a wide circle of friends, though most were not good for him. He could be anywhere at the moment, especially if he was on a high, the list of places would be long: bars, casinos, strip joints, clubs or at many other places. Kate wouldn't be able to speak sense into him there and then. She seemed to have a way with him. He seemed to listen to her. Kate had been the only one of them to make something from her life. Still a White-Collar—nobody knew why she'd not been promoted—she had a good job. A career she loved, something she didn't mind staying in. What she did she knew was important. She felt a breakthrough on the cards, something to make a real difference for people. It was close.

"Kate, I'm scared," her mother said, though Kate knew that much. It scared her too.

"He'll be okay," Kate assured her, though she knew there was no certainty of that. People like her brother didn't think of the impact their actions would make, didn't consider the damage it would do to those left behind.

"I think he's using again," her mother confirmed, words that caused Kate to sink a little lower in her leather seat, the insides of the vehicle still smelling as it had in the showroom.

"How?"

"You tell me," is all the desperate mother said. Drugs and depression were never a wonderful combination.

Kate swore under her breath, not sure if her mother could hear, though she didn't hear a comment in reply. She looked out of the window. The buildings were giving way to greener views as she reached the edge of the city. The car would pull off the main road within a few minutes.

"Do I need to come?" Kate asked, holding back from saying so until then, this the last resort. She'd been twice before in such circumstances, one at least mostly a false alarm. He'd been in his right mind by the time she'd arrived, a pleasant week spent together but a complete waste of time. It was a very long drive.

"Absolutely," her mother said, almost desperate to communicate that much, though she had never wanted to be the one to ask it of her daughter.

"That serious?" Kate asked, immediately. She'd never heard her mother sound so panicked.

"You know what it means if he carries through with it," she said, aware of the challenges that would come her way as a mother if her son took his own life. She didn't live in a very forgiving place. She would face the stigma for the remaining twelve years she had left. Her Jubilee Year privileges might even be denied. She was counting on that to survive, to have something to leave to her children, or child. She only had two.

"He won't," Kate said, trembling with those words, her car braking as it came to her junction, smoothly navigating the turn that it had made hundreds of times. Kate checked her calendar. The drive to her mother's house would take her three days––it was two thousand miles––and even if she found the charging points for the car en route, it wasn't anything she could do overnight. Work was paramount, though flying wasn't an option she would ever consider. She dreaded flying.

"Look," Kate said, her tone indicative that she was offering a solution, "I'll clear a few things at work and set off this Thursday." It was Monday. She should be there by Saturday.

"It's too long, Kate," her mother pleaded, knowing her daughter didn't fly, but Joe might not have five days in him. "You can't drive this one. It's too far."

"I've always driven," Kate protested. It had never been too far before.

"We don't have the time," her mother qualified her previous statement. "Joe doesn't have the time. Please, Kate, for your brother."

Kate looked at the date. Four days remained of the year. She shook her head silently, her hands beginning to tremble, sweat appearing.

"I can't, it's too dangerous."

"Katherine, everybody flies!" her mother scolded, now raising her voice for the first time, a forcefulness present that had not shown itself until then.

"You know what I think about it though." Her mother did. Kate told her every time she did that ridiculous drive. Her mother resented the fact, saw it as an excuse. She didn't blame Kate. If she had a mother and brother like Kate did, she would probably feign a fear of flying too, cutting down the trips––given the distance––to a bare minimum.

"If you wait on this one, if you aren't here until the weekend, then I'm terrified that this time it'll be too late." The tears had gone. There seemed to remain only blind reason, sheer logic in her mother.

Kate searched the onboard computer as the car continued to drive, now only a few roads from home.

"There's a flight tomorrow," Kate confirmed. Three days until the end of the year. One of hundreds still flying. Good odds in her book, though not as good as avoiding all flights altogether. "It'll get me to yours by dinner tomorrow."

"Thank you," her mother said. The ticket was booked and confirmed within seconds and Kate gave the precise details to her mother. She asked her to find Joe, to have him meet her at the airport if he could. Her mother promised to try. They ended the call.

Kate stayed in the car as it sat on her driveway, the journey complete, the engine going into shutdown. The street was quiet, several lights on inside the homes she could see, her own in darkness, though a security light would illuminate her path to the front door the moment she stepped a few paces from the vehicle. She loaded her boarding pass onto her phone and gathered her things together. She would have to clear it with the office. It hadn't been the first time she had needed to leave, and they wouldn't have an issue with it. The issue was her own. She didn't enjoy missing work. She was grateful not to be working for a Red-Collar firm now, who would press her for the reason, always gathering information on people. They would be less sympathetic, already factoring in Joe's behavioural challenges.

She was grateful to at least have some distance from them. It suited her, even if it put what she did on the second tier, one down from the major players, where funding and resources were plentiful.

She liked her life just how it was. What she hated was the metal deathtraps, one of which she now needed to use the following day.

7

The flowers which had surrounded the bed for the last two days were now obscured by a crowd of people. Vivian sat up in bed, the baby fed and sleeping, the young mother not yet up to feeding in front of a live audience, even if these were familiar faces. Relatives and friends, they'd all come as soon as they could, pleased for the couple.

The baby slept, his plaster showing, nothing mentioned by any of them, not mother or father, nor the hordes as they arrived. All wanted to know. That much was only natural. *How long does the sucker get?* But you could never openly ask that. It wasn't the done thing, nor could they have known yet. The plaster would stay on for another week, the family nearly always home by then. They would hold a party, as new parents always did. Another chance to celebrate something that really didn't warrant praise. The unveiling of the date––a *date party*––always seen as another excuse to drink. Drink away the truth, drink away the reality. It was perhaps the hardest moment in the entire process, when the new parents learnt how long their fresh offspring had on the planet.

Parents should never know the day that their children would die. It didn't feel natural, it never had. It never should.

The System disagreed. They allowed anyone time off work if that was what they needed to attend such a party. Most parents didn't even bother to schedule it at such a time that might require said action. They were too accommodating to the System, too accustomed to how things needed to be.

Vivian had pleaded with her husband the previous night, just the pair of them, to find out the date for their boy. That truth lay under the plaster. All they had to do was to take a peek, to have a look and confirm what they longed to be the case. Confirm what they dared to hope might be the reality. A long and healthy life.

Given the earlier protocols––it was number twenty-one which saw an end to all existing medical conditions at the time––usually a long life was guaranteed. Most people got between sixty-five to seventy years. Some even broached eighty, though these were rare. No-one present had ever even met anyone who would live as long as seventy-two.

There were several new diseases, however. All had occurred since the sealing of the protocol, all there mocking those now living, beating their scientists, testing them to the limit. The New World Council had meant to be a fresh beginning for all––the seal of a better life. Yet people still died.

True, crime was now unheard of––if it happened, nobody reported it. If it happened, nobody saw or heard about these crimi-nals again. Most assumed, as they were taught, that society had evolved beyond petty crime. That they were the most enlightened generation ever––each new generation taking on that fresh mantle.

Sitting on the bed, looking at the cheery faces, watching her baby sleeping, Vivian didn't know what she thought of all these ideals now, all that enlightenment. Her baby boy, not even seventy-two hours out of the womb, already had the date imprinted on his head that would dictate his departure from them all.

She would, naturally, be gone before then. It was every parent's basic prayer.

"Any hint on the name?" a friend asked. All knew the tradition that dictated the parents reveal the name at the date party.

"I think we can rule out your suggestion," Vivian said with a smile. That had been a girl's name, most assuming they were having a daughter. The couple had kept the sex of their child secret from the others, as they had the condition their little one carried. Vivian read up more on it that morning, the research ongoing, one report suggesting the lead scientist was nearly ready to report her findings. The process would then move on to human testing, and once results were confirmed, have the condition removed from the current list of incurable––and therefore life-length altering––diseases. It would give many future families a chance, not to mention their own child and potential grandchildren. Though not entirely genetic, having it in the family did skyrocket the chances of it being passed on.

"So we'll stick with baby Bryant for now then," the friend confirmed, that name written on several cards, a scattering of pinks and blues evidence that not everyone had heard they'd had a boy.

"When we're home, we'll let you all know when the gathering will be," Vivian said, her mind working for a better word, willing herself not to call it a party. She'd never liked the idea as much as those around her. Now even less. "And I'll choose a work day, mid-morning," she smiled, ever the provocateur. A few nodded in understanding, still others murmured between themselves in inaudible whispers. It didn't bode well to provoke the System.

THEIR SON LAY nursing at the breast, Vivian taking to feeding him like a duck to water. It was just the three of them now, her husband dozing in the chair beside the bed, Vivian stroking the head of her son, his little eyes scanning the room, though most often gazing up at her, as he drank his fill.

They'd dressed him in fresh clothes once the well-wishers had left, the clothes a gift from one couple whose children were already school age. His little legs poked out of the ends of the clothing, their baby somewhat larger than the average one-week-old, it would seem.

Vivian cupped his head in her hands, so fragile, so smooth. She felt the plaster: the baby showed no sign of discomfort, no awareness of pain. The nurse had said it didn't hurt, that the plaster was there to help the skin heal, that was all. It also gave the parents something to unveil at the party.

She played with the edges in her fingers, testing the resistance it offered on the skin. The edge came away easily enough, sticking back down without issue.

She toyed with the thought.

"What are you doing?" Her husband had evidently woken from his snooze, his hushed voice not overly startling her, but pitched at a point that communicated the concern he had.

"We need to know," she said. "We can't do this in front of everyone; not if it is bad news."

"It won't be," he said, less conviction there than he had hoped. Truth was, they didn't know. They'd not told anybody. It wasn't the done thing. Admitting to a condition within the family line was now tantamount to admitting to Nazi affiliation during the twentieth century. It blemished the family, put a permanent stain on future generations. And all because of a condition which was about to be cured.

She played with the plaster once more, her son showing little sign of it distracting him. This caused her husband to stand up from his chair, glancing around, looking out to the corridor before closing the door firmly. His actions seemed to give Vivian some encouragement.

"Stop," he said, coming back beside her, but not going as far as reaching out and taking her hand from the spot. His actions of moments ago had suggested he wanted her to proceed.

"We'll still carry on as if we don't know," she said, as if that were the crux of his hesitancy.

"You know it changes everything if it is bad news," he said, a change of tone from seconds before. He'd just told her it wouldn't be bad.

She looked up at him, seeing the same fear that she'd carried in her own eyes for six months now clear in his, and not for the first time. Ever since finding out the truth, they'd wondered. Had they

shared with friends, many would have encouraged them to termi-
nate the pregnancy––this the right thing to do. The loving
thing, too.

That didn't feel loving now, holding her son. Him on the nipple.
Feeding him. Embracing him. Her bundle of joy. Their offspring.

"We need to know," she said, resolutely this time, her husband
not voicing a response. A gentle nod of his head told her all she
needed to know.

Slowly she peeled the plaster, getting as far as she'd dared before,
though this time teasing it back further. Baby Bryant didn't seem to
notice much, the odd little breath taken. His drinking paused
momentarily, but he carried on, as did his mother.

She revealed the first number, which was always a one. The first
day of the month was always the start of another intake of Jubilee
Year people. Next came the month, a summer one for their son.
Usually that was seen as favourable. Nobody wanted their last days
spent in a cold winter. Then the year.

"No!" she screamed, the baby pulling away, her hand going to her
mouth. Her husband leaned forward, straining to confirm the
unimaginable, their worst fears realised.

"This can't be," he said, speaking to the ceiling as much as to her.
They both knew the System never made mistakes. They had assured
them that they'd received their messages.

Vivian pulled back her own hair, the date of her baby boy one
month earlier than her own date. She would start her own Jubilee
Year four weeks after her son––a boy twenty-five years younger
than her.

The baby cried, a nurse appearing in the corridor. Vivian frantically stuck the plaster back down, though the nurse came in through
the door before she had finished. Vivian's reaction alone would have
told the nurse something was wrong.

"Did you know?" Vivian demanded, turning towards the nurse as
she came into the room.

"Know?"

Vivian pulled back the plaster. Not usually anything a nurse would get to see. They never knew the dates, it wasn't their place to know.

"He'll be dead before I am!" Vivian screamed, tears now forcing their way out even while she tried to hold them in. This wasn't meant to be how it happened. She was meant to go first. She would be sixty-two, hardly ancient, but healthy and seeing her children grown up. People were meant to see that much. Now she knew she would bury him.

The shocked look on the face of the nurse told them both that she'd evidently not known. Not kept something like this from them.

"Vivian, I'm sorry. I didn't know, I can assure you," and she took the child, the mother trembling now, tears streaming from her face, her arms barely able to hold the boy steady. The nurse quickly stuck the plaster back in place—it was clear someone had tampered with the thing, she would have to redress it before they left—and held the baby on her own shoulder, preparing to burp him.

"Take me to them!" Vivian demanded, her husband stepping close, but she stood up, wincing slightly but no lingering pains from giving birth were going to stop her now. He pushed past him, stepping towards the nurse who took a step back herself.

"I can't," she said.

"You have to," Vivian pressed. "This can't be. This can't happen. They promised. They said they would listen. There will be a cure before that date. It's just a matter of years."

The nurse knew nothing about that side of things. She was just doing a job. A White-Collar like the rest of her patients. She received only medical information that related to a safe delivery. Nothing else was shared.

"Viv, calm down," her husband said, easing alongside his wife, the nurse placing their baby into the cot.

"Calm down? How can I calm down when they've done this to us!" she screamed.

"Your husband is right," the nurse said, stepping in, Vivian grabbing her by the collar and thrusting the young woman towards the door.

"Viv!" he said, reaching for his wife who pressed the petrified nurse against the wall.

"Don't you move!" Vivian barked at her husband, her finger pointing at him, daring him to step forward another inch. It seemed to work for the moment and she ordered him, "Stay here and watch our son." She turned her attention back to the nurse, ignoring the fear she saw racing in the young woman's eyes.

"Please," the nurse pleaded.

"Take. Me. To. Them," Vivian mouthed, slowly and deliberately, displaying a menace that neither had seen before. A woman not to mess with.

"They won't be there," the nurse whimpered.

"Take me!" she snapped back. Vivian watched her husband as she closed the door, leaving him with the boy. She encouraged the nurse on with a shove in the back, though she walked a step or two behind as she followed. It wouldn't pay to be openly aggressive in the corridors of the hospital.

They walked in silence for a little while, before turning a last corner, the notice declaring that the room they were aiming for was now in front of them.

"They've gone for the day," the nurse confirmed. Vivian ignored the information, pressing into the room, the lights coming on automatically, though this only confirmed the truth of the nurse's words. She moved away from the nurse, pacing around the room as if lost in thought, crying in silence. This was where they had dated her son, marking him for life; robbing him of decades of life, for no reason.

The nurse hung by the door, terrified but knowing she was in no danger anymore. She'd done what Vivian had asked her to do; the room had already been empty for several hours. Security would be in place by the following morning. She slipped away unnoticed moments later, alerting two officers to what had happened.

Vivian sank to the floor, only now noticing that she was alone, quickly getting to her feet again, but not leaving the room. She went to the machine, its purpose plain. How many times had it robbed humanity of years? How many times had it shaved decades from somebody's life? She ran her hands across the computer, not aware of its purpose there but sure something linked the two.

She went to a large mirror, too large to be just that. During the day she was certain others would stand behind the glass, watching, unseen from within the room where Vivian now stood, but surely able to observe all that happened.

Vivian pounded the glass in utter despair, the mirror thick, solid, unmoving.

"You bastards!" she screamed, more to the emptiness than anything else. They'd taken her son from her before she'd even got to know him. "You lied to me!" she boomed again, pounding all the harder, as noise from the corridor confirmed security personnel were closing in.

She turned to the door as it flew open, three Black-Collared men standing with batons drawn, the nurse behind them, terrified still.

"You need to come with us," the leader said, his tone definitive. He didn't need to shout.

"Not until I see a Red," she demanded. Red meant a Red-Collar, one of the elite. The ones who made the rules.

"They never come here," the man said. She'd rarely met a Black-Collar; they usually only went where the Reds did.

"I don't believe you," she said, the man taking a step forward, an arm in front of him as he ordered his men to put away their batons.

"I wouldn't care if you did. I'm here to see you transferred back to your room."

He hovered within arm's length, though he didn't take that last step for the moment.

"No, I demand to see a Red and we talk this through."

He knew she meant about the dating of her son; the nurse had told him that much.

"It will not happen," he confirmed.

"Then make it happen!"

He didn't budge. "Are we finished?"

She shook her head, tears replacing the rage that had temporarily displaced them.

"It's not fair," she wailed.

"It never is."

"No, you don't understand."

"I understand perfectly," he assured her, not elaborating quite what he understood, Vivian in no mood to tell him anything. He closed the gap between them both, his men staying by the door. At twice the size of Vivian, he felt in no physical danger.

They led her from the room, a few nurses watching the party move down the corridor, an anxious glance back and forth between them all but these things happened from time to time.

The lights stayed on in the room for a while, empty as it was. Standing on the other side of the glass, barely inches from the pounding fists of Vivian, had stood a man, alone, taking in the entire display.

The Red-Collar of his shirt appeared underneath the black sweatshirt he had worn into work that morning.

8

Blythe was at home, a house into which several families could have fitted, as he ended a conference call from his upstairs study. He'd had to put another few people back in their place. He replaced a few folders into his briefcase, a thank you gift for his latest promotion. It lay on his mahogany desk, which three generations of Harrells had used and which was now his.

Pictures of his two forerunners—his father standing before a crowd of people, his grandfather sitting in a pose—hung prominently on the wall. Heritage was everything.

Blythe was a third generation Red-Collar, and very few families could say that, even if others had the wealth now, others with equal influence.

Blythe walked bare-footed over his thick Persian rug, back into his bedroom. A family photo of him with his two adult sons hung above the bed, both boys in military uniform, their Black-Collars either side of his Red.

No photos of their mother hung there; Blythe's new wife didn't feel it was appropriate. The sons barely came to visit him anymore, leaving their father to his new trophy wife, a woman barely a few years older than his first child.

He opened the curtains, the sunshine bright, the high hedges at the front of the house only partially allowing a view of the wide tree-lined road that ran beyond. Two houses down and barely visible from his, save for the scaffolding, a neighbour was having an extension added. Three extra rooms in the attic creating another floor.

Blythe turned away from the window, strode the twelve paces to cross his ample bedroom and went out through the door, onto his landing which fed the six upstairs bedrooms and three bathrooms. Only his office ran off another room, the rest connected by that landing. A balustrade ran the length of the landing, looking down onto the entrance hall, the front door beyond. A curved staircase swept around one side of the space, taking him down to the ground floor. Paintings hung on the wall every few steps, these pictures in the family for generations. Blythe did not know what they might be worth now. His father had been the art collector. He knew the most valuable was worth three million. He assumed the other six were far less valuable.

The sound of the blender coming from the kitchen told him the whereabouts of his wife, Blythe leaving her to it for the moment. No doubt she was coming up with another interesting mix of ingredients. Pregnancy had thrown out several strange cravings, nothing his first wife had had with his two sons. He hoped this latest development wasn't an omen. Both boys had grown up to become something within the System.

Sitting in the lounge, the fireplace still hinting the activity it had known the night before, embers no doubt still hot deep within the ash, Blythe sat in his usual chair, a view to the garden beyond. The bay window from which he looked was the only window in the house that didn't need curtains. Nobody overlooked the property. But with a garden as beautiful as the one beyond, they had always insisted the view should remain unblemished.

If his sons were ever to marry—they were early twenties now, just setting off in their military careers—then any future offspring could never be let loose in that sanctuary. Blythe had worked endlessly on the garden once his boys had become old enough to no longer need it. He'd reckoned that had been at age twelve, when studies should be their priority. Over that last decade, he'd created a magnificent display, the best money could buy.

His wife hardly dared go there, perhaps wary of causing it damage. She claimed not to know a thing about gardening. Her family had always had gardeners take care of their grounds. She had grown up with a string of hired hands, though for Blythe the garden had become an obsession. The one thing left to him that seemed real, seemed alive.

He grabbed his device, reading a report that he knew was waiting for him. He ran through the list of names, most of them starred. He would have his team check the details for those names without a star, those people caught up in something bigger than their insignificant lives.

A message alert confirmed the receipt of yet another urgent summons, though this one turned out to be one few people received, nobody his age. It was an invitation to the Capitolium, for an audience with the Supreme Commander, the man who now ran the World Council. The very centre of power on the planet.

It was no great secret that the Supreme Commander would enter his Jubilee Year in a little under two years. The man was already seventy-eight. Blythe's name––a shock to some––was one on a very short list of successors. The invitation was evidently part of that selection process. A few senior officials––all on the panel selecting the next leader, none of whom were in the running themselves––had secretly informed Blythe that in their eyes, it was his to lose. He doubted he was the front-runner, but if he kept his nose clean, they were confident he had a great shot.

Blythe smiled at the message. The date dropped into his calendar. It was a plus one event; the timing took them into his wife's second trimester. She should be through the current phase, and not yet so large that movement became difficult. For many, she'd been part of the reason he now stood as the favourite. She came from excellent stock too; they all knew it. The daughter of one senator, it had been every bit a marriage of convenience as it had been of love. And Blythe loved his wife dearly, as he had his first wife, in her own way.

How that first marriage had ended was something he thought about often. He wouldn't make the same mistake again. He wouldn't let his wife make that mistake.

Blythe stood, leaving the device on his oak unit, strolling back into the hallway, then through a sitting room, before arriving into the open-plan kitchen. His wife sat in a soft chair in the conservatory, the doors that led out from the dining room standing open. A greenish concoction filled a glass on the table in front of her, the evidence of whatever she'd blended some moments before.

She smiled as he walked over, reminding him just how beautiful she was.

"What's that?" he asked, giving her a kiss on the forehead as he passed, taking the seat next to her.

"Kale and pea extract," she said with a smile. "Power food for the baby."

Blythe refrained from comment. He'd once done a smoothie detox and, after a month of similar recipes, vowed never to touch another one again.

"I got an invitation," he said. She'd assured him he would, something that still baffled him. Her sources were even better than his. He still didn't know how she did it.

"Congratulations," she said, her eyes all knowing, though she showed genuine pride all the same. "You know, only the top three candidates have received that invitation."

He didn't, and it showed.

"I thought it was the top ten?"

"It's three, trust me."

"Well you'd better keep the second weekend in March free," he informed her.

"It's already in the calendar," she winked, Blythe shaking his head in utter amusement. *And they say they forbid gossip.*

"What time is the hospital appointment?" he asked, changing the subject from his own possible promotion to the more imminent reality of their unborn baby.

"It's at three, we have plenty of time."

———————

THE DRIVE to the central hospital took a little over an hour, the couple able to chat, the technology delivering them to their destination without their involvement.

"Can you find me the names of the other two?" he asked her. This was something she was sure her husband had wanted to ask since finding out he was one of the final three in contention.

"What makes you think I don't already know?" she smirked. She didn't, but loved reminding him how connected she was, despite her relative distance from that world.

"You know?"

"No," she confirmed. "Would you really want to know? Would it help?"

He thought about that for a moment. Perhaps it wouldn't. If he knew one name, it would complicate matters, for sure. Anyhow, he would apparently meet them both in March.

"It's never a bad thing to know who one is up against," he said.

"I'll see what I can find out," she said.

The car pulled off the main road: the signage showed the hospital was only a few miles away.

"So, do you want them to tell us whether we are having a boy or girl today?" she asked, honing the conversation onto their coming appointment, now that they were getting close.

"What are your thoughts on the topic?" he asked, knowing she wanted a daughter. Perhaps knowing before the delivery whether that wish would be granted or otherwise would help with any disappointment there might be.

"I would like to know," she said.

"Me too," he lied. He really didn't mind. A baby was a baby. He had raised two sons, though he didn't mind a baby girl this time either.

"Then we'll ask the nurse to tell us."

The appointment would take in many things, besides the sex of the child. Neither parent had hereditary conditions in the family, both coming from *good blood*. You couldn't be a Red-Collar and have genetic defects. They would both likely live to see their grandchildren born, something only possible now given the decades of medical breakthroughs. Families now also started sooner than they used to. The years might be shorter, but they ensured the quality. For families like Blythe's, they lived in utter luxury.

As they pulled into a separate car park at the back of the building, Blythe helped his wife from the car. She showed no actual sign of being pregnant: only a slight bump. Like many in her walk of life, the baby would be delivered by caesarean, easily the most common form of delivery now.

They walked across the tarmac, in through the automatic doors which swung open for them, and up to the reception desk. Evidently they were both expected, the lady inviting them to take a seat before they had even given a name. As was customary, no other appointments were scheduled for that afternoon to give the couple space.

Only a minute later, a nurse appeared from the consultation room.

"Mr and Mrs Harrell, if you'll come this way please," she said, almost regally. She stood to one side, allowing the soon-to-be parents into the room first, the nurse allowing them both the time to look around before closing the door. "Please, make yourselves comfortable," she said, pointing Blythe to a chair and his wife to the treatment bed, where the scans would be performed. "This is your first child?" she asked. The hospital's information was usually accurate. It needed to be.

"Yes," his wife confirmed. She wouldn't mention the two adult sons Blythe had. This information would be on the computer. Everything matched up somewhere.

"Well, you have nothing to worry about," the nurse assured them.

"This procedure I'm about to do is perfectly harmless to your baby. It'll take certain measurements and readings. You'll also be able to know the sex of the child if you wish."

"We would," she said, Blythe nodding in agreement, the nurse having looked up to him for clarity.

"Wonderful," and she stepped closer. "If you'll just lift your top, we can begin."

———————————

THE NEWS HAD COME as a shock. Not the fact they were having a girl, which was greeted with tears from the delighted mother, but what came later. While there were no genetic conditions from the historical record, they had identified a newer and rarer condition. It fell outside the latest protocols, labelled incurable at present. It posed an immediate dilemma.

"Explain it in layman's terms," Blythe demanded, the nurse shocked and unable to use anything other than long medical phrases.

"It's new," she confirmed. "Within the last forty or fifty years."

"But they'll find a cure, right?" his wife pleaded, looking at the nurse and her husband for reassurance.

"At the moment, this disease is one of the half-dozen excluded from the safe list. I'm sorry to tell you, but it'll have a significant bearing on the life expectancy of your daughter."

The nurse had been in the room the other morning, a child with the same rare condition given far less time than most. The nurse recalled the parents saying that they knew research was close. It hadn't been close enough in their case, that much was certain.

"But there is research," the nurse added, both parents not saying anything as they took in the news. "Someone is close."

"Within life-close, you mean?" Blythe asked. That was the phrase the System accepted for such new diseases.

"Yes, I believe so. We had a child born with your daughter's condition this week. The parents are still here, I think. They don't yet know how long they have given their son."

"How long was he given?"

"Thirty-nine years," the nurse confirmed, unable to look either in the face.

Blythe paced the room, going back and forth, thinking it through. The nurse handed the couple the information they had available on the disease. His wife took the document, saying nothing. She wasn't about to thank the nurse. The nurse left the couple to themselves for a while.

"We aren't aborting," his wife said, not words Blythe had thought, though he knew the System would put it on the table. Greater minds than his would point out that nobody with his potential could keep his current trajectory if they went through with the birth. Such a man producing a child with anything less than seventy years of life was a scandal.

"I'm not suggesting we do," Blythe said. Having a child had been her dream for them both. She was still young. He'd already been there, but he couldn't deny her this. Now he wondered if he should have done.

"Here, take this," she said, shoving the information about the disease at him. "I don't want it." Blythe took it from her, scanning down to the name of the disease on the front page. Something he'd never come across. He needed to understand more, and being in a hospital, knew he was in the right place. There would be a Council facility onsite, perhaps even a fellow Red-Collar with whom he could speak.

"Give me a moment," he said, excusing himself, passing the nurse who had remained outside, Blythe telling her she could go back in, before asking for directions. Two minutes later he stood outside the door, a Black-Collar standing to one side, letting him in seconds later. As Blythe had reckoned, a Red-Collar occupied the room, a large glass window looking into the room where the inking machine sat. The room was in darkness.

"How can I help?" the man asked, taking in Blythe's Red-Collar, the two not knowing each other by face.

"What can you tell me about this?" Blythe asked, holding up the

information that the nurse had given them, the name of the condition displayed on the front.

"They sent you from Command?" the man asked, somewhat
alarmed. "Is this about the boy from the other day?"

Blythe said nothing as he took in the words, though nodded
slowly, the man taking that as an encouragement to keep talking,
evidently panicked by his appearance.

"You know, the System is always correct. I double checked the
numbers, even called through to your office," the man said, apparently assuming Blythe had something to do with the dating aspect.

"And?"

"They said the research hadn't yet reached an advanced enough
stage for consideration."

"I see," Blythe said, sounding as if the advice wasn't what he
might have hoped.

"It's not one of our research centres," he said, scrambling now.
"That always complicates things." Blythe knew it did. Anything
outside the control of the System—and therefore out of reach of the
World Council themselves—couldn't be trusted. That was why, eventually, any institution which wanted to make a real difference came
under their governance.

"What did the report say?"

There would have had to be a report filed by the parents-to-be.
They would review these files before they completed dating.

"Gave the name of a small institution, one researcher they
claimed was close to finding a cure."

"A within-lifetime cure?"

"So they claimed. But I checked," he said, feeling as if he was in
the firing line himself now.

"Relax," Blythe assured him. "I'm not here to discipline you."

The man breathed a little easier for the moment.

"Do you have a copy of this report they filed?" Blythe asked.

"I can send you a copy," the man confirmed. Blythe passed him
his card, the man's eyes instantly looking Blythe square in the face,
even more concern showing. Just then the lights came on through the

glass, causing both men to turn as two women came into the empty room, one a nurse, the other evidently a patient.

"God, it's the mother of the boy we were talking about," the Red-Collar said, coming from behind his desk, heading to the door.

Blythe stood at the glass, allowing the other man to leave. The woman started pounding the window, screaming that she had sent them the file. The nurse disappeared, the distraught mother left alone for the time being, sinking to the floor in tears. Soon three men appeared, one of them eventually leading the woman away, Blythe standing inches from the window the whole time, a small glimpse of the world out there, something beyond his reach. Something he didn't want to get involved with, a route he would refuse to take.

"WHO DID YOU SAY THEY SENT?" the wide-eyed security guard said that night as he stood next to the Red-Collar in the kitchen.

"Blythe Harrell," he confirmed.

"Bloody hell."

"Exactly."

"Didn't he sign the warrant that did away with his first wife for speaking out against the System?"

The Red-Collar looked around instantly. He did not know if anyone could hear them.

"You didn't hear that from me," he said.

9

The beginning of every month always brought people together. In a time when buildings were functional, space tight, the need for efficiency always crucial, these rules were never applied to the venue that so many were heading towards that morning.

The Colosseum: something every province around the world now had, host of all World Council formalities, and central to the Celebration Day events taking place around the world that day.

The elite came in their droves. The day reminded them all of what they had built, of what they were a part of. While attendance was not compulsory, they would notice anyone missing. These Red-Collars remained high up, in the best seats, away from those others present, the White-Collars each handing over their working-era outfits and ready to don the Gold of freedom.

As always, for a few Reds, this day would also see them making that change, as they reached the age where they too swapped one colour for another, though perhaps the change in lifestyle would be less dramatic for them, wealthy already, with never a struggle in life.

The end of life became the only thing that everyone had in common, though today was not about death, but life. Life to the fullest. It was the start of another Jubilee Year for those attending in the crowd below, and they gathered in that colossal venue to mark the occasion.

Herbert Bradley, teacher until the day before and now starting his last year, moved forward with the crowds as they all left the train station. The walk to the Colosseum was another half-mile, a straight run from the platform, the towering columns and circular roof rising into the sky before them. For many, it would be the only time they would have been inside the building. For some, the first time they'd even been close.

Loudspeakers along the avenue encouraged them forward, celebrating their triumph in life and calling them forward to their bright future. For so many present in that crowd, they would get the riches for that last year that their years of toil could never reach.

Groups of Black-Collars clung to the edges of the avenue, often saluting the passing crowd. They weren't there as a barrier, nor was there much need to provide protection. These people were not at any threat, not there, not so close to the centre of power.

Herbert wondered what these officers might do if he veered off the avenue. Would they move towards him and stop him? Would they become aggressive? Might the crowd ask what he was doing? He took in the faces of those in the same boat as he was and saw only excitement all around him.

It made him sick.

He pressed forward, the group perhaps in the thousands, many no doubt coming a long distance to be there that morning. He would have given anything to be in the classroom as usual, to carry on teaching for years to come. However, that option was not available anymore.

Music blasted from the roof of the giant building they continually moved closer to with every step, an instrumental number, their footsteps falling in time with the beat the nearer they drew. The crowd grew larger still, other groups perhaps waiting already, other stations bringing people in from different sectors. A mass of humanity, all healthy, all well. All dead twelve months from then, that very day in fact. There would be no such ceremony then, not on this scale. Not with this fanfare, even while they would fulfil their duty. Do the right thing.

Herbert doubted they would refer to that in the speeches that followed. Today was not about the end. It was the beginning of a fresh adventure, a final one, like nothing else they'd known before, they promised. The System made great boasts.

The crowds continued to mill around, though not long after Herbert and his group reached the shadow in front of the entrance, the doors opened, the music increased and the mass of bodies filtered through into the vast arena.

As Herbert finally made it in through the doors, his mouth dropped open, as did those around him. The view was spectacular. No picture existed of such a day, no-one who had experienced it ever talking about it. Herbert would understand why that was later, when the instruction came not to spoil it for others. He assumed some spoke, perhaps to loved ones.

Herbert glanced upwards, towards the oval roof open high above them, the blue sky visible directly over their heads. Underneath the roof sat the rows of seating, tens of thousands of faces peering down towards them, as if they were Olympians, this the Games.

Who these people were Herbert could not tell, they were too far away. Why they watched such a thing he didn't know either.

In the centre of the field, at the far end, a tall tower rose, the colours that hung around it and the flags that blew in the gentle breeze that of the World Council. A podium waited, empty for the time being, though soon a figure appeared, the large screens relaying his face. A face they all knew. The Commander of their province.

The crowd continued to fill out the space, the appearance of the Commander enough to send an excited murmur around the expectant audience.

At ground level, inside and circling the entire arena, there were booths. Perhaps two hundred, at least. Pictures and adverts spoke of their meaning, these the options and adventures that might await, these sellers no doubt there to entice and inform. Herbert had read about the options available to anyone in their Jubilee Year. They were growing by the year.

The swell of people pressed forward, closing the gap between them and the platform at the base of the podium from where the Commander would address them. A semi-circle formed, thirty feet away from the base of the column, from where people looked upwards.

The music died away, the man himself moving towards the microphone, his voice carried to every corner of the Colosseum as he spoke his first words.

"Welcome to your Celebration Day!" he boomed, a roar of delight going up, starting high above, and as if caught like a virus, quickly spreading to those on the ground. Herbert copied their actions, raising his hands into the air, though he voiced nothing. After a minute the public outburst died away, the Commander, smile embedded on his face, stepping back towards the microphone.

"It is truly a day to celebrate. A day to cherish, a day like no other. Before you leave this monument to human engineering this morning, you will have everything you need to live the most lavish year of your long lives," he said.

Herbert couldn't help feel that so many others had received more years than the System had afforded him. He'd spotted, however, several in the crowd, easily younger than he was. There were people with it worse than he had, that much was clear.

"Today you step into your destiny," the Commander continued. "Today you give back your uniform that you came here with," unable to name a colour of the collar, as there would be White, Black and Red-Collars present. "In its place, you'll each receive the honour of your Gold-Collar, an item of immense importance, of fundamental beauty. It will open doors you could never access before, I promise you. Wear it with pride. Wear it with honour. Wear it with freedom. You are people of esteem, your path before you a journey that many have taken before, and one which we will all take one day. I myself, far from a young man, will step into this great honour in less than two years, my successor giving this speech, my shoulders rubbing shoulders with people in your position. I will also stand where you are and look up to the faces above. This audience that is here to celebrate and honour you, this crowd here to acknowledge that what you are all doing is noble, is right, is selfless.

"For centuries this planet struggled. An ageing population, a changing demographic. When families had only one or two children, we ran out of carers. The cost to the planet was vast. For a time we turned to machines, robotic carers who might take the place of humans, but these too failed to meet the need. Economies collapsed, the burden thrown onto the surviving relatives, old people trapped in bodies and minds which no longer worked. Kept alive by drugs and medical advances, but no longer living. No longer truly alive. Just burdens to both society and more crucially their families. And then the burden transferred to the grandchildren, their parents and grandparents struggling, needing care, needing help.

"Our founders saw sense. Nobody was flourishing, nobody was free. The strain became too much, the burden unbearable. They made a move, took control of the situation, put a new System in place.

"We know what followed wasn't easy. We all know our history and the struggle that threatened to get out of control. But our founders prevailed. They won through, taking back control of our destiny. The first protocol ushered in the New World Council, and we have never been better off."

A roar from the stands erupted on cue at that remark.

"We have never been healthier."

Another roar.

"We have never had so much freedom."

Roar.

"Never have we controlled our own destinies as we do now."

Roar. It was filtering down to those on the ground, people catching on to the behaviour, caught up in the euphoria coming from the heavens above, people in the crowd cheering every phrase too.

"No longer do we have to struggle with the strain of looking after the frail."

Roar.

"No longer does society waste money treating the terminally ill."

Roar.

"We are free to decide our own destiny."

Roar.

"Free from the unexpected. Free from even the fear of death."

The crowd had now become electric, barely silent between each wave of hysteria, which pulsed through the mass like an electric charge. Herbert stood caught in its field, his body resounding with every wave, like a dancer in the middle of a rave.

The Commander paused this time to allow silence to settle in, his face beaming with delight to his audience. He pressed closer to the microphone again: the crowd obliged.

"What our founders achieved was to change our world forever. Every human being with a purpose, everyone with a job for life if they wanted it, and if not, then an alternative career path could be found. Purpose, employment, income. No longer did we need the financial drain of looking after the elderly. No longer were our healthcare systems around the world so different, so stretched, and yet, whatever the system in place, the cost of old age was always the same. With the medical breakthroughs in the early years and the signing of the most important protocols in our history, we entered this age of enlightenment. This age of freedom. We dated the first babies eighty-two years ago this coming anniversary."

Another tremendous roar, this one taking several minutes to simmer down.

"As we all know, there is not a single person alive today who doesn't know when their time is up. You stand before this distinguished audience as heroes, men and women stepping into this glorious reward, determined to continue the great legacy that our forebears carved out for us. Determined to live the best life possible, with abundant resources. Many of you might use what we will give you today to help those around you, something that is noble and good. However, do not forget to live exuberantly. You have worked your entire adult lives for this privilege. Your sons and daughters want for nothing, each certain of a Golden send off themselves. There is no need to leave your wealth unspent. Around you this morning, in the booths of only the best firms available, you each have the world at your feet. These experts will help you plan your adventure. They will show you the technologies you might not know about, the trips you could only have dreamed of, and the opportunities only now available to each of you as a Gold-Collar.

"Speaking of which, you will find behind me, at the north end of this splendid arena, our wardrobes. Before you leave today, you will have the honour to hand over your current shirts and receive your new ones."

Each person would receive two shirts. They could purchase additional ones if they wished.

"You will also each be assigned an advisor. I implore you to speak with them, if not today––and you probably won't all have time to do that, given the crowd––then within the next few days. They will help you manage this year. There are so many things you can do with little cost, but they are here for your benefit. They are here to make sure your money lasts, and to help you put it to good use. They do this all the time, and this month they are solely at your disposal. Use their wisdom. They are worth the investment."

He paused at that, Herbert glancing over to the booths nearest him, where these experts stood. They each wore a Red-Collar, as did many of the people in the experience booths, those offering trips and gadgets. He couldn't see beyond the forty nearest him, each person smiling at him as they looked his way. Ever the face of openness. Very much the face of the System.

All there for the money these people were about to receive.

"We will send you your money as you leave the Colosseum today," he confirmed. Herbert had read how that worked, the imbedded chip in each person informing the System who was there. Once they passed the sensor, their Gold-Collar visible, an electronic payment for one million units would be sent automatically to their personal account. It would arrive before they even reached the train station. The standardised average monthly wage stood at four thousand units. Even the best-paying jobs might only offer treble that. This money would give them a freedom they had never achieved before, those who had been only White-Collars, at least. For the elite, they had their own income streams, family money that sat in vast banks accruing interest all the while. More than they would ever need. The million they might receive that day just adding to the tens of millions already showing in their balances.

"I wish you the best year imaginable," he concluded, as the speech he gave every month drew to its end. "You now have plenty of time to explore the options before you. Make this year the best yet!" and he stepped away from the podium, a polite applause coming from the seats above, the crowd below already starting to move off to the various booths. Herbert spotted a large crowd making for the wardrobes, perhaps wanting to avoid the rush later. He spotted others heading straight towards the experts, both those offering experiences and those offering advice, the queue for which soon developed.

He didn't move for the time being, taking in the surrounding scene, the movement of people, the Commander as he slowly navigated his way from the speaking area. High above, people got up from their seats, the show over. He noticed several making for the stairs that led down to the edges of the arena, the same people soon spotted emerging through doors, manning booths further around. So these spectators were also there to present options.

Soon it was only Herbert standing in the field. He moved off to the side, circling around the backs of the crowds that were six or seven deep as they huddled around each booth. There was a person speaking to the crowd from the booth, giving their brief presentation, drawing in their audience. Herbert soon noticed his peers walking around with printed material, no doubt handed this from each visit, each expert there to sell their wares.

This was nothing but a trade show, those present the latest customers. Herbert couldn't believe what he was seeing.

Coming alongside the booth of advisors, Herbert could hear the discussions, people asking questions, all accepting the viewpoint that they would get more out of taking these people's advice than otherwise.

The fee for using their service was two-thousand units, payable within a week, convenient when these new customers would all be receiving their money that day. Two thousand felt a small price to pay for what they could get out of it. Herbert had heard several of these experts promise that, on average, their clients saved anywhere from twenty-thousand units a year by working with them. With each advisor now likely to pick up thirty or forty new clients that day, Herbert couldn't help but see they were the real winners. And they would earn that money every thirty days, with another batch of people starting their Jubilee Year at the beginning of the following month.

He decided against using an advisor. Herbert didn't want to play into their hands. He felt more than capable of handling his own budget.

HERBERT STOOD in a queue as he waited for his new clothing. Something that would open doors for him.

He couldn't have cared less. He didn't want to be there, he knew that. It wasn't the place; it was what it all represented. What they represented, these Red-Collars, their corporate smiles, their sideways compliments.

The System was giving away well over a billion units that day. Herbert couldn't escape the thought that this entire show existed to help them all claw back as much of the money as they could, as quickly as possible. Their money. The money these White-Collars had worked their entire lives for, money they were getting for saving the world, money not needed to fund nursing homes, to train care-givers, to cover longterm treatment plans. Money freed up from all that, lavishly splashed upon those now receiving their Gold-Collar, and yet the hand that offered it seemed only partially willing to let go. The other hand was there to grab it back again, like a cruel magician.

Here's your money, but I don't really want to give you that. And they snatched it back again, though this was no theft. Herbert looked around at his peers as he drew nearer the front of the queue. This crowd was willingly handing over control of their money. If not to the advisors—*what's two percent of your new fortune, anyway?*—then on the experiences themselves. Space flights, even a few nights on the International Space Station. Lunches in Paris, dinners in Milan. Desert adventures in Dubai, or lavish spas in the Far East. If you really wanted to see the world, then the thousand-unit-per-day world cruise would do that for you, taking ten of your allotted twelve months, and visiting every continent and corner of the world while indulging in the most luxury known to mankind. The queue for that booth was several hundred metres long.

Herbert didn't fancy that long at sea.

Car sellers were there in force, the most expensive option Herbert had noticed selling bespoke versions of the latest in the range, the cost an easy million units and some, yet still there were people standing there. Herbert knew these people must have vast wealth already. He spotted at least one person signing an agreement, having his photograph taken as if he'd won the lottery.

Herbert couldn't escape the fact that all around him, people seemed happy. And he understood why. He'd taught this to his students down the years, as all teachers had. This was the right thing to do. This was noble, proper. Yet here he was, and it didn't feel any of those things now.

It felt staged, false and deceiving. He didn't know why.

"Mr Bradley?" a voice called from in front of him, Herbert instinctively glancing towards the sound, seeing the smiling face of one man from behind his booth. Herbert recognised him immediately as one of his former students, perhaps from a decade before. He had expected there might be some there. Three had become Red-Collars, this man being one of them.

"Well, isn't this a surprise," Herbert said, feigning delight at the unexpected encounter.

"I heard you would be here," the man beamed.

"Did you now," Herbert smiled, no idea how a former pupil should know that his former teacher would be there.

The man looked with pride around the place. "Quite a sight, isn't it," he mused.

"It is," Herbert said.

"Have you seen the other two yet?" he asked. Herbert was initially unclear though soon he understood. All three of his former students who had become Red-Collars were there somewhere in the throng, the three evidently talking with each other.

"No," Herbert said.

"Look out for them," he said. Herbert glanced at the information on offer at the booth, which drew the other man's focus. "Care for a top of the range hot tub for home, sir?"

"Not sure I have the space," Herbert smiled, politely. Unless these things could sit on a small sloping roof without losing their contents, he didn't see where he could put one.

The man smiled. "I get this all the time. Stop thinking like that. You can upgrade," he said.

"Upgrade?" Herbert wasn't sure what a better hot tub could do to change the situation. "I still don't have the space."

"I'm not talking about my product. Upgrade your house."

"Move, you mean?" Herbert asked, not at all keen on the idea.

"Absolutely! Why not! You can afford to live anywhere now," he beamed, too cheerful for how Herbert felt about any of it. And there were areas where even a million in cash wouldn't be enough for just a few square metres. "Speak to some guys in real estate. It'll amaze you what's out there."

The idea sounded ludicrous. They all had twelve months to live. What was the point of spending so much time on moving house? Perhaps the cruise around the world wasn't such a bad idea.

"The point is, sir, you have options now."

"Options?"

"Yes," he beamed, that same salesman's smile he seemed to wear like a mask. His speech was smooth, polished, persuasive. University had evidently put that into him; Herbert couldn't remember the man speaking like that when he had taught him, though that was a while ago. He knew the family always had money. All three former students who had since become Red-Collars came from wealth.

For years Herbert had taught everything the System instructed him to teach, instilling in his students a pride in what they were doing. Encouraging them along in their thinking, something begun long before they reached his classes, the groundwork laid in their first years of school. He'd heard now that even kindergartens taught it. The moral choice. The noble cause.

What a mockery all that felt this morning, surrounded by the circus, confronted with the reality. The crowning of life, the supposed pinnacle of existence. Here he stood, with unlimited options, wealth assured. Yet he had never felt poorer.

10

B lythe sat in his office, the same cup of coffee by his side, the drink long since cold, untouched. He'd not moved in an hour, lost in thought and quiet prayer---even as a man who represented a System that said it had replaced God. They were the gods now, even able to determine when everybody died.

Yet, he prayed.

The couple had spoken little the previous evening, the sudden news of their unborn child's condition a shock; the fact that their daughter was otherwise healthy was no comfort. As things stood, their little one had a death sentence awaiting her.

Blythe had had a phone call that morning, a courtesy call he was told. They knew. Someone did, anyway. The call had been from someone close, a supporter at that. A man Blythe looked up to and a man guiding his young protege all the way to the very top. This man didn't want his project with Blythe scuppered by some genetically faulty offspring.

He'd strongly suggested the couple kill the foetus.

Blythe said they would not do that. He saw the logic, had no moral reasons against it. However, his wife had always wanted a daughter. They had wondered if they couldn't have children. Though she was young and healthy, he wasn't so young anymore. They'd been trying for years before the surprising news of this pregnancy. They might not get a second chance, and learning that this one was a daughter, his wife was adamant. An abortion was off the table.

The conversation had then moved on quickly, the caller apparently in the know about their unwillingness to abort. The news hadn't fazed him.

"Then do away with the mother," the man suggested.

"I can't," Blythe said. He loved her.

"We both know that's not entirely accurate," the caller said. He was referring to a previous occasion when Blythe had turned to him for help. Blythe's first wife had become outspoken and uncontrollable. She'd refused to allow her sons to go into the military. White-Collar graft was respectable work. She didn't want them poisoned by the System, she'd seen what it had done to her husband.

She'd not come from Red-Collar stock, the marriage one of love, of lust in the early days. How quickly that wall of affection had fallen. She'd become a liability. One night she never came home from a run in the woods.

Blythe acted the part of bereaved husband, taking his place at the funeral, wearing black and lowering his head, but there were no tears. No sense of loss. How quickly things carried on as before, the man back into his stride.

His sons were enrolled into military training seven days after they buried their mother. Blythe stood as a proud father that day, no hint from the happy smiles captured for posterity's sake of what he might have been going through. The ceremony had been lavish, his two sons switching from their White-Collars when handed their new uniforms, complete with the prestige that a Black-Collar came with.

After Blythe's brief comment the morning's telephone call had gone quiet for a while. Was the caller threatening him? The System knew. They had helped to arrange the death of his first wife. But outside of the inner core of the System, Blythe was only a good man, mourning in his own way the tragic loss of his wife, and doing the best for his sons. His reputation hung on such a viewpoint, the man of upstanding moral fibre. A man of fine legacy and a third generation Red-Collar.

Would his actions come out if he didn't do what they were asking? Could he even go there? It was different now. He loved his wife, and she now carried their child.

"I don't like the way this conversation is going," Blythe warned.

"I'm not threatening to use this against you," the caller said.

"Like hell you're not!" Blythe stabbed back. He knew a threat when he heard one. He'd used similar tactics himself over the years. He could see his current predicament made him a prime target for manipulation. It wasn't a position to which he was accustomed.

"I'm not, believe me," the caller assured him. "I'm just looking out for your prospects."

The man meant Blythe's chance of becoming the Supreme Commander, a role, if he were to believe what his wife had told him, for which he found himself on the final three-person shortlist. A role others had hinted was his to lose.

Was he losing it by taking his current stand?

"My prospects," Blythe repeated, drawing it out.

"You know exactly what I mean." The caller left it at that.

"Losing my wife is not an option," Blythe said, determinedly.

"That might not be your call, ultimately."

Blythe swore. "If they lay one finger on her, I warn you!" he spat. The caller was not roused by this threat, though it pleased him to have provoked such a response.

"Calm down, Blythe," he said, warmly. "I've got your back, remember?"

It didn't feel like that at this moment.

"Look, there's another option," Blythe said, the caller letting out a snort, though staying silent. A third way might just save them all a little more bloodshed.

"Go on," he eventually said.

Blythe explained what he had in mind.

Nearly an hour later, the coffee long forgotten, Blythe hadn't moved from his spot. That call had committed him to a path, forcing

him to take a route, to decide right there which way he would
this one. It was that or either of the first two options. He had to ti
third.

He'd read the entire booklet. It only painted the picture from the
medical side, a bleak one at that. Any publication on these newer
diseases had to vilify the condition. Anything that the System
couldn't control became the enemy. This was one of the latest six
enemies that had defied modern medicine. The booklet confirmed
no cure existed, with medical research––by that it meant World
Council research, for which this was their leading journal––not able
to give a cause, nor did they understand from where it came. It was
only partially genetic, in that if somebody had it, they might pass it
on. But it had only appeared in the last few decades. Nobody had
had it when the Protocols were first written, when science had
defeated the last of the ills and a healthy, clean new era had been
heralded. Protocol twenty-six had been set into law only weeks after,
every condition now tracked and known. They could predict life
expectancy to the month, perhaps to the week. A dating system
allowed scientists to predict the peak year, the final one before
health might then deteriorate, giving humanity the freedom to have
everything, to live to the maximum, before stepping aside, their time
over.

The new diseases that appeared had no genetic roots in any of the
previously known killers. It still mystified the scientific world. The
booklet offered little hope. It stated on its last page that this condition, the most serious of these recent waves of diseases, would have a
big impact on dating. If other factors were present––nowhere was
there a written list of what these were, though Blythe knew them
all––then it would limit the disease carrier to forty years, with the
expressed suggestion that the individual never had offspring
themselves.

Education backed up these ideas. Nobody was to marry someone
with such an early date. Having a child that would carry a disease
was inhumane, unethical, wrong. Nobody questioned what made it
wrong, nor asked why. Why was it unethical? Who set the ethics? The

schooling system was excellent at instilling this message in the young minds they educated.

Blythe turned to his device, the report there from the day before, from the man he'd seen at the hospital. He pored over every page, this report not talking of the limitations, the dangers, but talking of the research, and the sole researcher said to be making significant progress. The woman in question had told the couple when confronted that a cure within-life was easily possible.

The System had not taken this information into account, as Blythe knew. The researcher was outside of their control, a quick check showed that the reason she was not employed in an official System-sponsored facility was through no fault of hers but because of a relative. Blythe finished reading the entire report, finally stretching, leaving the mug of coffee where it sat, a plan of action forming in his mind.

This researcher was the key to their child's survival. He would make sure she got the funding needed to speed up the process, covering more ground in the next seven months than the years that had gone before them. If a within-life cure was announced during that period and before the birth of their daughter, the condition would be removed from the list of diseases. It would free their other-wise healthy daughter from this death sentence, the medication available to eradicate the disease from her body. She would have a long life, the family of outstanding stock. Seventy years or more would await her, wealth and fortune too. She would want for nothing, and if the child's father were to become the next Supreme Commander, she would be untouchable.

Blythe wanted a shower, having risen early that morning, spending time in the garden before locking himself in the office. Now he needed freedom from those four walls, the conversations racing through his head. What he'd just read had given him hope. He needed to freshen up, to wake up and come back and understand everything he could. A man in his position had plenty of power, plenty of opportunity to pull the strings, to move things in his favour. He knew perfectly well how to play the System. Every Red-Collar did.

It was how they prospered, how they stayed on top, unchallenged, unthreatened. Elite. *The elite ones.* The odds were always stacked in their favour, the world playing by their rules. Wealth won. It always had, and it always would. Their fundamental challenge was educating the world to be blind to this, to believe they all had the same chance. Yet the rich remained rich, the poor only ever that, and they would allow nobody from a disadvantaged background to become a Red, despite what the System would have them believe.

Hope had to be the carrot; but whoever heard of the donkey ever reaching forward and getting that carrot?

DRESSED NOW for the day ahead, Blythe had taken his mug down to the kitchen. He needed an actual drink, one that he would consume this time.

"How are you?" he asked, his wife pottering around, otherwise oblivious to his presence.

"Fine, I guess."

He knew she had slept as badly as he had, both minds no doubt going over the same things the previous night. Trying to process the news, trying to work out what to do. Trying to find a way out of this hole they'd fallen into.

"Look, I think I've found a way through," he said, keen to offer her the same hope he'd now been telling himself existed. Her immediate attention told him she was desperate to hear anything. He filled her in on what he knew for now. He needed to spend some time on the computer to dig deeper. He promised his wife that he would do everything within his power. They embraced, and she handed him his coffee as he strode back off upstairs, a smile now on her face, tears of joy running down her cheeks.

He left the study door open this time. She wouldn't disturb him, he knew that. He liked the extra sunlight offered from the bedroom, too. He drank half his coffee before sitting down, his mind getting into gear, working through his next moves.

He started by reading what there was on the researcher. It listed her recent life, various comings and goings, as much as the System knew about her, usually when she made a payment for something, entered an official building, that kind of thing.

A recent entry brought him up short, a memory triggered. Blythe frantically scrolled through his messages, scanning for the one he knew would have come in that morning. He located the message, opening up the file it contained with its long list of names present. And included on that list was this same researcher.

He swore.

11

———

Kate sat at her breakfast table earlier than usual the following morning. She wanted to get into work for at least a few hours, before heading to the airport.

She scanned through the news for confirmation of any further air disasters. She swore under her breath at the lack of fresh results, swore aloud at her brother for being such a dick, swore at her world which had now forced her into such a situation.

"It'll be okay," she told herself, though she was never one to take undue risks. She'd looked up all flights leaving the city for the rest of that month. There were hundreds. The odds were still good, even if decreasing all the time.

She knew one of these flights would not make it. It wasn't a might-not, or a perhaps-it-would-not. She knew. One plane which took off from her airport would crash that month. One had crashed every year without fail for the last thirty years.

There had not been a downed aircraft so far that year. There were four days to go, the options down to triple digits. One would be the unlucky flight. She'd been driving everywhere for years, her brother first telling her about his thoughts——some would say drug-induced fantasies——about a grand conspiracy. She'd been able to dismiss most of his ideas, but this one had stuck. She'd been watching, the subsequent years always bringing one news story about an air disaster, most often just one plane dropping from the sky. Five years back, two planes hit midair––that was a first.

People now heralded air travel as safer than ever, yet crashes still happened. In a time that had cured so many illnesses and diseases, a time that had almost completely cured unexpected death––people still died suddenly, though this was becoming increasingly rare––it seems safely transporting a few hundred people at a time from one place to another via a flight was still a bridge too far.

Joe had nearly convinced her of some bigger plot, before he moved onto other things. Seeing risks that weren't there. Kate didn't even know if her brother still believed what he had said about flying. If he did, perhaps he wouldn't have been such an idiot and made it necessary for her to fly like she would later? However, it had stuck with Kate. Of all the things that could have taken root, this had been the one. Kate had marked down every single crash for the last thirty years. One year, one crash. No survivors. Sometimes it was several hundred––the most being the midair collision which had killed all seven hundred and forty-eight passengers and crew members––the least cost in human life being two hundred and six.

There seemed no pattern. Most crashes happened in wintertime, that was clear, but not all. Several mid-summer accidents had broken the pattern. December had been the month of most occurrences, though not once in the last nine years. Except so far that year, there was yet to be a crash.

She cursed her situation once again.

Perhaps it was nothing, merely circumstance? Perhaps they were getting safer? Crashes aside––other countries had a similar record–– air travel was much safer than it had been decades ago. In the early days, the first part of the century, crashes were far more common. Now they were minimal. The air industry was proud of its record.

She knew they had to say that. Yet could anywhere be completely safe? It still made flights a risk, kept people alert.

Kate washed up her one cup and plate, her toast covered in strawberry jam that morning, her not uncommon choice of breakfast food. She had packed a small bag, though she would buy the essentials when at her mother's.

Ten minutes later Kate was out of the door, back behind the wheel. She didn't have to drive it, in fact she had never driven the thing, wasn't sure it had an override code, even as an option on this model of car. She was soon on her way to work. Hers was the fifth car in the carpark, each taking the spot they regularly used, ever the people of habit.

A different security man greeted her on the way in, the man polite, less with the small talk. Kate nodded and smiled and moved to her lab. Three others were in already, their group nearly at full strength, though they worked independently. Her imminent absence was not about to require them to pick up the slack.

"I need to have a word," Kate said, once she'd donned her lab coat, protective glasses hanging on a string around her neck. Her boss glanced up, walking into his office, Kate following him in immediately.

"Everything okay?" he asked, as Kate closed the door gently behind her before answering.

"It's my brother," she said.

"I see." He'd been the only person she had mentioned things to in the past, when she'd needed time off. She trusted him. He had her back. "How long do you need?"

"I'm on a flight later today," she confirmed.

"You're flying?" He knew she didn't fly, though she'd never explained why.

"No option," she said.

"I see," he said, a common response. "That bad this time?" Flying made the trip more manageable. She might even be back by the end of the week.

"It's hard to tell. My mother thinks so."

"Will you stay for New Year?"

"Yes," she said. She wouldn't double her odds by taking a return flight that same month. A new year and things transformed. There had never been two crashes less than a few months apart.

"Thanks for letting me know. You know you have my blessing. Come and go as you please. Only stay safe." She was good at what she did, and he was grateful to have her on the team. They all were.

She closed her eyes and bowed her head in silent thanks, turning without another word, not wanting to take up more of his time, nor give her colleagues more reason to wonder what the matter was. They would soon know she was going, that much would make sense. She trusted they didn't know why. She returned to her station.

At lunch Kate left the building, the trip to the airport about the same distance as to home, though the roads were faster. She would be there in thirty minutes. That gave her an hour to get to the gate.

"Mum, I'm heading to the airport," Kate called from the car, her mother answering after only two rings.

"I've not heard from him yet, but I'm trying," her mother confirmed.

"He didn't come home last night?" Kate asked, alarmed.

"He did, but left early. I wanted to catch him."

"Look, if he can't meet me, let me know. I'll pick up the message when I land and will get a cab from the airport."

"I'll meet you, love, don't worry," her mother said.

"You don't need to," Kate told her. She knew it wasn't easy for her mother to get out to the airport from home.

"I'm sure Joe will collect you," she said. Brothers were meant to do that kind of thing, right?

Kate ended the call. Her mother's words had done little to settle her nerves, but she hadn't expected them to either. She hadn't called for comfort; if Joe were okay again, she wouldn't bother to fly. The fact her mother hadn't spoken with him didn't tell her anything. She switched on the news, letting it read out the stories for the rest of the trip.

Kate cleared security seventy minutes before the scheduled time for take-off. Crowds swelled around her, Kate keeping to the side, away from the masses. Did they all not know the danger they might be in? She caught her thinking. It would help nobody to talk like that. She sounded more like her brother all the time.

She cursed him again under her breath for making her go through with this.

There were more children than she expected, their high-pitched voices perhaps rising above the general noise level more than most. Kate realised the school holidays would have started, these families either heading off somewhere on holiday or perhaps connecting with relatives, or on the way back from doing that.

Gold-Collars were visible, these wealthy few living out their last year, a jet-set mass. Children had their Blue-Collars, as always, and all the rest were White, like hers, save for a few Black-Collars dotted around the place. Kate wondered how the Red-Collars travelled, if not by air.

The large screens that hung above the waiting areas and shops showed her gate was to the right, a ten-minute walk with boarding starting in thirty minutes.

She had time for a coffee.

Kate meandered towards the gate, a fair choice of drinking options before her, the queues somewhat okay, though she would find one with fewer people. Children ran in and out of trolleys, playing tag or whatever it was they played now. Her brother Joe didn't have children, and neither did she. Kate knew very few people who had children. She'd forgotten how annoying and noisy they could be. She'd never had that maternal instinct the movies always suggested every woman got, eventually.

Several venues were exclusive, catering only for the Gold-Collars, their clients noticeably chirpy. Kate wondered how she would feel. She had years left. Perhaps she would be ready then? Perhaps the slower pace, the time to travel—though she wouldn't fly, she knew that. How far could she really get if she only drove everywhere? Most of them looked old to her. They sported tans that suggested sunshine, hinting at adventures they'd already experienced. With the beginning of a new month only days away, she figured for some of these people in front of her, this might be the last flight they would take.

She watched the faces for a while, standing in a queue only five deep, waiting her turn. Could she tell those just starting their year from those about to end it? And then what? What came after, if there was anything? The official view was that nothing came. Life was life and death was the end. The message had always been: *It's not the years in your life but the life in your years that counts.* A quote from a previous century, and while a former US President might have spoken those words, the world now lived them. They had formed the backdrop of nearly everything. These words had greeted her at the airport when she arrived, painted in large letters across the ceiling. Reminding people that it was quality, not length of life that mattered. *Live abundantly. Go wild. Travel. Enjoy.* However, do the honourable thing when your time comes. Don't be a burden. Nobody wants to struggle to the grave, becoming a strain on society, on those who love you. That wasn't care, that wasn't right. The Jubilee Year was there to reward everyone. Taken when you still had your health, giving you freedom that you'd never known before, offering the best year of your life.

"Ma'am?" the man behind the counter called again, Kate drawn back to the moment, her attention taken by the crowds of older people living out possibly their final days.

Kate stepped forward, ordering her coffee. Not another glance at the others. She went to find a seat nearby, ignoring the children, the planes through the windows beyond and the thoughts in her mind. She took two sips from her steaming coffee when her phone rang, robbing her of even a minute's silence, surrounded as she was by noise.

She pulled the device from her pocket, the number withheld.

"Yes?" Kate said, device to ear, coffee placed on the table in front of her. "Who is this?"

"Is that Katherine Vann?" the man's voice said, ignoring her question as to his identity.

"It is. Who's speaking?"

"A fan," is all he said.

"A fan?" She had no fans, and if this was some kind of sicko, she didn't want to speak to him a second longer.

"A fan of your work. Your research."

"How do you know about my research?" she asked. The voice wasn't anyone from work; few knew anything about her studies beyond the safety of where she spent most of her life. She'd yet to publish her findings, though her boss was excited. He might have mentioned something to somebody? That was possible. She'd never had someone call her about it before, however.

"That doesn't matter," he said. The accent was strange to her. English, though everyone spoke that now. It was crisp, which spoke of belonging to someone well educated. He had a natural sophistication to his tone which soothed the listener, begging them to hang onto every word.

"Well, I can't really speak for long. I have a flight to catch. Can we speak next week when I'm back in the office?" She worked hard to pronounce every word, defying her background.

"You're catching flight AB92?"

"Sorry?" She didn't know her flight number. He repeated the number, stating the destination. She knew that part, anyhow. She confirmed she was about to board.

"Don't get the flight," he said.

"Excuse me?"

"You heard me," he said.

"Can I ask why?"

"I need to see you. Today, at work."

"I'm sorry," she said, dismissively. Well spoken or otherwise, it wasn't his place to tell her what to do. She would be back in the office the following week. They could continue their conversation then. "I'm away from the office this week."

Flight number AB92 is now boarding at gate number twenty-six. The automated announcement rang out from the speakers high above her. Kate glanced across the concourse as people gathered at her gate.

Thankfully, it looked like no kids were on her flight. Small mercies there.

"You must not get on that flight," he urged, this time more force-fully, something in his tone connecting with a deep-rooted fear inside her.

"Why?"

He didn't answer.

"Why?" she repeated as if that were the reason he had not responded, standing up now, the coffee left on the table for the time being.

"You know why," he said, leaving it at that.

"What do you mean?" but the call ended, Kate glancing at her phone, the confirmation there. Her cover picture appeared a second later, a photo of her mother and brother standing next to a statue. Ahead of her at the gate, people were already boarding. There were no children, not even any Gold-Collars. Given the masses at the airport that morning, the contrast was stark.

Last call for flight AB92 rang out, eventually. Kate sat there finishing her coffee as the last of the passengers boarded, all the while pleading for a family or three to come scampering to the gate in a hurry, kids screaming, a baby or two crying their eyes out. Or the laughter of a group of older people, their Gold-Collars displayed proudly, as they talked in twos and threes about the adventures they'd had or the ones still awaiting them. Any of these and she would have stood, would have joined the last people, even against her better judgement, and boarded that aircraft.

This is a last call for Katherine Vann on flight AB92. Your flight is now ready to leave from gate twenty-six. Last call for Katherine Vann.

Kate didn't move, instead drawing her phone out, opening up the message settings. Her mother wouldn't have left from home yet. *Mum, I've missed the flight. Will get a later one when I can find a seat. Keep Joe safe and I'll see you as soon as. Kat.* She pressed send.

Five minutes later, she watched the plane taxi away from the gate. The cabin crew had shut the door leading to the plane a minute or two before with their last passenger deemed a no-show.

Her phone rang again. This time it was her mother.

"What's happened?" she asked.

"It's nothing, okay. I'll let you know what I've rearranged."

"Okay," she confirmed. "I'll see you soon, right?" She sounded nervous even asking.

"Yes," Kate assured her. "I promise."

The call ended, Kate dropping the phone back into her pocket as she stood, still trying to work out what to do, when it rang again. With a huff she reached for it, expecting it to be her mother once more, worrying about something else, though it was again an unknown number.

"Hello?"

"Well done," the same crisp voice from before said. "Go home for the night. You don't want to be at the airport today. There is a flight at eight in the morning which will work for you," and before she could speak, the call ended.

Against her better judgement, she walked back to her car and was travelling home within minutes. She checked the tickets, and sure enough there was a flight the following morning at eight. There were still a few seats left, meaning she wouldn't need to cancel her return flight home. She confirmed the ticket.

IT WAS all over the news when she arrived home an hour later, Kate rushing to the television.

"The flight, carrying three hundred and seventy-two passengers and crew, reported problems thirty minutes after take-off. At four-fifteen this afternoon, it vanished from radar screens. Aerial shots from our traffic helicopters show the extent of the devastation. Some viewers might find the following scenes disturbing," the reporter said, the feed switching from the studio to the onboard cameras, which swept over fields on top of which the plunging jet had evidently landed.

The ticker at the bottom of the screen ran the following message on a loop. *Flight AB92 has crashed shortly after takeoff, killing everyone onboard.*

Kate swore.

"Do we yet know anything about the cause of the crash?" the same voice in the studio spoke over the still roaming images of the debris field.

"Experts are on the scene and are locating the black box, the flight recorder, which will give them the state of the aircraft at the time of the crash. They have said this aircraft, while old, was serviced only last month, and was in excellent condition. This is the first time this model of aircraft has ever come down and experts have said there is no need to feel alarmed. Flying remains safer than it has ever been, and while we are yet again at a scene of mass devastation, the authorities have promised a full investigation."

Kate had seen that through the years such investigations rarely seemed to draw many conclusions, and if there were safety concerns, these had never been made public. Perhaps they were being kept from general circulation?

"The airport remains closed for the rest of the day, causing travel chaos for many who were planning to set off for holidays at a busy time of the year," the studio-based reporter said, the camera back on her, the scenes from the crash site now ended. "With New Year just days away, authorities have promised to get things open again quickly, perhaps as soon as tomorrow."

The news moved onto another story, Kate switching it off at that point. She didn't know what to think. Getting to her brother now seemed more important than ever, not only to talk him out of doing something stupid—that still played on her mind—but even more crucial than that. He was right. He had to have been. That call from the stranger telling her not to board the plane. That man had known, whoever he was. He knew the plane was going down.

As yet, there was no mention of this being a terrorist attack. Such incidents were unheard of in the modern world. The Black-Collars would not allow even the chance. If it became apparent that human intervention caused this, Kate would know that her caller had been part of the plot. She would go to the authorities herself. Perhaps they might have the chance to trace the call, even if she didn't know the number?

Her mind raced. What if the crash was described as another tragic accident? What then?

12

B lythe sat in his luxuriant garden, on the bench his first wife had bought him for his thirtieth birthday. It needed a fresh coat of varnish, but apart from that, seemed to hold up well.

Footsteps along the gravel path leading from the house told him that his wife was coming his way, and she reached him moments later, sitting down next to him.

"They called to say you didn't go in today," she said, a mix between concern and puzzlement detectable in her tone. He had been out of the house for hours.

He said nothing.

"Blythe, this isn't like you, what's up?" She knew several things that it could be, the baby the most obvious. "Is it what we talked about?" She had been clear on her views regarding the scientist.

"I called her," he said.

"You did what?" and she stood, facing him.

"If she had got on that flight, our hope, the only hope of coming through this, would have been dashed."

The news that day had been of the latest plane crash.

She shook her head.

"What did you say to her? Did you tell her?"

"No," he snapped, as if he would have been that foolish, though he had done as much as that, he knew deep down. "I said she couldn't take the flight."

"She didn't ask you why?"

"She is afraid of flying," Blythe added, something he'd picked up in the notes.

"Afraid?" That didn't make it any clearer.

"It's her brother, the reason she's not already under Council control," Blythe said. "He filled her with doubt, told her about the crashes. She doesn't fly because I think she believes him." His wife stayed silent at that. There was nothing for her to say. Nothing good to say, anyway. Now this researcher knew for sure that whatever her brother had suspected, had foundation.

"Who is the brother?"

"A nobody. Off his head most of the time. It would seem on the edge, too. She was flying to talk sense into him. The woman's mother had called the day before, begging her to come and help. Terrified that this lowlife son of hers would finally kill himself."

"There must be more to him than that?" she asked.

"Perhaps," Blythe confessed. If the man suspected anything about the crashes, then somebody was speaking to him, feeding him these conspiracies. Gossip was unheard of amongst most people; they knew the consequences.

"So she took your word and didn't take the flight?" his wife asked, coming back to the unlikely scenario they'd reached earlier. "You must have said something."

"I didn't say it outright, okay," Blythe admitted, his wife already dreading what she might be about to hear. "When she asked me why, I just said *you know why.*"

"*You know why!* You said that to her, a woman with a conspiracy theorist for a brother?" He nodded. There was no hiding her shock. She swore. "And you're sure she wasn't still on that flight?"

"After what I'd told her?" he seemed surprised she had even asked. He'd checked the files, knew the details of what the scientist had decided. "She went home, as I suggested. Has a ticket booked on a flight in the morning." Blythe had arranged a complete communications tap on everything Kate Vann owned. "She's not told anyone yet that she should have been on that flight. Didn't even tell her office that she missed the outbound journey."

They'd still not discussed the wider implications. Somebody in their position, especially a man like her husband with so much to lose, couldn't get involved in anything like this. Shouldn't have said anything, opening the System up to minds unfit to understand the bigger picture. It put the entire Council at risk, if word got out. If this woman or her brother said anything, it would finish Blythe. Not only would it ruin his chances of ultimate power, it would ruin him too. They might even deem his actions treasonous and shoot him on the spot.

The fact they could both be together in the garden now meant the System didn't yet know, which was something. It seemed the scientist had said nothing, though Blythe's wife feared that would definitely change once the woman arrived to her mother's.

She sat back down, the pair in silence for a moment, each lost in their own thoughts.

"Do you think this scientist will make the breakthrough we need her to?" she asked.

He thought his actions showed he believed she could, given what he had just explained. "I think she is close, yes, and close enough for the System to get behind her with more money."

"But you said she wasn't under our control?"

"She's not," Blythe confirmed, knowing his wife meant Council control, to which the elite felt intrinsically connected. "I'll make the funds available, I have the authority."

"Will it attract attention?"

Nobody in their situation wanted that kind of scrutiny from the System.

"I think it's a perfectly natural move. We all want an end to these new diseases. It's natural that, given our news this week, I would look to speed up anything that would give us hope."

Red-Collars were nothing if not people who looked out for their own interests first. His actions were understandable within their world, even if he hoped no-one ever learned of the way he had gone about it all.

"I can see them buying that," she said. "Have they given you any advice regarding me?" She looked at him, knowing even if they had, he would likely not tell her. She knew what had happened with his first wife.

"I won't let anything happen to you," he said, and she believed him. For the sake of their unborn child, she would trust him. His actions that morning, wild and dangerous as she saw them, had been to protect the life in her womb. There would have been better options of containing the risk if he'd only been thinking about his position within the Council. She knew he was looking out for her.

That was not always enough, as they both knew.

"At the hospital, I didn't tell you on the day, but there was another family there who'd given birth to a son. He had the same condition as our daughter."

"You met with them?"

"No," he confirmed. "But I saw the mother through a window. She'd come looking for someone to speak to, I think. Stood there screaming at the mirror, demanding to see the man in charge." He paused. He didn't know how to express what he was feeling. He'd rarely felt like this: confusion, questioning everything for perhaps the first time.

"What is it?" she asked, placing a hand on his knee.

"This woman was no different from us, really. Not when it boils down to the fact that she just wants a full life for her son."

His wife looked away. There had always been a chasm between those with wealth and the rest of the world. It had never been something she dwelt on. Some people just had more than others. They were better than the rest, deserved what they had. It was what she had always known.

"It's how the world is," she said, removing her hand from his knee, looking at the tidy rose garden in the distance, the bushes cut back. They would be radiant come summertime. The pruning helped them grow. Life went on. From time to time, people had to know they were expendable, pruned for the greater good. For their good. Why her husband had been so foolish she still couldn't fathom.

"Is it though?"

She'd never heard him once question how the System ran things, knowing full well such words would be foolish. A failing to accept the obvious. A failing to see that what they did, they did out of necessity; it wasn't callous.

"I mean, take our situation," he began. "A few days before we find out about our daughter, this mother has given birth to a son with the same condition. She's been researching it for months. I only knew about this scientist because of the woman's report she filed with the System. Anyway, for them, it wasn't enough. We considered them unworthy, the research not seen in the right light. Their son will live with this verdict for his relatively brief life."

"It's how it goes!" his wife said.

"But it isn't. We get to choose. Now that we know, just days after this poor mother had her son dated––with our baby due seven months from now––we can make sure the research progresses. We can make sure our own child gets the years we want her to get."

"And you would benefit everyone in the future with this break-through," she said, as if pointing out a greater good that they should both be proud of, though seeing no fault in anything else.

"All because of our position," he stated.

"Darling, there have always been people who have and people who don't," she said, as if discussing a minor difference that tipped the scales marginally in their favour.

"It's wrong," he said, his wife turning as if he had sworn violently at her. They never used words like right and wrong. There was no wrong, only the honourable way forward, only the correct thing to do. Morality didn't feature in the System. There was no moral code, only their code. The System, controlled by a small few with a wider circle of wealthy people benefiting enough to keep it all moving. The mass of humanity kept under heavy watch, with firm control. Conditioned to believe in the greater good. Living in the wealth that the

Red-Collars allowed, striving for a wealth of their own. All heading for their own glorious retirement, which they saw as their reward for a hardworking life and their duty to the planet. The System had given them everything. Employment for life, medical breakthroughs and support if they should need it, and a rich future to allow every citizen the same opportunities in retirement.

They brainwashed them to see themselves as equals. Yes, there were different standards, but they all ended as equals. That was what mattered, they believed. Nobody could cheat death.

Blythe knew that to be rubbish, nothing but a mask which the System used to hide the truth from the rest of the population. He'd learned so much in recent years, things he'd not even told his wife. Things that had made him question it all for the first time in his life. He suddenly wasn't so blind to the injustice as he had been even a week ago.

"Be careful talking like that," she warned. Even in their own garden, it wasn't safe. Even for someone--perhaps especially for someone--predicted to be the next Supreme Commander, such talk could destroy their reputation in an instant. Friends would suddenly no longer call, colleagues turn away from you as you entered the room. Isolation would then lead to a rejection by all. The outspoken person seen as an outcast, a leper. Unsafe and unclean. Blythe had overseen the removal of several pieces of deadwood in his meteoric career, on his unchallenged rise to the very top.

"They aren't listening here," he said, somewhat confidently. He'd never given them reason to, something that might not remain the case for much longer. He knew that. He would have to be careful.

She paced a little around the grass in front of them, running her hands through the thick yew hedge, planted decades ago, now taller than she could see over.

"Will you call this scientist again?" she asked, caught between the feeling that it would be a reckless move and that without doing so, their little girl might not have a chance.

"I'm not sure I need to meet her, no," he said. "Her lab will get the funding, though."

"Will it be enough?"

"That, I must see," he said, the realisation that funding alone might well not be enough. He would have to make sure the research got heard, and that they presented the reports in enough time for it to clear every hurdle quickly. That would require a hands-on approach, something he could do. Their daughter's life depended on it. So did his career.

"And this brother?"

Blythe didn't respond immediately, instead joining his wife on the grass, the couple wandering around their garden for a little in silence. He knew the brother was a tougher situation. He could cause them all a lot of problems, particularly if the sister told him everything. Blythe knew there was no reason she wouldn't. His own reckless actions had given her an insight into how things worked. He'd given that to her. He hadn't had a choice.

"I'll have a team watch him," he confirmed after a moment's thought. They would report directly to him, the team unaware of who the man they were following was, or how it involved Blythe. They would follow orders, as always, and not ask questions.

13

Kate walked past the gate she'd been due to fly out from the day before, which remained empty and closed, perhaps as a sign of respect. If she had walked through that door, boarding that plane as she had intended, taking the seat assigned to her, she would now be dead. That much was clear.

Overnight, nothing new had come out regarding the reasons for the crash. There was no mention of human error or intervention, nothing said about terrorists taking over the plane or anything like that. Experts were reporting it as a mystery the last she heard, the television on early that morning though the need to leave for her flight meant she only caught a few minutes.

She gripped her coffee, there to see her through take off, though she had a renewed sense of calm that morning which hadn't been there the previous afternoon. She didn't feel scared, not now. Not after all that had happened.

The gate was busy, people seemingly unmoved by events from the previous day, determined to carry on as normal. Which is what always happened. Life moved on. What struck her immediately was the number of families around her, the airport as busy as ever. The cancellation of all the remaining flights from the previous day couldn't have helped matters. Now these families were taking the same flight as her. The earlier takeoff no doubt helped with this. Perhaps it was better children flew in the morning? But there had been plenty of children the previous day also, and they had seemed happy enough.

Kate spotted at least two groups with their Gold-Collars in the crowd at her gate.

As the plane taxied down the runway, preparing for takeoff, Kate sat in her seat, this time by the window, four rows from the back. Given that every seat was occupied on the flight, it seemed nobody had stayed away. She sipped her coffee slowly, glancing out of the window, as the plane first got into position and then, with the surge of the engines, raced along the runway. Soon they were soaring, the cabin crew already on their feet, offering drinks to those who wanted them.

As Kate stepped off the plane, her phone confirmed that both her brother and mother were there waiting for her. She'd not seen them for a while, work keeping her busy, their lives going in different directions. It appeared only her brother's mental state now warranted a return to her childhood city.

She spotted them before they saw her, Kate carving through the throng of people until finally standing in front of them.

"Hello dear," her mother said. She'd never been one to be overly affectionate.

Kate glanced at Joe, who offered to help her with the case.

"You doing okay, bro?" she asked. It was clear he wasn't—why would she be there otherwise?

"Fine," he replied, following his mother as they set off in search of wherever they'd left the car this time.

Kate sped up to draw level, the three walking in silence, mostly going with the throng towards the exit.

"Thanks for picking me up," she said, now alongside her brother.

"No worries," he said, adding. "It's nice to see you." He turned and smiled, their eyes meeting momentarily, though she soon saw that same look she'd seen in him so many times. Isolation, fear, terror, she'd never quite been able to place it.

"You too," she said. She meant it. They were all she had, as sad as that was. Them and her work. She actually couldn't wait to speak with Joe, though she would wait until it was just the two of them. Their mother would only call what Kate had to tell him conspiracy talk. She wouldn't approve of Kate egging him along with his delusions.

With lunch finished, Kate glanced at her mother, who seemed keen for the two siblings to have a good talk as soon as possible. She'd come to the end of her tether with her son. It was time his sister had a go at getting through to him.

"I'll do the dishes," their mother said, collecting the dirty plates together. It was her sign that Kate should suggest a walk or something to do with Joe. They both watched their mother move into the kitchen.

"Want to show me the vegetable patch?" Kate asked, well aware her brother would be eager for her to see it.

"Sure," and he stood, fully aware she didn't really care much about the carrots and lettuce he had grown that summer in the small back garden.

Two minutes later, they stood in silence. There was little to see.

"Mum's worried, you know," Kate said, moving the conversation in the direction both knew it needed to head. She wouldn't add that it terrified her too.

"She always is," he commented, which was partly true. He knew what he'd said to worry her this time, however. Enough to warrant a visit from Kate.

"You know what I mean."

Silence ensued for a moment, both allowing the air to fill their lungs, which was fresh, a threat of a snow shower soon.

"Look, I need to talk to you," Kate said, the change in tone dramatic. She glanced towards the kitchen window as she spoke, their backs to their mother. The window was closed. Their mother couldn't hear what the siblings were saying. Kate smiled at her mother before turning back. She was watching them, probably worried out of her mind.

"Go on," Joe said, resigned to another telling off.

"Did you hear about that crash yesterday?" she asked. It would surprise her if he hadn't, though in his state of mind, perhaps there were more pressing things going on.

"One crash a year, just like I told you," he smiled, the first inkling that he still held to the same idea that he'd shared with her over a decade before.

"I should have been on that flight," Kate said. Joe turned towards her at that.

"For real?"

She nodded.

"Bloody hell," he said. He shook his head in disbelief. He'd never come across anyone who had lost someone in a crash. "That was bloody lucky you missed it then," he laughed. Of all the things he'd come across recently, that took the prize.

"It wasn't luck," she told him, her voice low.

"Come again?"

"Somebody called me," she said, desperate to tell someone what she knew. "A man. It was minutes before boarding. I was there, at the gate. Had my ticket. Somebody knew, Joe."

"He told you the plane was going to crash?"

"Of course not!" she said, looking her brother in the face, shocked he could think that if she'd known such a thing, she could have done nothing about it.

"Then what?"

"He told me not to get the flight. When I protested, he said I knew why."

"You knew why?" He didn't seem to follow. He doubted Kate knew that the flight was going to crash.

"Your theory," she said. Joe still didn't seem to get it. "Since you told me your little conspiracy theory, I've stopped flying."

"Really?"

It bothered Kate that he hadn't even noticed this, but she let it drop.

"I've been watching, too. Every year without fail there is a crash. One crash. Thirty years and counting now."

"And?" He knew that much.

"And somebody didn't want me to board that flight because they already knew it would not make it."

Joe nodded.

"You believe me now," he said, turning to face his sister. "You believe what I meant about this secret world that exists around us?"

"Joe, I'm not saying I believe all that, but this I know. I should be dead. Had I boarded that plane as I intended to, you would both be receiving news of my death this morning."

"And compensation," he pointed out, though why he did, she wasn't certain. Payouts in these situations were often generous, reportedly. "I'm glad you made it though," as if realising how that might have sounded.

"I'm glad too," she said.

"So who warned you?"

"I don't know. It was a stranger, an unknown number. I was at the airport."

"You took a stranger's advice?"

"He was very convincing," she said. "Knew what he was talking about, as we now realise too, I should add."

"Okay," he said, getting the point. "So what else did he say?"

"Not a lot. Said something about being a fan of my research."

"Your research?"

She couldn't believe it. She must have told them half a dozen times already what she did for a living.

"At the lab," she said. No point in elaborating now. "He knew what I did," which was evidently more than her own brother. "He told me not to fly, told me to go home for the night and said I could catch the flight that I did this morning. I'd booked the ticket before I even heard about the crash."

He considered all this for a moment, his body demanding an illegal substance or three, but his mind required clarity for the time being.

"Was this man somebody you work with?" he asked, thinking quickly.

"Not anyone I know, no," she confirmed. She'd gone over the same thought herself the night before, running through the list of people who worked at her building—which wasn't long—and knowing it wasn't any of them. "I think he's on the inside." It was a hunch she'd settled on as she dropped off to sleep the previous night.

"In the System?" he quizzed.

"Possibly a Red-Collar, even," she said, partly in awe at the thought, partly in disgust. The Red-Collars were supposed to be the elite, people of renown, looking out for and sustaining the System.

"You spoke with a Red?" He'd not come across anybody who had. They didn't live anywhere near his part of the world, that much was clear.

"It's my best guess," she said. "He sounded different, too. Well educated."

Joe nodded. He'd heard plenty of stories around the pubs at what these people got up to. Even Joe didn't believe them all, which was saying something.

"You'd better be careful," he warned.

"Why?" The man, whoever this stranger was, had just saved her life.

"If they find out you know, they'll come for you." Joe had heard plenty of rumours of those types of things happening. People asking the wrong question and suddenly they would vanish.

"But I know nothing," she pointed out.

He shook his head. "You know more than most. You know that plane crash was no accident," he said, which was true.

"So what do we do about it?" she asked, looking into her brother's eyes. She saw his old self there now, a man with purpose, with energy. With a reason to live.

"Let me think about that one," he said, heading back to the house. Kate smiled at her mother as they passed the window. She grinned back as Joe passed, her way of thanking her daughter for once again setting her son back on track.

14

E ducation within the System had been standardised the world over, intakes based on when somebody was born, each year graduating from the formal education in the year they turned eighteen.

That meant that some of those present that day were already adults and had been for several months. Others might only reach the age of adulthood a month after the ceremony. Twelve years of schooling had led them to this point, and their parents sat in the stands of the stadium as the four thousand school leavers streamed into their rows.

This would be the last day that they wore their Blue-Collared shirts that had seen them through their education. They would each get a White-Collar that day, most staying in that classification for their entire working life, a few moving in time into either or both of the other options available, if they got the opportunity.

The military band continued to play at the front of the stage, the endless rows of students drifting into position, before the delegation from the Council made their way onto the stage, the men and women looking with enthusiasm out onto the sea of young people.

"Ladies and Gentleman," the Red-Collar said, standing at the microphone and looking at the stands either side, "students and teachers," and he addressed the crowd in front of him now. "It is my great honour to welcome you here today to this most joyous and celebrated occasion. Another school year has come to a close and for you, the oldest groups in your respective schools, it is time for you to finish your education.

"You have all completed your exams, years of hard study culminating in yet more fantastic grades," he smiled. Students would receive their results together with their White-Collars at the end of this presentation. Career options and promotion hinged on what those results might be. "Today you start your new journey. A journey that will see you pay back into our society, see you rewarded for your diligent studies and see you make a living of your own and a life of opportunities. Who you each become is up to you. All can lead a fruitful life, that much we ensure, and a very prosperous retirement," he reminded them. With a group that large, there could be as much as thirty years' difference between dates from the latest to the earliest, even while they were all now the same age. Background really did count for a lot, the schools present covering various areas of the city, some wealthy, most struggling. Those wearing uniforms, which made them look more like an army than students, made up the private schools. The masses in smart clothes came from the state schools, each student obliged to buy the same blue hat that would join the other four thousand as they threw them in the air at the conclusion of the speech.

"Today marks an important turning point. As honoured members of our global society, you join the vast ranks of people who have gone before you. We need your skills across many industries, your hands and feet filling gaps as others step from work into their Jubilee.

"For you all, so bright and young with long lives ahead of you, such talk of old age is futile, I know. The world is improving rapidly. Who knows what inventions your minds will come up with? Who knows what businesses you will be a part of, or what factories you will assist, establishments which form the bedrock of our society? There is a place for every one of you. Be creative, whether that is for jobs or businesses, in opportunities or the next must-have luxury products. The world is before you, the Council is behind you and we all applaud you," and with that, every parent present and the entire delegation on the stage rose and clapped, as they had all been applauded like that once themselves.

The students looked around, taking in the scene. They'd all been told about it, that much was sure. For five minutes the applause continued, the four thousand young people silent, their senses alive to the feelings this situation produced. Eventually the stage went quiet and those watching from the stands retook their seats.

"Each of you will carry forward this legacy. Many of you will one day return to a stadium like this one, looking down upon your own sons and daughters, applauding with us all as we congratulate another group. Some of you might even be up here, on this stage, wearing your Red-Collar with pride."

He paused there for impact, a murmur going around the audience, many of the students looking up towards the stage in hopefulness, though it was the uniformed groups who gave each other a smug grin. Their parents were the ones in those positions, and these opportunities usually followed bloodlines more than any other factor.

"You've had it said to you many times but let me utter it once more," he said, coming in close to the microphone, looking around as he spoke now, taking in the faces, making eye contact briefly with several students on the nearer rows. "Do your duty," the three words perhaps most repeated of any they had heard those previous twelve years. "Do your duty in work, fulfilling the roles marked out for you. The ones you were born to do. Do your duty in society by following the rules, by respecting the systems in place. And do your duty in death, by working until it's time, by celebrating in health and by stepping with your heads held high into your wonderful Jubilee Year."

He allowed silence to follow as his words bounced around the corners of the stadium for a few more seconds before they went silent. Every eye looked up at him. They waited eagerly, the speaker in no hurry, wanting the weight of his words to sink in, though aware that if these students didn't already know this to their core, then there would be no changing it now. He smiled. He'd waited long enough.

"It's my huge honour to once again announce that you have all officially graduated!" and with that the students jumped to their feet, as four thousand blue graduation hats rose as one into the sky, some only rising twenty feet, others twice that. The parents and waiting photographers took their shots, as if a flock of bluebirds had lifted off together.

Down they came again, the mass of falling hats meeting the stretching arms of the students, some having multiple hats fall their way, others needing to go off in search of an abandoned one.

The stage had emptied: the students moved away from the chairs, the queues already long as they grouped to collect their shirts. Parents started feeding down from the stands, in search of their children in the melee of bodies.

It took another hour for the last of the students to collect their shirt, most students changing and handing in their Blue-Collar. Screams started rising up from around the stadium, results celebrated in various groups as the grades came through. For many, they had got the marks they required. Somewhere around forty percent of students went into university. Others would miss out, either their grades not good enough or there being no need or desire to go that route.

Remarkably, only ten percent of those who would become either a Black or Red-Collar had ever gone to university. Education was only one way into that elite club.

15

I t wasn't clear where the phrase *mercy flight* originated. It didn't appear in any record that existed in an official capacity. No school taught such a thing, the integrity of the education system unable to fathom such a practice.

Within the corridors of power right around the world, those who held office would never dare whisper the phrase. They knew it existed, everyone in power did, though none of them spoke about it.

Four decades ago, the new era pressing into the second generation already, the wealthy saw they had a problem. In a System that didn't allow weakness, how could a family like any average Red-Collar preserve all they had and yet face the same unexpected challenges that befell the common folk?

Some of the longest standing families had a problem, their patriarchs getting old: men and women who might become terminally ill or develop dementia before their assigned date. Even those born within the System, dated and prepared to live out their years and live them to the full, wouldn't always remain healthy.

The solution would eventually be found by a group of people who, while they knew they had wealth, understood they would never get accepted into the inner core. This was those with new money, those families the world over who got lucky. Perhaps it was something they invented, perhaps a clever piece of technology. In the early days it might even have been illegal earnings, gathered before these became impossible, the protocol that regulated all currency making cash a relic. Earning illegal revenue after that point had to become smart. So they did.

The Jubilee Year sellers boomed, people well placed and in the loop aware that the abundance of wealth offered a startling new opportunity. With just twelve months left, people didn't bother with saving it. Most might leave a tenth for their families, perhaps a little more in rarer cases. More often than not there was nothing left in the bank, the possessions that were purchased often sold off for a fraction of what they had cost, the depreciation of these items deliberately huge.

Quickly this black economy grew, and the System got in on the act. They knew the fight was on for these millions, money that, if they could recoup it, stayed within their trusted families. Allow too many new businesses in on the action, and they might see their wealth travelling far and wide. The Jubilee Year was ultimately an experience they sold, nothing more. A reward for a life well lived, the carrot kept far out of reach. *Live well and do your duty. Don't hoard, don't save, and don't attempt to make the lives of your loved ones better at your expense. They would all get their chance. Everyone equal. Enjoy yourself, go wild. You've earned it.*

Everything cost, however. For the newly rich, these costs didn't seem a problem. They had a million units. More than they would need, as they were repeatedly told. It paid to seek advice. The System soon tightened up, strictly regulating who they approved or not. Only those approved sellers could be present at the Celebration Day, these events happening each month, all around the world, billions paid out each time. Statistics showed over ninety percent of this money was eventually paid back into the System, the single digit leakage a small price to pay ultimately for the benefits they all reaped. If they could claw back more, they would.

Devon Scott was thirty-eight and wealthy. He'd bought his way into the Red-Collars a decade earlier, taking on the empire in which he'd been a henchman. Putting a bullet through the skull of his former boss had been the only credentials he'd needed to take over.

He quickly established his right to be there and now, years later, those within power let him be. He served a purpose. Not one they would or could ever acknowledge––he wasn't looking for fame or honour––but something they needed. He was a necessary evil, as had his predecessor been. They suspected foul play in the swift handover, though they sought no proof. They would let the dogs fight amongst themselves for the scraps.

Devon's scraps amounted to millions of units a year. He'd branched out into other areas too, things that would get him into huge trouble if the System ever understood the extent of his operation, though that would compromise them. They needed him for what he offered them. What else he might be up to, they did not know and if they had any suspicions, they weren't showing signs of doing anything about it.

How his clients found him––he always viewed those he worked with as clients, he there providing a service, they receiving something they desperately needed––Devon did not know. People talked, regardless. Word amongst those with the most to lose soon spread, his name the point of call when things didn't go to plan.

The latest client to find his way into the offices of Devon Scott was Humphrey Edward Boothroyd Senior whose son sat on the Senate committee, a tremendous honour.

"Please, sir, take a seat," Devon invited, well aware of the man's son, who appeared on the television often. He'd done his research on Boothroyd Senior, since the man had first made contact. No-one approached Devon unless they had no option. He already felt a few steps ahead of them.

The old man lowered himself into the chair. He was sixty-nine and looked much older. The records showed that Humphrey would not reach his retirement age for another six years. He looked ready to stop already. They always did.

"Thank you for seeing me," he said. No Red-Collar ever wanted to see this man, not under any circumstances. Devon knew that. He wasn't there for their wellbeing. This wasn't charity. It was business.

"I always find time in my very busy schedule for such esteemed clients as yourself," Devon smiled, appearing every bit the cheap secondhand car sales man his reputation among those of influence and wealth suggested him to be. He was, however, a fellow Red. Niceties needed observing, the pretence kept up until they had each agreed upon the outcome.

"You know why I am here?" he asked, as if he might need to go over things in more detail than he felt comfortable doing. Humphrey had used the facility linked to Devon's business to run the tests, which kept the results away from the System. Away from the public record. The results were probably in one folder on the desk in front of him.

"I know what you need from me, even if not the details. You can spare me those. How long would you have left?"

Humphrey eyed his prey somewhat sternly, perhaps assessing if such a question even warranted an answer.

"Mid-seventies. Far more years than I've got," he confessed.

Devon said nothing. He knew that much anyway; it was why they always called him. He always kept things between himself and his clients. Nothing went on record. His firm would make all the arrangements, even reach out to the compensation firms as an extra courtesy.

Devon opened a fresh pad, the new client's name already initialled on the front cover.

"Tell me who you are leaving behind," he started, Devon running through his list of preliminary questions, jotting down the answers as Humphrey gave them.

"Do any of these people know that you are speaking with me today?" It always paid to be clear on that one, Devon aware of who he could speak to after the event.

"Only my wife."

"And she agrees with what you are doing?"

"It's my decision," he said. "It's for the good of everyone."

"It's not my place to say otherwise, don't worry," Devon smiled. "What's your window."

"That's the difficult bit," he winced. He'd left it longer than he should have, he knew that. He'd been unwell for a while, fearing what he suspected but too frightened to do anything about it. "The clinic says not long."

Devon opened another file, scanning through the various options there were present.

"How long?" Devon pressed.

"A month. Maybe three."

Devon didn't need to say the line that it never paid to be cautious. If he was doing this, the sooner the better.

"I have space this month." Devon waited for the look of panic, a look that suggested it was too soon. He got neither.

"Which day?"

Devon gave him the date and where he would need to be.

"I'll do that then," Humphrey confirmed. Devon swivelled around on his chair and turned on the computer screen, the display appearing moments later. He tapped away at a few keys, reading from his notebook twice.

"I've got you in," Devon confirmed a few more keystrokes later. It always paid to have that sorted before they discussed the details of money. "Will you definitely take this flight?"

"I will," he confirmed.

"And you've read and signed the contract we sent you?"

Humphrey delved into his bag and reached for the contract, dropping it onto the desk between them both as if it were contraband. Devon picked up the file, the client's reaction not at all uncommon. He flicked through the pages, seeing the signature at the bottom of each, before ending on the last page, the most important of them all.

"You haven't signed the last page, Mr Boothroyd," Devon pointed out, well aware the man would know he hadn't.

"Well, about the fee," he began. They always wanted to haggle.

"It's non-negotiable," Devon confirmed.

"Nothing is non-negotiable, young man!" he snapped, not the first time that a client had spoken to Devon like that, and he knew it would be far from the last.

"My fee is one percent of assets, non-negotiable." Most families got the money back in the compensation, though in Boothroyd's case, with a fortune of thirty-eight million units, that might not be the case. It would be an excellent payday for Devon, however.

"That's preposterous!" he said, banging his fist on the table. "You are taking advantage of me. This is nothing but theft!"

"I'll remind you, sir," Devon said, calmness personified, far from the only time he had delivered such a line, "you came to me, not the other way around. What I do is at enormous risk to my business."

"And I have no option, is that it!" It was true, he didn't.

"Not if you want to keep this from the Council, you don't."

"Are you threatening me?" Humphrey's face was getting redder the more he spoke.

"I don't need to. Another month and the System will know. You'll get hospitalised; it doesn't matter what you then do. Seek treatment or step aside, you will have forever tarnished your family record. Your descendants will be stigmatised. Their status reduced, your legacy eventually coming to ruins. Do you really want to leave that in your wake?"

Humphrey shook his head in rage, his cheeks flapping a little, unable to come up with a suitably scathing riposte for this gold-digging charlatan. He soon broke out into a coughing fit, Devon rising eventually to fetch the man a glass of water, the cough the reminder Humphrey needed that he didn't have long. It was why he had come to Devon for help in the first place.

"The fee is one percent non-negotiable and paid upfront," Devon reminded his client, passing him back the form and holding out a pen for him to sign with. Humphrey refused the pen, his one final act of defiance, instead drawing one from his own pocket, and ever so begrudgingly, his fingers shaking as he tried to control it, he signed his name on the final page, not even looking at Devon as he pulled away. He slowly returned the pen to his inside pocket and took another sip of water.

Devon was the first to stand, going over to a cupboard at the side of his office, pulling from it one hanger, the contents of which were covered in black packaging.

"Take this with you," Devon said, passing it to the man, who didn't know if he wanted to touch whatever he was being handed. "You'll need it on the day in question. You'll wear it to the airport."

Humphrey reached out and took it, something mentioned in the contract he had just signed. He slowly got to his feet.

"I'll need the money paid within twenty-four hours," Devon reminded his client. "Failure to do that and the deal is off."

"You'll have your bloody money!" he snapped, dropping the clothing into his case, shutting it up before moving towards the door. He didn't shake hands with Devon, who stood there with his hand out. Devon smiled as the man passed. They rarely shook his hand. They were too proud to admit they needed him. He knew they were grateful, really. They wouldn't keep coming to him if they weren't.

———

HUMPHREY WOKE EARLY, his wife already up, a special breakfast promised. It was still dark outside.

His cough had kept him up all night. Lying in bed didn't seem to help him. He knew he was ready for whatever awaited him.

The hardest thing was not being able to say anything to the rest of the family. They couldn't know, his wife had told him. They weren't ready. She promised to make sure they were all taken care of, Humphrey unable to say anything more on the subject.

He ambled downstairs, his wife spotting him and coming over to help him into his seat.

"I've cooked you your favourite," she beamed. He had little appetite, didn't feel like eating anything. It didn't seem worth it.

"Thank you," he said, leaving his plate untouched.

"I'll drive with you," she confirmed.

"You really don't have to," he said.

She looked hurt at that comment. "Darling, it's the least I can do." She wouldn't cry.

They spent an hour eating very little of what she had cooked them both. She didn't have an appetite either.

Once showered, she helped him dress. She passed him the clothing that Devon had handed him; the size confirmed ahead of time, the fit right.

It looked wrong on him.

"You look very smart," his wife lied.

"I look stupid," he confirmed. It hardly mattered. It made it all easier.

"I'll get the car ready," she said, leaving him to the last touches.

When he climbed in beside her twenty minutes later, he could tell that she had been crying. Neither of them said anything. Humphrey glanced up at the house as they pulled away, a building he'd inherited from his father, home for so many years.

The automated voice confirmed that they would reach their destination in two hours.

They spent the entire drive going over old memories. The couple recalled holidays they had taken when the children were young, events they had been to, anything to take their mind off what lay ahead.

Finally, the car made a last turn, bringing them into the front of the airport. It pulled over smoothly and the doors opened on the near side. Humphrey climbed out, his wife coming around the side.

"Remember, you can't say anything," she warned him.

"Neither can you," he smiled back. They hugged. She gave him a long kiss on the forehead, hiding from him the tears that were springing up in her eyes.

"I'd best get going then," he said. "Goodbye darling," and he headed for the doors.

She would cry the entire journey back home.

Inside the airport, Humphrey drifted across the concourse. He located the gate he needed to be at and waited on a chair. He recognised several other passengers by sight, and could pick out the rest from the way they waited. Their lack of baggage, their age, the look on their faces.

Flight number AB92 is now boarding at gate number twenty-six. The automated announcement rang out from the speakers high above.

Humphrey glanced up. Two ladies in airport uniforms stood behind the counter and checked the boarding passes of the first passengers in the queue. The few faces Humphrey recognised nodded in silent acknowledgment as they spotted him, none of them saying anything, all in the same situation but none of them about to speak about it.

He walked down the tunnel, having shown the lady his boarding pass. They had him on the second row, business class. He found his seat easily, settling into position, ignoring the belt. There didn't seem any point.

He watched as several younger people boarded the flight after him, all probably in the same position that he had found himself, though the telltale sign of their hand luggage bags suggesting they were just the innocents caught up in a much larger scheme. *Collateral damage*, nothing more.

As they reached cruising altitude on board the older aircraft, due for decommissioning, the gas had already put the passengers into a deep sleep. Take off could be handled by the computer. There were no pilots on this flight, no cabin crew.

The plane disappeared from radar not long after, plunging thirty-thousand feet to its designated field where it exploded on impact, leaving nothing for the salvage crew to find. The black box would be inconclusive, as always. Just another tragic accident.

For the two hundred and eighty Red-Collars on board and the ninety Black-Collars, the crash would keep their secrets intact. A secret that would otherwise have cost each family dearly.

Devon's firm had taken another huge pay day, his network of

people vast, the money put to good use. It would be another seven months before the next flight, half the seats already taken with clients of his. He hoped to fill the other half with his clients too but these were fully commercial flights. There were always a few people who booked themselves onto the same flight. They would get compensation, all the victims would. There were costs to every operation.

16

It had been a while since Blythe had been to the Capitolium, his invitation meaning he didn't need an escort. The Black-Collared men on the front gate let him through once the scanned identification card proved who he was.

One day it might be his office.

Six others were waiting in the conference room as he arrived, the men and women on first-name terms with each other, greetings offered as Blythe moved across to the drinks machine, pouring himself a coffee.

He caught up with a few of them, at least one of whom Blythe knew to be on that three-man shortlist for the top job.

The Supreme Commander came in moments later, showing some signs of his age though he brushed away any concern that might have been offered. The room knew not to go there, waiting for him to take his seat at the head of the table, before they all settled behind the other available seats. Four sat on one side, three on the other. Nobody would be foolish enough to take the empty seat at the other end of the long oval table.

"Thank you for joining me again today," he said, addressing his inner team, most of whom had been with the System for decades,

Blythe by far the youngest and newest to it all. The Supreme Commander liked him, however. Trusted him more than anyone else present, which he didn't mind showing. He'd secretly given those who chose his successor Blythe's name as his choice, an endorsement that would go a long way.

Blythe pretended he didn't know he had been given such an endorsement.

"I know two of you have concerns," he said. Two of those present—the only female Red-Collar there, together with the only Black-Collar present, a man who headed up the military—had raised much noise over the last week. The son of a Red-Collar, a boy of eleven, had been shot by the military, the instruction coming from on high, though not from either of the two who now raised the issue. They were both close to the people involved.

No names were mentioned. As usual, everybody knew exactly who the Supreme Commander meant.

"Rules are rules," he stated. "We felt an example needed setting, even amongst the elite," the two who had tabled the complaint itching to speak.

"I know the decision came from this room," the Black-Collar said, his men on the scene having first called him, though the overrule had gone against his advice for the men to stand down. The man's own son had been one of the two friends playing with the victim of the shooting. He knew the family well, they were friends. He didn't believe this situation should have ever happened. Shouldn't be permitted for their ranks. He felt above it all. And the Supreme Commander knew that.

"It did," the Supreme Commander confirmed, never going to give the name of who had made the call. It wouldn't have been him, the other two knew that. "I was aware of what was happening, I will add."

That took part of their fight from them, neither willing to go in as strong as they thought they would have. It would only threaten their own position in that group. They looked at Blythe, who didn't react. They didn't trust him. They then looked at the others. None of them would look them in the face.

"I feel I need you to explain your decision," the woman asked, somewhat boldly if truth be told. The Supreme Commander didn't have to answer to anyone, his position taking him beyond questioning, a role for life, the selection process such that only those who epitomised the System and all that they stood for were allowed into such a powerful role.

He looked at the woman with tender eyes, however. He saw the opportunity to remind those present some things he hadn't been able to say in a while.

"Seven decades ago, at the foundation of this new empire, we celebrated the medical breakthroughs and our technological advances," he began. "As a people we had so much. The war had taken many things from us all, but our resolve to press forward had never wavered. Our forefathers had the mandate and went about rebuilding the world as they saw it. As they envisioned it. And for a while, we lived in peace. There was no differentiation. Everybody was equal, the ideals of our new world as our founders had originally dreamed. One people, one nation, no borders.

"As you will know from your history lessons, these years were short-lived. Humanity doesn't do well without a struggle. When all were equal, nobody could thrive. Nobody could succeed. We became lazy. The crops went unharvested, food became unreliable. One thing was missing. Fear. Our forefathers learned that, without fear, people didn't really reach their potential. Without the fear of failure, people didn't bother to succeed. Failure fuelled the Industrial Revolutions that humanity had known over the centuries, leading right up to the dawn of our era.

"Equality had to go, a bad idea," he said, turning his nose up, clear that had he been in position then, he would not have made such a mistake. As Supreme Commander, he was one of the most wealthy people who now lived. He was easily the most powerful. Everybody feared him, and while he now used his team to outwork his plans, he'd not risen to such a position without being known as a ruthless man in his youth. "Thankfully, our forefathers saw sense, as we all know. They brought in the collar system, a genius concept. It gave humanity something worth striving for. There were no Red-Collars originally. We couldn't just allow the wealthy to take these positions but soon they were the ones who took over. Our military enforced the orders and laws of the World Council, and society got back on track.

"Our education reforms allowed us to train our children from a young age. We are now living in the good of that decades later. The System works," he finished.

"And this situation?" the Black-Collar asked.

"The boy was on the street wearing the costume of a Red-Collar," he answered, pride in his voice. "There were others watching. Believe me, if there was a better way of reminding people of the rules, I would have taken it. People need to know the fear of breaking our sacred rules. Without it, we have nothing. Without it, we lose everything."

"This family lost their son," the woman said. She had children too. As a Red-Collar, she wanted to know they were safe.

"A tragic loss, for sure," the Supreme Commander said, "but a necessary sacrifice. We must aggressively keep the rules. We cannot show favouritism. It will be the downfall of us all."

The woman thought about arguing the point. Nobody would have known in this case, the street exclusive, the families all wealthy and elite. Letting one eleven-year-old walk away with a reprimand would hardly have caused a revolution. But she said nothing.

"I take it I'll hear nothing more on this issue?" he asked, addressing mostly the two who had raised the complaint. They both said nothing. However, after a while they shook their heads, his gaze had not shifted from either of them, his stare pushing them until they felt uncomfortable. "Very good," turning away at last.

He continued onto other business, the meeting taking over an hour before they broke for lunch.

***

. . .

"I'LL HAVE a word with you if you don't mind waiting behind," the Supreme Commander called, Blythe staying in his seat, the others moving out through the door, none of whom looked back towards them. When the door shut, leaving the older man with his young would-be successor. The Supreme Commander was the one who spoke first.

"These are strange times we are entering, Blythe, you need to be ready."

"I'm sorry?"

"My handing over of power. I saw it when I took office. It won't be easy for the person who follows me. Those who were overlooked for the role don't always settle back easily into things, especially with change. A new leader will always put their flavour on what follows."

Blythe considered that point for a moment. The Supreme Commander had been in power since Blythe had been in school. Blythe had been ten or eleven when the change had happened. He couldn't remember anything about the time, not really. His father might have mentioned some things, his father close to power, but Blythe had been too young to understand. He knew history taught them that every kingdom was most at risk when the leader in charge gave their crown to another, whether that was willingly or otherwise.

"You are in a special position," he reminded Blythe. "Some tell me I've gone soft to have so openly backed you."

Blythe didn't know what to say. His mind raced to his own actions that week, the possible exposure of something to the outside world that might lead to unrest, or worse.

"You already have seen more of the workings of our world than most people have ever seen, but you can go higher still. There are things even you do not know," he said, Blythe well aware that was true. He wasn't sure if he should know it all now, either. "Few people ever get to be considered for the job I've had the honour of filling for these decades. Even fewer are on the shortlist now. You and two others form that list. One of these three names will take things on, and I want that person to be you, Blythe, you know that."

"Why, sir? Why me?"

The Supreme Commander considered that for a moment, sitting back in his high-backed chair, allowing his mind to fill with an answer Blythe required. The words he needed to hear.

"Nobody else in this room today could have made the call you did regarding that boy, for example," he said. "I've always known you were different. I've known the rules meant more to you than to your peers. You're a very special man, Blythe. A rare breed."

Blythe didn't dwell on that thought. He'd known the family in question, known the name of the boy he'd ordered to be shot. He'd seen the same thing that the man in front of him had seen, the absolute need to follow procedure, to set an example. To remind them all just how fragile things could be if people crossed the line. Nobody was exempt, not even an elite family in their private road with their large house and weighty bank balance.

"You'll make a splendid Commander," he promised. "There'll be tough calls to make and I need my successor to make them. You've got what it takes, Blythe. Keep your nose clean, keep doing what you do, and I assure you, you'll be the man the Committee selects to fill my boots."

"That'll be my greatest honour," Blythe said, his mind in utter confusion now. If anybody found out what he had done, it would finish him. Perhaps they already knew? Perhaps word would reach the ears of the man in front of him before long, Blythe's failings made clear. He knew his rivals would want nothing but to discredit him. Yet they would have a point. Even by his own standards, what he'd done that week had been foolish. It'd been reckless. If it had been anybody else, if Blythe had discovered someone in his ranks had broken the rules so severely, he would have ordered their immediate arrest. That would have been only the start to their troubles.

But what if he were to become the Supreme Commander? Could he really do that job the way his predecessor believed he would? Might he only disappoint him? Would he even still be in the running when the handover came? There were many months left until the man retired and stepped aside. What if it all came out before then?

His mind raced back to that earlier thought. Could he change things for the better if he came to power? Would he have the authority to do so, and while he knew he would, would he have the credibility? When push came to shove, would those under his control carry out an order if it worsened their own position? If it made them less wealthy, less special, less elite? And given what the history books taught them, should he even think like that? Didn't people need fear to keep them in line? Wouldn't they just become lazy and unproductive all over again?

"I'll see you later, Blythe," the Supreme Commander said, his arm inviting Blythe to join the others as he pointed to the door. Blythe stood, thanked him, and left seconds later.

17

---

eborah and Jonny Willard were a mother and son team getting into a new rhythm as they left the house once again on a Monday morning. She would head to the school that she had worked at for many years, a teacher to first-grade children, and this was the first day of school for them. She had an extra spring in her step that morning as she locked the front door and walked to the car.

It thrilled Deborah when Jonny was promoted into a Council facility. He'd been working in his new role there for three months now, that morning the start of his third cycle, so he knew well enough what lay ahead of him as he set out on foot.

"I'll see you for dinner," Deborah said, taking the car. He could walk to work from where they lived, it wasn't far.

"Later," he said, bounding down the driveway, the family living in a modest but fairly new semi in the heart of a bustling suburb.

By nine, both were in their respective workplaces, Jonny standing before his boss, Deborah standing in front of her class of terrified looking six-year-olds. The welcome assembly where the Head Mistress had greeted the entire school had gone as smoothly as ever, though Deborah couldn't wait to make her new intake feel a little more relaxed in their classroom, now that it was just the thirty-five of them and not the whole school.

"A new cycle begins today, lad, so you'll be on clean-up duty all day," Jonny's boss informed him, a man who'd been working in that facility for years. "Take these trolleys to the back room immediately, would you? We need the space."

The back room held the incinerators. Five trolleys already occupied the room they were standing in, the lad wheeling away the first, whistling as he walked the empty corridor, the paintings hanging along the white walls all of nature. One was a forest scene, a couple were of snow-capped mountains, two had mountain lakes in them and the final one had a desert expanse. Jonny turned the corner at the end of the corridor, the hum of the trolley he was pushing giving out an off-key tune, though nothing musical. He tried to ignore the noise, silently hoping this was the only trolley in need of a little oil. Arriving outside the back room, he pushed on through, the large door swinging open, the heat yet to build in the space. It would, before the day was over. He left the trolley to one side, its contents not being consigned to the flames just yet. He needed to fire up the ovens first, which he did with a flick of several buttons. Deep underground, the incinerator directly underneath the room that housed the controls, the telltale sound confirmed the vast machine was springing into life, hungry no doubt for more fuel. It would take a little while to warm up completely, Jonny spinning round on the spot now, ignoring the first trolley, as he walked back the way he had just come to collect the next one.

"WELCOME to your first day at school," Deborah Willard said, their new teacher taking in the little faces. She loved teaching that age group most of all. They said hello in unison, most managing her surname, though it wasn't the easiest to say. She corrected them soon enough.

"You all have an amazing adventure ahead of you," she started. Deborah opened her handbook, the material supplied by the Council. Something read to every child starting school that morning. She put on a pair of glasses as she positioned the booklet into its optimum spot. "We all have a duty," she began. "It's a joyous thing, a wonderful thing. Many years from now, when you are all old and wrinkly, you each get to step aside. *To rest from this life, when things might get difficult. You see, we aren't all as springy and jumpy as you are now,"* she smiled. *"Who can jump?"* and hands shot up, though soon they were all jumping as high as they could. *"And who can run fast?"* More hands shot up, though this time the children realised that they didn't need to show her. *"And what would it feel like if you couldn't run anymore?"* Deborah smiled at them, her eyes passionate, her tone engaging, drawing the children in with every word that she spoke.

Nobody replied for the moment. *"It would be sad, wouldn't it?"* she encouraged.

"Yes, Miss," they said enthusiastically.

"It would," and she glanced back at the handbook again, her hand trembling a little. It hadn't been the most promising start. *"So some clever people came along and helped us. They said that when we can't jump and run, when our joy leaves us, we don't have to worry. Do you know why that is children?"*

A few hands shot up at this, which made her smile. Deborah pointed to one girl on the front row. She had yet to learn their names.

"Because we can die!" answered the enthusiastic little girl.

"Excellent!" the teacher said. "A star for you!"

BY THE TIME Jonny had wheeled the third trolley all the way to the back room, the temperature in the incinerator showed that it was now hot enough to devour what he had to feed it.

"Go on then, get on with it," his boss called, Jonny not aware that the man had been standing behind him. Jonny quickly positioned the trolley into place, dumping the contents down through the hatch, the trapdoor below not allowing any heat from the fire to waft up, making it safe to stand there, though the room would warm up soon. He did the same with the second trolley.

"You know how these fold together?" his boss asked, having watched the lad successfully deal with the first two batches.

"I do," Jonny confirmed, dropping the second empty trolley into position, *so it rested flat on the first one, allowing him to push a maximum of ten back with little effort.*

"Good. Get that last one in over there and then those other two back in dispatch. Then take the five empties back to the main hall. They'll need them later."

---

*"D*YING USED *to be a thing people didn't talk about much," Deborah said with a smile, as if telling them a fairy tale. "It used to scare us. But we are not scared any more now, are we children?"*

"No, Miss," they said en masse.

"Excellent," she beamed. "Because we can choose, that's right. And when we do that, we help everybody. We help our families. Who enjoys helping their families?"

All their hands went up at once.

"I do too," she continued. "What does it feel like when someone doesn't want to help you?" She called on another child who'd raised his hand at this latest question, the reward of a star already meaning they all wanted in on that action.

"Not friendly," he said.

"Excellent, a star for you too, Oliver." He beamed all the more. "Yes, it's not friendly when people don't help. And we all want to help, especially those we care about. You want to help your mummies and daddies, don't you?"

"Yes, Miss."

"And they want to help you. So do your grannies and grandpas. And do you know what those clever people give to your grannies and grandpas when they choose to be kind?"

Their little eyes glowed in wonder, yet not one hand was raised.

"They give lots of special treats! Do you like treats?"

"Yes!" came the roar.

"I love treats too, and these clever people will give us all treats. Each one of you. No-one gets left out. And all we have to do is to be helpful," she continued.

JONNY HAD DROPPED in the fifth load, the contents of the trolley sliding down into the fire. He placed the empty trolley onto the other one, wheeling the five back together.

He didn't particularly like the main hall. He'd been there last month; they'd not asked him to go there the first time this happened. He figured they needed to know if he could manage the job first.

His boss glanced his way as Jonny passed the office. Jonny paused in the room where he had begun that morning; the double doors that led into the main hall stood in the centre of the wall leading directly from where he now waited.

He pushed the five empty trolleys in front of him, pressed hard as they connected with the doors, giving enough extra force for them to open. A sea of trolleys sat before him, the main hall vast.

There must have been hundreds.

"Leave those by the side," someone called out, spotting Jonny with the empties. He didn't look up, not taking in the scene. He preferred the trolleys on the other side of the wall from where he'd just come, as he'd seen those first five. Covered neatly, all tidy.

Though these people before him now were not conscious, he could see them. Lying there. They were not yet covered, some yet to die.

This was the death room. These were those whose date had arrived, this the start of another month, this the day another thousand would die.

They had administered the drugs in another room. Jonny hadn't been there, his role didn't require it. That was for others to do. He didn't want to mingle with the living, and actually only senior figures could be there. It made things less complicated.

Here the trolleys were placed in rows to allow the drugs the time to take full effect. When the person had died—and medical staff constantly patrolled the aisles, checking the machines, there to confirm death—they would zip up the bag. That was Jonny's sign to wheel away the trolley. It would take him a few days to complete the task, the main hall chilled, the bodies good for a week.

The quicker he could complete the task, the better.

They zipped another dozen bags, Jonny moving over without invitation to shift them, taking the first and pushing it into the room from which he'd just come. He did the same for the other nine, so they had the space they needed in the main hall.

Jonny refused to look at the human sized shape underneath the black plastic that lay on each trolley. This was just a byproduct, he reminded himself. The packaging left behind when humanity had moved on. He didn't know where these people might have moved on to, didn't know if he believed in any of that. It was just packaging—he reminded himself constantly—as he repeated the journey he had done five times already that morning and would do many more times before the week was out. He took in the pictures as he always did, imagining himself in each of the settings as he moved down the corridor, thankful that this trolley didn't sing to him as the wheels moved round and round.

D*EBORAH WALKED AROUND THE TABLES*, *the children colouring in some pictures that the Council had deemed essential first day material.*

It showed a family waving fondly at their loved one who walked off towards the Colosseum, the sun blazing, the scene of glory. The actual picture hung in one of the official buildings, the artist now long dead, though famous because of his depiction of what was to come. He'd titled the work The Golden Era, *and it rapidly became the focal point of much that the schools would cover. The six-year-olds colouring in that adaptation that morning around the world were far from done with that masterpiece yet. Its ideology would follow them all the way through school, and if the teachers at every level had done their jobs correctly, would launch them into their working life with the belief that they too had this great responsibility. They would raise children in the understanding they had, they would encourage their own parents when the time came and, when old themselves, when their Jubilee Year beckoned, they could remember this picture with pride, as they too walked off into the glory that lay before them.*

THE BOSS STOOD *with a huddle of others, none of whom Jonny yet knew by name. They seemed to wait for him, though as Jonny reached them, they continued to discuss something amongst themselves, not even bothered with his presence. One final trolley stood in that room, Jonny's pace slowing. He would then return the ten empty trolleys and collect another ten loads from the main hall.*

Jonny started moving the final trolley away, his boss glancing his way briefly, the lad moving off back down the same corridor. The pictures only captured his attention for so long. He was long bored already and yet had hours of this ahead of him, and for the next few days.

The furnace would take a further week to cool down. Most of his job after that was preparing for the following month. They would spend two weeks cleaning out the ash pile. He didn't mind that, there was nothing left. He didn't think of it as human at all.

The huddle of people moved behind Jonny, following him at a distance as he ambled down the corridor, Jonny glancing back, his boss ignoring him, though most of the others were watching him.

A groan.

Jonny let go of the trolley, swearing under his breath.

"Problem, lad?" his boss called from twenty metres behind, angry and authoritative. Perhaps he felt shown up in front of the others?

"No, sir," Jonny said, trembling inside. The groan had come from underneath the plastic in front of him.

"Then on you go," he urged. They were closing in on him, Jonny giving the trolley a shove, the wheels moving again, the lad's eyes on the contents of the trolley for a few seconds. Then the bag sat bolt upright, screaming as it did so, Jonny leaping back in instant fright.

The mass of people who had been following Jonny, including his boss, were soon wetting themselves with laughter.

Jonny swore at them all, his boss eventually coming forward, patting Jonny on the shoulder and unzipping the bag, letting out the prankster.

"Gets 'em every time," he smirked as he climbed off the trolley.

Jonny didn't know what to say, still trembling from the experience. He couldn't see what was so funny, but the others could hardly stand for laughing.

Jonny had gone very pale.

"Probation's over, lad," his boss said, with a smile. "We only do this to newbies like yourself as an initiation. We've all been through it." That didn't seem any comfort right now, his heart rate still up.

"Need a change of underwear?" someone called from the back. Jonny felt like he might do. He didn't comment.

"You okay?" his boss called, stepping forward, seeing Jonny turning a little greener now. He'd stepped too close to avoid being covered in vomit, Jonny's insides turning over.

18

Kate walked with her brother along their favourite track. The siblings used to run around these woods when they were little, before the world got complicated. Before they moved on different trajectories.

She'd not stayed up late the night before, unlike the others. She'd seen in plenty a New Year in her time, and away from home, only her brother's friends in attendance, she went upstairs to bed early. She certainly felt the better of the two of them that morning. She'd seen the pain on her brother's face as the sunshine first hit them when they stepped out of the front door. She did nothing but laugh at him.

Thankfully, amongst the fresh air and those childhood memories, his head had cleared a little, and they were talking more naturally, the two not so far apart really, despite their different lives, despite their different paths. Kate had also seen him come alive more in the few days that she had been there than in a long while. It was as if her being there, the things she had told him, had awakened him. Had reminded him he wasn't going crazy, that there was truth buried under so many lies.

They had avoided any such talk so far on their walk, the morning too fresh for such issues, the year too virginal.

"How's mum doing with all this?" she asked.

"With me you mean, being a total flop?"

"No," Kate said. It wasn't what she meant at all, though she didn't have words to reshape her question. "You know what I meant."

"You know as I do that my black moods scare the life out of her," he admitted. He knew their mother worried, had seen her drinking increase when he wobbled. She never touched a drop when he was sound.

She drank most days now.

"She loves you, that's all," Kate said. She knew that was their mother's biggest weakness, a heart too forgiving for either of them. A firmer hand, and perhaps her brother might not have turned out as he had. The lack of a father around the place had not helped. Neither sibling ever spoke of him, whoever he was, wherever he now lived. Their mother had never told them, and they'd stopped asking decades ago. The System would know and the Council could tell them about their birth father. They would know where he lived, what he did, everything. His DNA existed in both siblings. If they were ever to have children themselves––time was running out, neither in a place for that to be possible soon––then their children would have their lives lengthened or shortened based on the history on both sides of the family.

The System knew everything and as adults they were fully aware that they had every right to make enquiries, and it was their right to know. They'd never even asked, never once discussed it between themselves, never asking the other if they had gone to check, if perhaps their sibling knew the name and location of their father. They wouldn't ask. He was dead to them, had been all their lives. Not that they hated or despised him. They had only known absence, only had their mother. She'd done her best to become both parents to them, even if she'd not been able to do that.

It didn't seem to matter now. They were who they were, and her brother would not get any better by dwelling on what he didn't have.

"That's her problem," he smiled. Both knew she had a soft spot for him. He'd always been able to get away with more than Kate had, and while that might have been the second child thing—Kate had heard her mother tell her once that she'd not had a clue what she was doing when she first had Kate—the rules never seemed as hard or readily enforced with her brother. That would have had a lot to do with the timing of the breakup, their mother pouring all her love into the baby boy at the time when she was having it withheld.

"Kate, are you going to tell mum about the flight?" he asked, homing in on what he wanted to discuss. They'd been together for a few days now, the three adults crammed into the house that was a squeeze for two, and she'd not said anything else yet, besides what she'd told him.

"Do you think I should?"

He didn't know what to say to that. He couldn't tell his mother himself, this needed to come from Kate. Needed to come from the sane one. Uttered from his lips, his mother would let the words wash over her again, perhaps panicking inside. She would then pour herself a potent drink when she thought he wasn't looking.

"I think eventually she must know," he said.

"But for now?" Kate asked, picking up his tone, which suggested he was thinking along the same lines as she was.

"For now, we have more pressing things to discuss."

"Like what?" and Kate stopped walking with that question, her brother turning at her words, the pair surrounded by their childhood habitat as if the years had never happened.

"Finding out who your mystery caller is, for starters."

She didn't know how that would even be possible. "I don't have a number."

"You won't need one. He'll make contact again, I'm certain."

"Why?"

"You said he talked about your research. It'll have something to do with that. You were working on a cure for one of the six diseases, right?"

This startled her more than anything. He'd never shown the slightest inkling that he knew what she did, so much so she had assumed he didn't understand it. She'd only had these discussions with her mother over the years. As she moved closer to a cure, it had been her mother to whom she'd excitedly broken the news.

"Yes," she exclaimed, more happy about his knowledge than anything else he might be about to say.

"Then you get back to the office and watch. He'll make contact, somehow. Funding will come through, someone will visit, the Council will reach out."

"The Council?"

Her brother seemed disappointed in his sister at that comment, shaking his head as if she just didn't get it.

"Come on, Kate. Knowing what he knows, he's Council, for sure. My guess would be he's high ranking, too." She didn't know how he understood so much about how that side of things worked.

"You think I'll hear directly from him again?"

"That, I don't know," he admitted. It would be highly abnormal if she did, though that being said, what the man had already done by warning her not to get on that flight had changed the game. Her brother was certain this stranger wasn't playing by any of the usual rules. "Perhaps not directly, no, not immediately. Not unless we mix it up a bit. But you'll hear indirectly, that much I can guarantee," he said.

"Indirectly?" she quizzed, her mind still repeating what he'd said at the beginning of his response when the latter question had pushed its automatic question.

"Like I said earlier. They'll reach out somehow, offer help. Probably something that will benefit the whole lab. It might not even be obvious that you are the reason. He'll be smart about it."

"So I might not even know?"

"You'll know," he smiled, his clever sister for once being rather slow on the uptake. "Anything that changes the future of your working environment, we'll know," bringing himself every bit into this new conspiracy, whether or not she liked it. They were partners in this, the only two in the know from the outside world. Someone had broken the rules, someone had changed the game, and they knew. What he couldn't figure out was why.

Kate came back to the nagging thought she had from what her brother had said seconds earlier.

"What did you mean by mixing things up a bit?"

He seemed confused by her question before recognition set in.

"I could reach out to my contacts, see what they can find out. You might have options too," he added.

"Hold on there," she said, grabbing his arm so he couldn't walk off. "First, who do you possibly know who could discover this type of thing?"

"People, okay," was all he said.

"People?"

"The network, the people who got me onto this thing."

"Your conspiracy buddies, you mean?" she said with disdain, shaking her head at him with that comment.

"But this proves it, doesn't it? It's not all rubbish, just a product of unstable minds. The stuff about the planes falling from the sky is real, like they said."

He had a point. She couldn't deny that. She was still alive when she should have been dead. That was design, not luck. Someone had deemed her too important to lose. How long that might protect her from the System, she didn't know. She doubted this stranger who had warned her was acting within the bounds of their rules.

"Okay, I'll give you that," she conceded. "But what did you mean that I might have options too?"

"Your research," he began, a smile coming onto his face at his own piece of masterful thinking. "Do you have access to anyone carrying this disease, for your research purposes?"

"No, not direct access, I request it," she confirmed. Her lab wasn't Council controlled, which she liked, though it limited what she had available at her fingertips. Anything of a heredity nature she had to request, the information naturally sensitive.

"But they have given you such a list before, right?"

"Yes," she confirmed. It would not have helped her research had they not given her access to the information they knew about those carrying the disease. It was how she'd mapped what she saw as the cure. As far as she could tell, nobody else was close. She hoped to be the one to publish the paper that would set in motion the removal of this disease from the list of incurable conditions.

"Then that's where you start. Request a new list, you'll want to be up to date, anyway."

"And what will that show me?" she asked.

"Nothing, I expect."

Kate wasn't coy with the expression she gave her brother at that confirmation.

"Then what's the point?"

"It'll make your next move a little more natural," he said.

"Which is?"

"Would they give you a list of those testing positive for this condition in the womb."

"In the womb? Why would they have these records?"

"You work in your field and you need to ask me that?"

She smiled. If there were such cases, the System would note them down somewhere. The challenge with the disease that she was researching was that it didn't easily show up pre-birth. She'd only ever focused on a cure; had she focused on screening, then it would have lead to most babies being aborted when testing positive for the disease. She knew others in her field of research went that route. The principal research centre under Council control sphere headed that charge.

She deemed it as missing the point. Science was there to cure, not limit. Merely aborting the embryos wouldn't advance science. There needed to be a cure, something they could administer in life which would undo the damage the disease had caused, giving the person their health back. She was sure that these people would then be immune to passing it on. Humanity needed this immunity. You couldn't fight a disease by killing these babies before they were born.

"It'll be hard to find," she said.

"Would you know who to ask?"

She nodded.

"Then ask as soon as you get back. My bet is, your stranger has a child recently tested with this condition. You find a list of those carrying children with this condition, all still pre-birth, and I'll bet you anything your mystery man is in some way connected to one of these names."

It made sense once she allowed his words to sink in. Whether such a list existed, she didn't know. Getting hold of such a list might prove tricky, though given her unique position, if anybody on the planet right now was to request such a list, she doubted if there was anyone else as well placed as she was.

"I'll check," she confirmed.

"When is your flight home?" he asked, looking at his watch, their mother expecting them home for lunch in half an hour. They would need to hurry.

"Two days," she said, looking worried. "I'm not sure I want to take it, new year and all, a resetting of the clock."

He smiled. "After all this, you think there is any danger in taking that flight?" he asked.

She hadn't thought of that. "I guess not."

"You guess not?" he laughed. "Kate, you're now the safest passenger on the planet!"

Once she started sticking her nose into places that perhaps people might not want her looking, she didn't know how long that protection might last.

19

B lythe couldn't help but look at everything he passed in a critical light, the streets and buildings around him something few people saw, even fewer had access to. His position allowed him that, though he passed on by, heading to his usual office, the usual select people surrounding him, all with their own ambitions, all with their own vested interests.

Blythe wasn't sure he knew what his were anymore.

As he cleared security at the entrance level to his building, he put his game face on. Banter was loud, Blythe the funny man as usual, making a point of remembering names, reflecting on something someone might have once told him, sharing an in-joke with another. He bounded across the space to the lifts, some greeting him, many knowing to avoid eye contact.

He stood alone in the lift as it carried him effortlessly to the top floor, the elite of the elite.

Blythe spoke to nobody as he made his way to his personal office, a spacious place with views sweeping across the city, the landscape the pinnacle of human engineering, breathtaking to so many. He now only saw buildings and control, the System he represented using the brick and glass, steel and concrete to mask over what really mattered.

Build a high-rise office building. Let people die from curable diseases.

Hand out a million to the retiring heroes. Do everything possible to claw back every penny from those unworthy saps.

Hail the era of freedom and openness. Hoard and pander to the rich and powerful.

Boast of a world without crime and death. Control all by fear and suspicion.

Blythe pulled away from the window; he'd seen enough of that view. He refused to look towards the centre of power, a home that might one day be his new office if he were to become the next leader of this apparently free world.

He walked back out of his office, towards his team, a group of ten people who worked directly for him. He would have to decide who he took with him should he be changing location in the next two years. He was certain some of them were not there because of their support of him.

"I need everything you have available on Miss Katherine Vann," Blythe said, dropping a one-page document with the woman's photograph and basic details that he'd printed from the database. It listed her current work address, a job she had held for many years. Aside from that, the information was on a need to know basis. He now needed everything.

The woman took the sheet of paper.

"You'll have it on your desk within the hour," she confirmed.

"I want all we know about her research," he said to the next man, walking on down the room, his team stopping what they were doing with his entry into their section of the office.

"I want anything we have on the family," he said to the rest of the room.

"And our current operations?" someone asked.

"Everything on hold for the moment," Blythe confirmed. His daughter's future depended on him being selfish for the time being, and he would be far from the first person to abuse their position for themselves. They all did it, he was certain. Perhaps not the people in that room now, there just to do a job. But the elite, for sure. "This has to be your sole priority."

"Is she a threat to the System?" the same man asked, someone Blythe had suspected had been not fully onboard with him since his secondment there. Blythe would soon have the troublemaker moved on, probably thrown out of the Capitolium completely. These were only Black-Collars, the lot of them. If they didn't understand the privilege of being allowed into such a trusted position, then they would be reassigned. None of them would ever make the jump to Red, something that they would all be hoping might be possible. Working directly for Blythe Harrell, the odds-on future leader, was meant to be a step in the right direction.

Blythe suspected that some of his team members were planted there, placed to monitor him. It mattered little now. He had the ear of the Supreme Commander. Soon he would be unstoppable.

Blythe circled the desk, all eyes on both him and the man who'd asked the last couple of questions, his most recent one hanging in the silence like a potent smell. Blythe stopped behind the man, who didn't dare turn around, though he knew that Blythe now stood behind him. His screen showed evidence of the things he'd been working on for the last few weeks. He clearly felt aggrieved at having to stop all that so suddenly.

"I'll tell you what is a threat," Blythe said, lowering his head as if to whisper something between himself and this man, though speaking at a volume that allowed everyone else present to hear every word. There was total silence from those watching on. "Thinking above one's station. That's very dangerous, very unwise." The man didn't move, Blythe not showing any sign of shifting his position from behind him just yet. "Do you think I would ask you to do something if I suspected this woman of walking on a field when the sign said to keep off the bloody grass!" and Blythe shouted those final words so loudly that it made the entire audience, including the man inches in front of him, jump.

"I'm sorry, sir," the man said, frozen for anything else to do or say.

"You will be if you ever question anything I ask you to do again, is that clear?"

"Yes, sir," the man said, his eyes furious, focused on the screen, Blythe still behind him.

Blythe looked around at the others, who had done nothing else but watch the entire encounter.

"Well?" Blythe asked, as if they needed any further encouragement, and as one the room returned to normal activity, while they went about their task with renewed focus.

BLYTHE HAD NOT BEEN EXPECTING a visitor. He had been sitting in his chair, a coffee half finished on the edge of his desk, the view of the sunshine on the glass topped buildings beyond. A pile of reports lay next to the mug, a thick one on his lap as his door opened. Blythe glanced up in apparent frustration at the disturbance, and at the lack of a knock which never went unpunished. The realisation that it was the Supreme Commander drew all rage from his voice.

"I'm sorry to disturb you," he said, shutting the door behind him. Blythe had never had him visit his office before, it always the other way round.

Blythe stood, reeling from what it might all mean, coming forward and shaking his hand.

"Never an inconvenience," Blythe forced out, pointing him towards the sofas in one corner of the office.

"I'll stand, actually," the Supreme Commander said, going to the window, a brief glance at the desk that was messy and rather full of files, though it was the view that seemed to captivate him most. "You get a wonderful panorama from up here."

"It's quite something," Blythe agreed cautiously. He knew the man had not come to him to discuss real estate options.

"It makes one really appreciate what a wonderful city we have when one can look down on everything like this," he said. "It's nothing but a marvel."

"The greatest city on Earth," Blythe agreed. He'd always known that. The centre of power and an architectural masterpiece.

"Indeed it is. That's the trouble with beautiful things," he said, pulling away from the window and randomly leafing through the files which sat on Blythe's desk. "Once a man gets captivated by beauty, it's hard for him to look at anything else." The Supreme Commander settled on a document that carried Kate's face, albeit a younger image, but one that carried her best likeness. A simple charm.

"You think my investigation into this woman has something to do with my romantic feelings for her?" Blythe accused his guest, always the one to say things directly, leaving nothing open to interpretation. It was why the man he was speaking to rated him so highly. It was why Blythe would make an excellent successor.

"She is an exquisite little bitch, now. It wouldn't be the first time such a thing had happened."

"I'd not noticed," he said, which was true. The only image he had of Kate on file was less flattering, the sheet of paper he'd given to his team that morning. It was the name he'd been solely interested in, and her connection to the research that would save his unborn baby.

"If you say so." Pause. "I know things cannot be easy for you at the moment," he added, somewhat cryptically.

"Easy for me?"

"Your wife, your new wife that is," he said, the reminder they both needed that he knew all about the downfall of the first wife and the reasons behind that. "She is pregnant, is she not?"

It was clear he already knew that much.

"She is, yes."

"Pregnancy changes women, as we both know. You have two grown sons. I need not tell you what we both know."

Blythe got it. The Supreme Commander assumed that in Blythe's case, because his wife was about to balloon up, he might be ready to look on somebody else. He really didn't know Blythe as well as he thought he did if that was the case.

"I think you are going to tell me anyway," Blythe said, closing the gap between them a fraction.

The Supreme Commander dropped the file back onto the desk, walking to the sofas now, not saying anything until after he had carefully lowered himself into position. He then waited for Blythe to take a seat, which he did seconds later, facing him.

"Stay away from this woman, Blythe," he warned.

"It's not what you think it is, I assure you," Blythe said determinedly. The fact this man was even there, in his office, aware of who he was looking into, told Blythe all he needed to know. One of his team had called him, and Blythe didn't need to think hard which of the ten it would have been.

"Does your wife know?"

That felt like he'd gone too far already, and it now showed on Blythe's face as he struggled to contain his voice.

"She knows all about this woman, I assure you!"

That seemed to take the fight from the man, confirming it was something else, something which he would need to understand in order to see why Blythe had poured such resource into the investigation.

"Why would that be?" he asked, this time not accusingly. He seemed like he genuinely wanted to know. Blythe didn't know what to say. He couldn't tell him the truth.

"I had a call the other day," Blythe said, scratching around for ideas, his mind racing fast, putting a plan of action into place. Basing his story on a version of the truth would make it more believable. "A disturbance at the hospital. Nothing major, but we were close. We had an appointment ourselves that day."

The two men studied each other in the silence that followed, Blythe swallowing hard and putting the next bit of the story into words.

"I went as a courtesy, really. A low ranking Red-Collar needed help," Blythe said, dismissively. "A patient had demanded to see him."

"A patient?"

"A parent. Some mother. She'd given birth that week, I believe.

They were still in hospital. We had dated their son the day or so before."

"And what does this have to do with this woman?" he asked, pointing to the desk. He meant Kate, and Blythe was getting there, his story piecing together to sound a little more credible.

"What I observed troubled me. This mother stood in the room where her baby had been marked, and she knew. She knew we had given him little time. I was next door with the Red I'd gone to help. Witnessed the whole thing. This mother pounded the window. I don't think she realised that anybody was there. I know the Red did not go to see her."

"I should hope not," the Supreme Commander added. Walls and distance needed keeping between them and the common folk.

"It was what she shouted to the window that caught my attention. She said that she'd filed a report. Screamed that the disease was within-life curable."

"This mother had given birth to a defect, is that it?"

Blythe despised the term as much as he did the man who was now using it, as if they were talking about a broken washer or plug. His own child had this condition.

"Her son had a disease, yes. One of the six."

"Well then, she shouldn't have been upset. We've done her a favour."

Blythe hated the man all the more. All that wealth, all that education, all that power, and yet he could be as ignorant as anybody. More so, in fact.

"Except it's curable," Blythe said, going out on a limb.

"Impossible," the Supreme Commander said. He had monthly briefings on all these aspects. The best research centres in the world were working on these killers, and they weren't anywhere near finding a solution, especially something within-life. That was why the mother aborting the faulty foetus where a diagnosis was made was the only sensible option. Such a diagnosis was only available to certain people, worldwide testing awaiting approval. Blythe had been lucky in that regard, his family's status enough to ensure it included them.

"This woman, the scientist Katherine Vann, she's close," Blythe confirmed. "The mother knew this. I think she'd been in touch, heard it directly from her. She'd filed a report before the birth of her child, months before, with enough time for us to consider it, to prepare for the dating. She believed we would have taken it into account."

The Supreme Commander sat there and listened. He knew well that any report or research filed by any agency outside of Council control bore very little weight. All the best scientists worked for the System. He doubted that his team had even glanced at the report. It wasn't worth the time of day.

"We cannot change the dating," he said, something Blythe knew to be the case.

"That isn't the point." Blythe fought to control his temper the best he could, given how the conversation seemed to be unfolding.

"Then tell me the point, Blythe. What is this all about?"

"Don't you think this mother in question should have been able to see justice for her son?"

Blythe didn't like how he'd worded that, clutching at straws as he was, though from the look on the face of the man opposite him, he'd not seen right through him yet.

"Justice," the man repeated, as if weighing the word in his mind, feeling it for what it was worth. "Is it justice when one mother has a son at all when, for some parents, they are never able? Is it justice when a person who does a nothing job, meaningless, yet has the same medical care as a lawyer or as a company executive?"

Blythe didn't tell the man what he thought about that. He'd not even said anything of how the elite behaved. Justice was a mirage; it didn't exist.

Ten minutes later he was showing the Supreme Commander out of his office, the ten assistants in the other room looking up as one as the pair emerged, Blythe ignoring them all for the moment. He would deal with them later.

"I suggest you drop this one," the Supreme Commander warned.

He'd given Blythe his speech about the importance of those institutions under Council control. In his book any offer facilities were not worth listening to.

Blythe didn't comment.

LATE THAT EVENING, the Supreme Commander stayed alone in his office. A call an hour ago had confirmed Blythe had not changed his approach with his team. They were all still pressing deep. The Supreme Commander had told his man to keep his head down. Blythe's suspicions firmly focused on another member of the team, a man who'd never seen eye to eye with Blythe but was loyal. He did what Blythe asked, even if he felt it his place to question the orders. It was better that this man became the scapegoat should things escalate. The Supreme Commander thanked his source and told him to stay low for the next week. To do nothing to raise suspicion.

He sat behind his computer, the only mainframe on the planet that had access to everything. He typed in the name Katherine Vann, the System soon confirming the specific woman in question. He glanced at her life. The woman's brother was the issue.

Katherine was brilliant in her field. Anyone else and they would have been recruited already into one of the leading labs, or the facility she worked from brought directly into the System. It was clear from a quick glance through her findings that Blythe had been right. A within-life cure was within reach, and he read through Kate's own notes from her personal computer that she suspected it might be possible within as little as twenty years.

However, she'd been red-flagged years ago, as had her research and the laboratory where she worked. The brother was a known conspirator, twice warned about involvement in undesirable networks. He had remained outspoken and uncontrollable. How the Supreme Commander now wished the brother really had already topped himself. Little pieces of information existed, now that he looked into them, that he might have threatened suicide several times before. Kate had travelled back home a few times over the years, always at odd periods of the year. She'd driven every time aside from the last trip.

Her flight, one day after the most recent air crash, stood out immediately as odd. He'd read in her own notes that she feared flying. There was one file which recorded every crash that had happened for the last thirty years. He'd seen how, among his other offences, the woman's brother had been suspicious about the nature of those crashes.

He dug deeper, pulling up Kate's personal data records, the System extremely efficient at tracking every citizen. He saw the report of her car that had driven her to the airport the day before she had flown. Closed circuit cameras from the airport had her scanning in a boarding pass—she wasn't collecting somebody from a flight.

He brought up a new screen, his authority allowing him access to anything without question. It showed her booked onto flight AB92, a flight the Supreme Commander didn't need to look up. She was meant to fly out on that doomed aircraft.

He watched on the video feed as she waited to board, ignoring the other people at gate twenty-six, his gazed fixed on her for all the time she stood there. Then she'd taken a phone call.

He pulled up her records, and here the story became increasingly interesting. While it noted receipt of an incoming call, nothing showed on the record. That could only have been removed by a high ranking Red.

She didn't get on the flight. Her own phone signal, which had been working and tracking her the entire time, soon confirmed movement back the way it had come, the woman's car confirming the return to home only eighty minutes after bringing her to the airport. Not long into the journey she had made a ticket purchase for a flight leaving the following morning.

She knew.

Whoever had called her at the airport had told her. Had Blythe been that man, and if so, had he now betrayed every trust ever placed in him?

20

A s dating parties went, the one for Vivian and Stuart Bryant and the revealing of their son's date couldn't have been more of an anticlimax.

The couple were crying before even the first guests had arrived. The day was meant to be one of celebration. The friends, family and colleagues who had made it to the party were there to congratulate the family on the new arrival. Tradition had it they would reveal the name of the child and remove the plaster on their baby's head, giving everyone there the same first glimpse of how long the little one had to live.

His parents already knew. It was three weeks less than his mother, something that rarely happened now. Vivian knew it should never have happened.

"What's wrong?" a friend asked, the first to arrive, seeing Vivian slumped in a corner, evidently drinking, despite all the advice, despite the breast feeding. The baby lay asleep in his cot for the time being.

"It's not good," she said.

"You know?"

Vivian nodded.

"Why?"

Vivian explained the nightmare, the friend listening carefully, spotting a few more people approaching the house up the driveway.

"Look, only reveal the name today," he said, "trust me. Say you want to do the date thing as a couple later." It wasn't uncommon for that to happen now, even against the weight of tradition. Not because these rebels felt there was anything to worry about, but just that it had become something different. A way of not conforming with society at large.

There was a ring from the front doorbell.

"Wait," Vivian called to her husband, Stuart coming over to the pair. "Tell him," Vivian urged her friend.

"Vivian said it isn't good, but there is an option," the friend said. "Only nobody can see the date, not today. Just reveal his name," and the doorbell rang again, as if the household might have missed it the first time.

"Okay," Stuart agreed, glancing at his wife briefly before speaking, she seemingly on the same page as he was now. "I'd better get that."

Two hours later they were saying goodbye to their guests, Charlie feeding on the breast. They'd had that name picked out for months, delighted to reveal it to their friends and family. The story behind the delay had been enough to offset the slight awkwardness at not revealing the date. Vivian's mother had mockingly pushed the idea aside as this generation's peculiarities, but they'd soon all respected the decision.

Now it was just the couple and their son Charlie. Stuart fiddled with the name of the man that Vivian's friend had written for them on a piece of paper. They'd both been able to grab a snatched conversation with him during the party, the friend confirming there was someone they should contact. He'd written the name down before leaving.

VIVIAN ARRIVED with Charlie in a sling around her shoulder at the address they had been directed to the previous night. Stuart had made the call, but they'd told them just the mother and child could come. They seemed cautious about attracting too much attention.

Vivian checked her information again, the area not as modern as most parts of the city. In older times, it might have been called a dump, the kind of area nobody in their right mind would visit, filled with criminals. She guessed such areas still were, even if those types had gone upmarket now.

Shown into a well appointed reception area, Vivian took a seat in the comfortable waiting room, a few other people dotted around the couple of dozen seats. Nobody looked at each other, all ignoring the mother and baby as she walked in and took her seat.

It took thirty minutes before they called Vivian through.

A large, muscly man with a fake smile greeted the young mother as she stepped into the office, Vivian taking in the man's Red-Collar instantly, eyeing him with immediate suspicion.

"I'm Devon," he offered, holding out his hand. "Please, take a seat."

"You're Devon Scott?" Vivian asked, the man not anything like she had expected. She'd never met a Red-Collar before, either.

"In the flesh," he beamed. "I take it this is the little one in question?"

They'd mentioned something about Charlie the day before, the conversation guarded. Only when Vivian had given the name of the friend from whom they had got Devon's name and number, did Devon open up a little more.

"This is Charlie," she said.

"And he's a week old?"

"Five days," Vivian corrected.

"Good," Devon said, seemingly happy with that news. "May I see what's underneath the plaster?"

Vivian paused, not knowing if this was some test, some cruel trick. "I cannot help you unless I know the date," he clarified. She'd come to him for help, not the other way around. Her friend had promised this man could do something about their situation. He'd urged the couple to get in touch immediately.

She pulled back the plaster: the baby gave out a little cry as the tape came free. It wasn't as stuck down as it might have been. Vivian had already removed it once.

He took in the numbers, confirming what he'd been told.

"Isn't that a terrible sight," he mused, pausing for a second after that, as if allowing the moment the silence it demanded.

"But you can help?" she asked, pleading now. That was the only reason she'd come.

"I can," he confirmed, with a smile, sitting back in his chair. "You can cover him up again, if you like, but it doesn't matter too much. You're safe within these walls."

She dropped the plaster loosely back into place.

"There are two things I can do for you, both of which have to happen for this to work. We need the second immediately," he began. "First, I will use my network to hack into the mainframe within the System and alter the date that they gave your son this week."

"You can do that?" Vivian asked, open-mouthed. Dating was final, they all knew that.

"Anything can be manipulated if you know what you are doing," he confirmed. "But this leads me to the second thing. The numbers tattooed onto your son's head." Vivian touched the plaster instinctively. "These aren't so easy to alter."

"But you can?" she asked.

"Most certainly," he said, appearing every bit the man who'd likely done this many times. "But we need to act fast, and this can only happen over two stages, I'm afraid. If you want it to look authentic, it will take time."

"What do you mean authentic? Aren't you just altering one digit or other, making a zero into an eight, something like that?"

"No," he said. "For starters, it looks fake. They'll know. For seconds, the difference in the ink, the time they applied it, will stand out. And finally, as is your case, given the numbers available, it would only buy him eight more years."

She wanted well over eight.

"Then what do you do?"

"I'll explain, and before I do, know that we've done this many times in this very facility and have you ever heard of this in the news?"

"No," she said.

"Because we're good at what we do, that's why. It stands up."

"Go on."

"And your child will be okay," he added.

"Good. What is it?"

He paused at this. She couldn't help feel he was uncomfortable, as if this was the part he didn't enjoy. The reason for that soon became apparent.

"We'll perform two operations, one of which needs to happen today," he confirmed, holding a finger up for silence as she motioned to speak at the word *operation*. She'd been told it was merely a simple procedure. "My expert team of surgeons will cut the patch of skin away from your son's head that has the date on it," Vivian's face going dead white as these words.

"What?"

"It's perfectly safe. At this age, the skin heals wonderfully. Your son's skull is still supple, it won't form into one solid bone for months yet. While the skin will take time to heal, it will heal. It'll return to its baby soft form as with the rest of his body. They are very good at this now."

"He'll have a hole in his head!" she protested.

"Not a hole, no. They are only taking enough off to take the date away. What's important is that you keep the wound covered. Keep him away from people."

"People will expect to know the date soon."

"They can't," he urged. "Nobody but you and your husband can know anything about this. Is that clear?" It was important Devon settle this before they went any further. There were many things he did for the elite--the mercy flights being one. This he did only for the masses. The World Council would not be at all happy to find out that this was going on underneath their noses.

"Then what do we say?"

"I'll leave that up to you," he answered, unhelpfully. "Perhaps your son is unwell, or you take a trip somewhere. Just make sure he has the time to heal."

"And what about my regular appointments?" The hospital had these scheduled every week for months, a programme they put all new parents through.

"Especially not them," he said. "These classes and checkups exist to stop this very thing from happening. Use whatever excuse you can, pull any strings available. Do not let them see your child before we've finished with him. Is that understood?"

She nodded. She didn't know what they would do, but they would think of something.

"How long does it take to heal?"

"Could be six weeks, could be ten," he said. "There are treatments that can help, but time is the best healer."

"And there won't be any sign of the date?"

"Not a trace."

"And scarring?" She'd heard stories of adults who had tried to change their date. Anybody with a scar anywhere near the digits on their head was routinely questioned. They quickly arrested those who had been found guilty of deliberately trying to alter their date. Nobody ever heard from them again.

"In children as young as your son, there won't be any. He's lucky to be so young. That is why it's important you've come now, and before anybody else knows the date."

"The hospital knows the date," she said.

"They process thousands of babies a week, and I've told you, I'll change the date. They won't know this one has been changed, not from my side. I promise."

He went a little silent for a while, aware they hadn't discussed the reason for the short date. His team could alter what the System saw, but apart from that they couldn't work miracles.

"We need to discuss the reason they dated your son like they did, though. That doesn't go away, and they don't make errors, as we know." What was usual was a family wanting to hide a known and curable condition. These diseases would impact life expectancy—granted, not as much as the client in question—but were fully treatable within the medical system. Anybody falling ill before their Jubilee Year had that guarantee.

"They've made a mistake, believe me," she said. His clients always tried to convince him of that.

"I see," he said, thinking she would leave things at that.

"I've seen the research, I know what I'm talking about," she added. "My son has a rare condition, one of the six new diseases."

"Those are incurable," he stated.

"Currently, yes. But one institution is close."

"Within-life, close, you mean?"

"That's what the leading researcher told me personally, yes."

"Yet they didn't factor in these findings?" he asked. He'd heard nothing about such a breakthrough, he knew that much. These new diseases had been big news. Any change in their curability would have been bigger.

"They had the report, but said it didn't make a difference," she confirmed.

"Such things are often complicated," Devon said.

"The research is sound," Vivian countered. "Twenty to thirty years and it will be curable."

That was news to him.

"Okay then," Devon said, laying that aspect to rest. He'd still not told her about the second procedure, which was a lot more straightforward. "Back to the solution in front of us," raising two fingers as if counting off what they'd covered so far. "We have the initial operation which can happen now, and I suggest today, and," lowering the second finger as he got to this point, "we have the corrective procedure that'll finish the process in six to eight weeks."

He stood up, this explanation best done with a visit to the laboratory they had onsite, something they'd spent a lot of money to put together.

"Follow me," he said, Vivian somewhat surprised. She rose slowly, Charlie still asleep in the sling. They went through two doors that led off from the back of the office. Soon they were in the white-walled corridors of the clinic, several members of staff visible, all greeting Devon and Vivian warmly as they passed, each as professional and courteous as anyone Vivian had ever come across. Devon stopped outside a room marked *Chemical Supplies*.

"Believe me, we don't want the wrong people stumbling into this room," he joked, glancing around the corridor, the coast clear as he opened the door, switching on the lights once they'd stepped into the darkness. Vivian's mouth dropped open. If she'd not just walked with him from the office to where they now stood, she would have sworn that she was back at the central hospital, this the dating room that had tagged her son.

"It's amazing," she said, taking in the equipment, the set-up identical. The only thing missing was the mirrored wall, the same one that Vivian had pounded in her distress when she'd last been in a room looking like this one.

"We used the same team who designed the original," he said proudly, as this was an important piece of information. She only cared that they could do what they promised. "The computer is here to make sure we match the new date to the one we put into the System. We must discuss that. There are rules we have to consider. We can't make him live until he's too old, now."

"Just a good life, that's all," she said. Anything above her own years. Long enough for him to have his own family if he chose. Vivian able to see her grandchild born before she retired.

"Well, we can do that. Once your son's head has healed, this machine will ink your boy with new dates. It'll look fresher than most babies initially, but soon there will be no noticeable difference. No scarring, no poorly altered numbers, no computer record that doesn't match. It'll be perfect, I guarantee it."

She let out a long breath.

"Thank you," she said.

"Well, there is one more thing," he added, as if thanks might be too premature. Her stomach turned. The cost. She had been told this didn't come cheap, and looking around her, it wasn't a cheap set-up. This was the business, top of the range, no shortcuts.

"How much?" she asked.

Devon smiled, leading her back out of the room. The door locked behind them.

"Let's go back to my office, shall we," and he started walking before she said otherwise. Again, the nurses they passed greeted her fondly, and were nothing but respectful to Devon. It appeared he didn't seem to be a wicked man to work for.

Settling back down into the chairs they had been in before, Devon reached for the paperwork that she would need to sign.

"The good news is for you right away, there's nothing to pay," he smiled. She looked at him in disbelief, her mouth opening as if to form words, but he raised a finger as was his practice to keep her from speaking. "But," everything about what would follow, telling her she might not like it. "This treatment doesn't come cheap."

"I don't understand. You said there was nothing to pay."

"Most people cannot afford the fee, so we never charge it upfront. It's an investment for the future."

"The future?"

"We deduct our considerable expenses from the mother's payout," he confirmed. She got it at last. She would receive a million units when she entered her Jubilee Year, money she couldn't easily spend, most of it more than she might need.

"That's years from now," she said.

"I said it was an investment."

"Then how do you make your money?" she asked.

He looked shrewdly at her for a few seconds. "That's really what you want to know, is it?" he quizzed.

"How much?" she said, finally.

"Half your Jubilee payment," he confirmed.

"Half?"

He said nothing, his eyes bright, his smile remaining. She knew she didn't have a choice. She would give anything to allow her son a full life, both she and her husband would.

"Okay," she whispered, though he needed to be clear.

"Okay, you agree, or okay, but its too much to pay?"

"I agree. We'll do it."

He thought about asking her to confirm with her husband, but people like them didn't come to his office with options. They were desperate people, with time against them. His team needed to get to work on the boy that very day. The longer they delayed, the riskier it all became.

He handed her a document. "You must complete this paperwork right away," he said. She glanced at it all. "We will log the payment on your permanent record as a donation to a charitable cause." Nothing that would link back to him, but not a charity. It would be a couple more decades before this line of work started paying, but when it did, it would avalanche. "We'll need that agreed and confirmed by you before we start the treatment," he smiled.

"I'll do it," she said, ignoring his smile and waving the comment away. The quicker she could get on with it all, the better.

"I'll prep the medical facility to get everything ready," no hint that he would allow the pair to leave that day without having carried out the first operation.

He made the call, Vivian signing the consent form as he did so. He finished speaking to his team, remaining silent while she flicked through a few more pages.

Getting nearer to the end, he spoke up. "We must come up with a new date for your son," he said. The date they decided on needed to be on that page of the contract which she would sign twice to state she agreed with the amendment.

"What would look least suspicious?" she asked. Charlie would live with it through school and beyond. For some children, having the furthest date into the future would attract attention, though too early would mean they were picked on. Average would do. He tapped away at his computer for a few moments, double checking two points.

Soon he tore a piece of paper from his notepad and scribbled down a number that upside down initially looked illegible. Devon handed her the note, which right way up made sense.

"How about that?" he asked. She smiled. It would give Charlie until his late sixties.

"Thank you," was all she said, entering the date onto the contract in the space provided, and then signing it where needed. She completed the last pages before passing it back to him. Devon didn't need to check it. He'd seen her sign the most important parts.

"I'll get the team to update the official records this coming week," he said.

His desk phone rang, Devon picking it up instantly, hearing the confirmation he needed, before replacing the handset.

"They're ready for you in the clinic," he said. "We just need to confirm the payment." He passed her the device that had these details waiting. She'd done nothing like this before, the change she was agreeing to confirming her desire to leave half of her retirement fund to the designated good cause. She pressed on the fingerprint pad and confirmed the agreement with her pin codes. She passed him back the device, Devon glancing at the confirmation. His own son would be the one to benefit from that money; Devon himself would have gone by that point, though he had plenty of money coming in to make his own life exceedingly comfortable.

"I'll walk you through," he said, standing. A minute later a nurse had met them, Devon leaving Vivian in their capable hands, wishing her all the best and getting to his next meeting.

21

K ate had been back at work for two days, the dust hardly settled from the time with her brother, when the funding notification came through.

Her boss called the whole team together, announcing it over a lavish lunch bought in for the occasion, and hailing Kate as their champion. She would get four junior researchers to work for her, and the boss clarified that if she needed anything else, all she needed to do was ask.

Still reeling from the news, Kate went about her usual afternoon tasks, buzzing from what it all meant. Her brother had called it perfectly. She couldn't wait to tell him, though she wouldn't dare call him from the office.

"Congratulations, Katherine," her boss said once again, always using her longer name, though she mostly went by that name in those settings. Whenever she submitted her research, she knew it would be as Doctor Katherine Vann. Now that timeframe might have dramatically shortened. "I couldn't be more proud of you."

"Thanks," she said. She'd worked hard at this for a decade already. She knew she was close before the funding. Now it would be a matter of months, if that. "Look, I'll need a list of current known cases. With testing, having fresh samples to analyse is vital." She had more than enough samples on ice in storage.

"You ask them for what you need," he said. The sudden change in attitude from the Council towards his research laboratory had shocked him as much as anyone. Where there had been distance, now they were rolling over to offer them help.

"I will," she smiled, focusing back on the glass jars in front of her, willing him to move on. He did, eventually, Kate allowing him to leave the room before she put down what she had in her hand, and went directly to her computer.

She put in a request to the Council for a list of all living people who were carrying the disease. Once they had sent that through, she would move things on another stage.

BLYTHE SAW the request come in from Kate, though only because he was watching her laboratory carefully. It was below his rank to even bother with such a mundane request. He noticed the message was soon picked up, somebody perhaps on the lower floors of his building taking in the request from an outside agency.

They spotted the payment made that morning, Blythe having used his network to green-flag the establishment, meaning there were no issues with complying with any sharing of information. Blythe spotted the list sent out within two hours of the request.

He smiled.

KATE, who was the last person in the office, had not expected it back that quickly. She had assumed it might be days before they sent her the list. She saved it to her personal devices.

She chanced the second one.

Please add any known pre-birth cases to my list she typed and pressed send. She didn't expect to hear on this one anywhere near as quickly.

Shutting down her computer, she hung her white overalls back onto their usual peg. She collected her bag together and left the building.

A different security guard was on duty that day, one who she didn't recognise. She said nothing as she walked past him, her mind on the call she would make during her ride home.

"The scientist has left for the day," the Black-Collar spoke into his handset seconds after Kate left the building.

"Understood," came the crisp reply.

"You were right," she called, her car barely out of the carpark before she'd dialled her brother's number. He'd answered on the second ring. "The funding came through today. They have already sent me the first list."

He swore. There had been a part of him that had feared there might be no further contact.

"And the second?"

"I asked for it as I left the office, making it sound like an afterthought," she answered. She might have it waiting for her in the morning, for all she knew.

"Welcome to the big time," he joked. "Do you know what you'll do if you hear from this stranger again?"

"No." She'd not really thought much about that. She'd far from processed the day. The news of the funding should have been enough to take in. It was all she thought she'd needed. She should be content with that. At least she could finish her research. There would be nothing stopping her now.

"Once you have the list, send it to me," he said.

"I can't."

"It'll be okay," he assured her.

"Have you said anything about this to mum?"

They hadn't said anything to her before Kate had flown back. The siblings had talked during their daily walks, but none of it needed sharing with their mother. She just felt happy to have seen the positive impact Kate's visit had had on her son. Their mother didn't want to get involved, wanted to let them both talk it all over. Kate, however, knew she would never approve of what they had spent most of their time discussing.

"Not a thing," he said.

"And you, how are you doing?"

"I'm good," he said. Kate knew this whole situation had been the confirmation he needed. He'd known deep down something wasn't right, and when he'd been unable to work out what that was, it had caused his own depression, caused him to view himself as the problem, death the solution. Now he had a new outlook. He didn't know what that would mean, but his sister had been the one to open his eyes to the existence of at least some truth to the conspiracies he had nearly lost his mind to over the decades.

"Really?"

"Yes," he promised.

"Well, I'm glad this worked out like that," she said.

"Me too. Look, stay safe and let me know when you hear anything else."

"I'm still not sure I should," she said, cautiously. She knew within her role that confidentiality laws allowed her access to stuff, but passing it on to non-medical personnel, especially people such as her brother who had many shady connections, was way outside the rules.

He didn't argue with her for the moment. He would let things play out a bit for the time being, see what she received. He would circle back to this idea if she had the hard evidence.

"We'll chat soon, okay?" he asked.

"Sure," and she ended the call after they said goodbye to each other. Kate sat back as the fields came into view, her exit not far away now.

If she'd known just how things might be about to change, she would have had second thoughts about taking any further steps.

22

———

"What is it?" Blythe's wife stood in her nightgown, her husband in the doorway to his office which led from their bedroom, but he hadn't moved. Wasn't in either room, just standing there, motionless, otherwise deep in thought.

"It's nothing," he said, in a dismissive fashion, though she knew him too well.

"Blythe, don't do this to me, not again. We know where it'll get you."

He did. He knew he couldn't brush her away, so he opened up to her, right there, a few minutes after waking up, the day still new outside. He told her what was troubling him, the fullness of his thoughts.

He told her that his boss had asked questions.

They sat around the breakfast table thirty minutes later, each with a coffee in hand even though she'd not drunk coffee since becoming pregnant. She nursed the cup for the warmth it offered, her lack of drinking it unnoticed by the man in front of her, lost in his own thoughts.

She had never seen him this troubled before, nor this concerned for their own position in the elite.

"Kate made a request yesterday for information from the System. She's pressing ahead with the research, wanted an up-to-date list of every person carrying the disease."

"Well, that's great," she said, pushing his otherwise all-too-familiar attitude regarding this researcher to one side. He'd never met the woman as far as she knew. She believed him, anyway. Yet he constantly referred to her by only her first name; as if they knew her. As if she'd been to see them many times, perhaps even as a friend.

She was the woman who would save the life of their daughter, that much was true. His wife didn't feel threatened by this mystery woman. She knew why her husband was showing this interest. He was looking out for them. Doing the best for the family. His best, however, might put them all in danger.

"It is, isn't it," he responded weakly, as if he didn't know that at all. He'd expected Kate to take action. They had given her vast resources to put into her work now. What else was she supposed to do with it? And yet, it brought him closer to conflict. And he knew what her next move would be, even while he'd not said anything to his wife.

Blythe had decided not to see Kate, not directly. As long as she completed and then filed her research within the next six months, as long as a within-life cure was tabled and entered into the System, he'd done his part. He could vanish back into the shadows, watch from the sidelines, continue his rise to the top. Nobody could ever prove anything about what he'd done, Blythe was sure of that. He'd been careful, used every privilege he had, and while that presented certain problems—there were few people who had such privileges—they still couldn't prove what he had done.

There would only be assumptions. That wasn't enough to destroy him, wasn't even close. He would fight back with everything, even if it came from his boss. The old man was on the way out, a new sheriff in town. Eventually Blythe would run the show. They wouldn't be able to touch him then, even if they had the evidence.

"You don't sound so sure?"

He smiled, but didn't answer, continuing to turn his cereal that he hadn't eaten in ten minutes over and over with his spoon. Soon he gave up entirely, downed the last of his coffee, and stood without saying another word. She watched him, mouth open a little, though she knew not to call after him. Knew to leave him to it.

Half an hour later, he left for the office.

BLYTHE STOOD at the large window in his office. He'd been there barely seconds when the notification flashed through on his screen for the information that Kate had requested late the previous night.

He blocked the information that was going to be sent to Kate in response to her request, something that the person who had issued the information would not know he had done. The information was a brief list. It had one name on it.

His.

The most pressing issue for him now was exposing the snake within his midst, the person planted there who was leaking information to his boss from within his own team. Blythe felt like he had a good idea of who this was, the one man in that group who just seemed to rub him up the wrong way, the one member of the team who, if anyone was going to answer back, it would be him. The others just obeyed, kept their heads down and got on with the task. This troublemaker would question, would even accuse.

Some would call it the makings of leadership, someone rising above their peers. Blythe only saw it as divisive and dangerous and if the sneak was feeding information back to the Supreme Commander—perhaps angling for a promotion himself, perhaps even gunning for Blythe's job—then Blythe would give him hell, opening up with everything in his arsenal, and blowing the man out of the water. Perhaps literally, too.

"Gather around everyone," Blythe ordered, walking into their room a few seconds later, all heads turning his way. Blythe would throw out some information, monitor them all and if, as he thought, one of them was about to report him to the boss, he would know.

IT HAD BEEN three days now since Kate made her request from the lab for the information on that second list. Unlike the first time when she asked for something, the response instant, she had received nothing back this time.

She stood at her screen in the lab that morning, the inbox still empty of anything worthwhile, a team of people around her working hard now that funding had allowed the lab to prioritise her research, yet she felt empty.

By lunchtime, Kate had had enough of the impasse. She looked up the number for the department from which she'd made her first request and decided on calling them. She dialled the number, the handset to her ear before she had time to talk herself out of it.

"Hello?" came the answer.

She introduced herself, though they knew who was calling soon enough, the number flagged up as coming from the laboratory, the only reason a non-Council establishment would have had their call answered.

"I don't understand, you should have received that information the same day," the technician said, somewhat puzzled. He'd handled both requests on the day Kate had made them, turning around the first within hours, the second within minutes.

"I never received the second set of information, and this one is perhaps the most crucial," Kate confirmed, not going to elaborate on why it mattered so much to her.

"I can see it going out from my server," he said, his voice breaking off a second later.

"Problem?" Kate asked, automatically. She'd picked up that much.

"They blocked it," he said, not really considering whether she should know that aspect of the System's inner workings or not.

"Blocked?"

"Yes, I think the System flagged it or something. I've not seen this happen before, so I must look into it. Leave this with me, and I'll contact you as soon as I know something." She wouldn't count on that.

"Thank you," she said. "It would be very helpful for my research to have this information," laying it on thick. "It could take months, perhaps years off the timescale. We might even cure this disease pre-birth if I had enough test subjects."

"I'll let you know," he said.

THE TECHNICIAN IN QUESTION, once he'd finished speaking with Kate, went over everything again on his screen, making sure he'd not done anything wrong. He hadn't. His own log confirmed he had sent the file a few days before, two hours after he'd successfully sent the first one.

A command in the log history confirmed that it had got held by the server, flagged as delicate information. That action could happen one of two ways. It could have been automated, the most likely option, and one easily remedied. Or it had received human intervention, and this would have been more senior than his own rank allowed. That scenario led to a few different issues and would open the technician to discipline if he continued without clearance from above.

However, he worked closely with those at the very top, and would pass along his findings, needing to know what they knew about it.

The Supreme Commander was handed the notification of the issue four hours later, his underlings having looked into it and unable to decipher what had taken place.

It took him no time at all. Alone and standing behind his own terminal, he could see that Blythe had made the block, the man's name flagging up in the document and his action to stop it from leaving the office taken moments after.

So the couple were on that list; it gave the Supreme Commander the ultimate piece of this puzzle, the obvious reason why his protégé might have got involved with somebody like Kate Vann. And it had nothing to do with her looks. It was much more crucial than that.

"Get me Blythe Harrell's current location," he called through to his team. Blythe had been a hard man to track for years, taking his boss's own suggestion and using his rank and privileges to block the automatic tracker that every human being had on them at all times. However, with eyes in the office where Blythe was now located, it only took a call through to his contact to confirm that the man in question was where he was expected to be.

Blythe spotted the call coming in from Control moments later. No message passed on to him. The fact it had come in to someone Blythe assumed was nothing but a loyal team member surprised him the most. He logged that piece of information, waiting for any message, hoping that he was wrong about this person. Twice he spoke with them that day, giving them the perfect opportunity to remember their shortcoming and mention something he needed to know. They were nothing but polite, their smile solid, their eyes loyal.

He left that day knowing he'd found the snake in the grass, but he would do nothing about it for the time being, biding his time. Just knowing who the person was might prove useful to him at a later point.

23

K ate had not heard from her brother in two days. He'd not told her he was coming to stay with her, wanting to be closer to the action, to be closer to her.

He'd been at the airport for hours, paranoid beyond measure but not going to take any risks now. Not now that he knew, not this close to such a breakthrough. He'd put word out to a few of his friends; they were gathering others, promising to get in touch with him once he'd gone south.

Two flights had left already that would have taken him to Kate. He would have been standing with her already, the two together again. He'd not been sure, though. He felt exposed, at risk. They might try something, for all he knew. He'd not flown in a long time, the year fresh, the clock reset. What had nearly happened with Kate could not happen to him, not now that he knew for sure, not now he knew the truth of the theory.

He didn't have a car, however. Driving so far was out of the question, even if he had the option. That only left flying.

Nobody asked him what he was doing at the airport. He was clever, he didn't stay in the same place for too long and never returned to one he'd used already. He watched people, mostly, the first two flights opening, the gates busy. He'd purchased a ticket for the first one, this done late, there still being seats available. He let it go without him, leaving him in the airport. Leaving him time to watch, to pick his perfect option.

Families had been on the second flight. While they rarely killed children in plane crashes, they had been on some flights. An entire family lost in a moment. They were not his hedge of protection, however. Nor were the Gold-Collars, who were present in their droves at such a place, which made perfect sense. They were all busy seeing as much of the world as possible. He spotted many from different places, the airport a natural hub to connect to other flights. Gold-Collars had also died on these crashes over the years, the news tragic––any unexpected loss of life always was, and the Council boasted that they now controlled their own destiny––but these were people in their last year. Some in their last weeks. Their relatives would get a partial payout, but this would be significantly lower than the payouts for younger passengers, especially families.

However, in all the years, in all the crashes, not once had there been a report of a Red-Collar being on the aircraft. Nor had there been a Black-Collar. Not that these people were not at the airport. He'd seen plenty of both. They'd just never been on a plane that went down, and now he knew why. Kate had revealed that to him. What he couldn't work out was why.

He would not take a flight unless he saw at least one other passenger present from either of these two categories, but ideally a Red. Then he would board, then he would grab that ticket and be right behind them. He would not know where they were sitting, but it didn't matter. The plane would be safe, he felt certain. The System would not kill one of their own.

Many hours after first arriving, he spotted what he had been hoping for. Two Red-Collars stood at gate thirty, the fourth flight option since being at the airport that would fly him to his sister Kate. Wanting to make sure, he went up to the couple who seemed alarmed to be spoken to by a stranger but confirmed the man was at the right gate for the destination he'd just asked them about. They were flying there too.

He purchased one of the final remaining seats within seconds, his boarding pass saved to his device automatically, and he now waited.

An hour later, he stood in line, some way behind the Red-Collars—he would not board until they had—and watched as they got to their turn, the couple joined by other friends before boarding.

As the aircraft moved along the runway, gaining speed all the while, Kate still knew nothing about her brother's plans that day. He'd not wanted to tell her, not wanting to inform anybody watching her that he would come. He sat between two other passengers and closed his eyes as the plane lifted into the air. He would try to sleep, try to push the worries and concerns from his mind. The plane would not crash; they weren't about to kill him.

It'd been hours since his last hit, the drugs beginning to wear off now. His hands shook as the aircraft continued to rise into the sky and he used his entire will power to ignore what his body was demanding. He would try to sleep.

———

It was already dark when Kate looked through her security camera, the knock at the door unexpected, the sight of her brother looking back at her even more surprising. She opened the door immediately.

"What are you doing here?" she asked, though he didn't answer, as he stepped inside, closing the door behind her. This seemed to concern her even more. "What's wrong?"

He shook his head. "Nothing, just being careful, that's all," he said, his eyes a little bloodshot as he glanced around the place. He'd never seen her new home. New to him, anyway. She'd lived there for nearly eight years.

"You didn't even let me know you were coming," she said, following him into the kitchen, as he continued to take in the house.

"Didn't want to alert anybody to my whereabouts," he responded.

He opened her fridge, as if he lived there, as if he'd been there many times. "Where's the beer?"

"What?"

"Beer," he said, pointing at the mostly empty fridge, something that rarely got very full, if truth be told. She'd not been to the shop for a few days. "There's none here."

"I don't have any," she said. She preferred wine anyway, but wouldn't say that. She didn't have any of that on offer, either.

He swore.

"Do you have anything to drink?" he asked her, Kate knowing what he meant, but pointed out the obvious, anyway.

"There's water in the tap and a kettle over there. Are you going to tell me what the hell my kid brother is doing turning up on my doorstep like this?"

He ignored the offer of a hot drink, and had never drunk enough water, though he answered that last question.

"I've come to stay with you," he confirmed.

She didn't know what she felt about that. It was one thing for her to visit their family home, staying with her mother, talking sense into her brother. It felt an altogether unique thing for him to be there in her world. She worked most of the day, longer hours than she would ever want him to know. What would he do all day?

"You flew down?" she asked, surprised if he had.

He nodded, having grabbed a slice of bread from a loaf on the kitchen side, ripping it in half as she spoke and stuffing it into his mouth. She watched crumbs fall to the floor, having cleaned the day before, her frustration getting the better of her now.

"God, Joe, you're such a slob," she scolded, going over to a cupboard and taking out a plate for him. She passed it to him, the other half of the piece of bread he'd taken already following the first into his mouth. He grinned at her, taking the plate, bread hanging from his mouth. She shook her head in disgust, going over to the drinks cupboard, where she had the sort of alcohol he'd been asking about moments before. His eyes lit up as she pulled out a bottle of whisky.

"Now you're talking," he said, taking the glass from her when she had poured them both a measure, and he washed the bread down with the liquid soon after.

Kate watched him closely as she sipped her own drink, his eyes edgy, tired from the travel, but it was more than that, she could tell. She picked up the slight shake in his fingers too, the glass he was holding not steady. He held it out, regardless, pleading another fill-up. She obliged, only filling it to half the amount she had a minute earlier.

"Well?" she asked, a finality in her voice that demanded a proper answer from him this time, a tone suggesting she wasn't messing around any more.

"I needed to be where the action is," he confirmed. "Need to stay close to you."

"Close to me?"

"Have you heard from your mystery man yet?" he asked, ignoring her sense of concern in what she'd just said.

"No, and I told you I would let you know as soon as I did."

"It's been a while though," he said, as if he was as much a part of her research team as those with whom she worked.

"You didn't need to come all this way for me to tell you that though, Joe."

"True. The guys want me with you, watching your back and all that."

"I can look after myself," Kate said, somewhat annoyed now.

"Can you?" he asked.

"And what guys wanted you here? Who have you been speaking to?"

"They're good people. My type of people," he clarified, which told her all she needed to know. The conspiracy gang, the same people who had been feeding Joe lines––both the verbal and illegal kind–– for decades.

"And what, they want to start some revolution?" she laughed, knowing his group of druggy misfits had never been up to much, the narcotics in their bodies making them merely outlaws in their own heads.

"Maybe," he replied, a little too coherently, a little too confidently for Kate to dismiss it as simple male bravado.

She let it drop for now.

"Want something proper to eat?" she asked. If they were drinking whisky, then he'd better have something more substantial in his stomach than one slice of bread.

"Have you eaten already?" he asked. It was nine at night. There was a frying pan on the drying rack, a dinner plate next to it.

"Yes," she said. She wasn't about to say that she'd been thinking about going to bed when he'd knocked on the door, work forcing her to get up early in the morning.

"I'll be okay with a sandwich," he said, putting the plate on the side and then grabbing another couple of slices from the bread bin, before buttering and adding a few layers of cheese to it while she waited. She walked into the lounge once he'd finished making it, Joe grabbing the bottle of whisky as he carried his glass and plate through, the bottle hanging somewhat precariously though he soon lowered it expertly onto her coffee table.

"Nice digs," he said, taking a seat on the sofa, putting his legs up on the table as he devoured the cheese sandwich. She said nothing to any of this, sipping her whisky from time to time, working out whether him being there was remotely a good idea. She didn't have a spare room, didn't need one. He would have to sleep on the sofa. It was hardly wide enough for him to be comfortable. She would also disturb him in the morning, which wouldn't be good. She didn't fancy having to tiptoe around. She resigned to offering him her room, though that had to be a temporary solution.

He put his plate back onto the table, in the spot where his feet had been. He'd spotted her glancing at them twice, and soon moved them onto the floor, gathering his glass of whisky and the bottle in his hands as he sat back, looking across to her. He topped up his glass again, Kate waving away the need herself, half her contents still swilling around in the tumbler she cradled on her lap.

"Mum knows you've come, right?" Kate asked. It wouldn't have surprised her if Joe had not mentioned it to their mother.

"She knows," he said. "She wanted me to come."

Kate had not spoken with their mother for a few days, an action she regretted now. Perhaps she would have had some warning.

"I'm not sure what more I can tell you," she said.

"You got that first list immediately, right?" he asked. It had been something she'd told him was the case, anyway.

"Yes, same day."

"And you asked for the next one right away."

"I did." She'd not told him about the conversation with the technician who had sent her the first list. She quickly caught him up with those events.

"He said they had blocked it?"

"Yes, seemed genuinely confused, too, like he couldn't explain it."

Joe smiled at that. "Proves it would have told us this man's name," he said, as if that were the only explanation, the only possible reason. She could think of others, though the idea had formed on the edges of her mind for a day already. She was, however, less prone to believe that type of thing than her brother.

"Do you think I'll still get this list?"

Joe shook his head. "If the man's suppressed it, you won't get it now."

Hearing that made her frustrated, the first sign that, just like her brother, she too wanted answers. She wanted to know who this man was, wanted to know what he knew.

"When my friends arrive, we'll see what they can find."

"Your friends?" Kate said, alarmed that there might be other knocks on the door before the night was out.

"They won't come here," he smiled, as if that were her only concern. "It'll be a while. I don't think any of them will fly, too dangerous," he said. "But they'll be here, eventually. They'll know who to speak to, they have these types of contacts."

"What contacts?"

"People, sources. Don't worry about that side of things, you just need to keep doing what you're doing. If this man wants to contact you, he will."

"You said I wouldn't hear anything."

"That doesn't mean he won't reach out. He doesn't want you knowing his name, that much is clear," he said. That point felt far from clear, merely hearsay, speculation, assumption. "But he probably knows you'll keep trying, anyway. That might expose what he's done with you."

"Expose?"

"He warned you not to take that flight," as if needing to remind her of this fact. "That can't have been normal procedure, as we both know. I bet this guy will do anything to keep his identity secret, and that goes both ways."

"Both ways?"

"If you keep pushing, it'll alert the System to the issue. They'll see the block stopping that list from reaching you. It might even lead them to him. There is no way anyone in the Council will like someone doing things behind the scenes, using their powers to limit the flow of information like this."

She wanted to know how he knew all this––or how he thought he knew. It might all be rubbish. Something based on old knowledge or no knowledge at all. But she realised who would have fed him this information. The same gang he'd been around since before Kate left home.

"So you think he'll make contact?"

"I think if you keep pushing, you'll hear eventually."

"Keep pushing?"

"Follow up again if you don't hear by the morning. Get them to explain why it's taking so long."

"He's told me why it's taking so long."

"Ask again," Joe said, waving away her protest. "Keep pushing until you have that name. Either they send you the list, your mystery man unwilling to put his head in the firing line by continuing to block that memo, or he makes contact directly, heading off the potential danger he could be in."

Kate glanced at the clock on her lounge wall.

"Joe, it's getting late. I need to be in the office before nine tomorrow. I've got a meeting." She stood. "You can have my room. That way I won't disturb you."

"You sure?" he asked, eyeing the sofa sceptically, unsure it would even fit his torso comfortably.

"I'll grab my things now," she said, bounding up the stairs seconds later, Joe topping up his glass one final time, returning the bottle to the kitchen, grabbing another four slices of bread which he buttered and added cheese to, before pressing them together and slicing both sandwiches in half, the mound stacked on his plate. He heard Kate coming back downstairs soon after, clothes in her arms, some bedsheets hanging over her shoulder, which dragged on the stairs as she came down. He stood in the kitchen's doorway as she dropped her clothes for the morning over the single sofa, before proceeding to tuck the bedding into the edges of the larger one. She evidently didn't have a spare duvet apart from the one she used on her own bed, and would make do with two blankets. The lounge was fairly warm, anyway.

"You can go up now," she offered. Kate didn't need him watching her, and she wanted to get to sleep fairly soon. "I'll brush my teeth and take a shower, but give me ten minutes and the upstairs is all yours." Kate followed her brother up, carrying his case, as he had his hands full with the plate of sandwiches and a glass of whisky. She showed him into her room, the bed neatly covered, the curtains already closed. She left him to it, going into the bathroom seconds later, the water coming on not long after.

Drying herself quickly, she opened the bathroom door, hoping he'd not yet gone to sleep—it seemed unlikely as it wasn't so late. She'd forgotten to get the hairdryer, needing to make sure her hair was dry otherwise it would look ridiculous come the morning. She wouldn't have the time or patience to fix it then.

Her bedroom door stood open, Joe not there. He'd taken the plate and glass back downstairs—she hoped there would be some whisky left in that bottle. She rummaged through her drawers, pulling the hairdryer from the bottom one. Her brother's case was open on the floor, nothing removed from there besides a clear plastic bag, the contents obvious, on her bedside table.

They were a packet of little white pills. The drugs she'd known he'd used for too long now.

When they passed on the stairs, she didn't mention what she'd just seen. His hand held a glass of water in his no longer trembling fingers, his eyes lacked the bloodshot nature of earlier, alive now and looking bright.

"Sleep well," he said as she passed. "Thanks for giving up your bedroom for me." Kate said nothing as she reached the hall below, moving towards the sofa as she heard him go into the bathroom.

She lay there for twenty minutes thinking about her brother. If he was still using drugs, it worried her. He'd always been fanciful at the best of times. These drugs only pushed him further into that world of conspiracy and counter-conspiracy. Did he even know what the truth was anymore? His presence was the last thing she wanted when she'd just got the breakthrough she needed at work. A time when focus and drive were most needed, the culmination of all her research, all those hours now about to reach the breakthrough she had longed for. A breakthrough that would see her name and reputation grow, that would get her noticed.

Was that now all at threat?

24

Blythe said nothing to the remaining nine members of his team as he left his office, pulling the door closed behind him.

That lunchtime, when there had still been ten of them, he'd publicly screamed blue murder at the man. He had betrayed them all, he'd said, even though Blythe had been the sole target. Two military personnel had forcibly removed the spy, Blythe glaring at a man he had trusted as they led him out of the room, the others shocked at the scene, though the guilty party didn't protest once. He knew the game was up; they had exposed him. He didn't feel in any danger, knew he would be okay. They might even promote him after this.

Blythe had not answered a call all afternoon, his team knowing not to bother him. Then Blythe had seen the communication. He didn't know if they had meant to hide it. The Supreme Commander, a man who Blythe had looked up to, a man who had said he trusted Blythe to step into his post, had instructed officers to watch Blythe. Had instructed men to move in close, Blythe's actions deemed a threat to world security.

Blythe had fled from the office that very minute.

Pulling the door behind him, his computer terminal locked and secure, Blythe didn't glance towards the others, not even sure if they spotted him go. They would all know better than to mention anything, all know better than to call after him and ask him where he was going. They wouldn't dare after what had happened earlier.

Blythe avoided the lifts, taking the stairs, sure that the security personnel in his own building would have that same communication concerning him. If they saw Blythe leaving in the afternoon, with no meetings shown, no other reason for his sudden change of plan, then they would know. They would stop him.

He took the fire escape on the other side of the building; the door slamming shut as he left. There was no going back now. He took a taxi home, Blythe warning the driver not to register him as a passenger—something that was illegal—but coming from a Red-Collar, who promised to tip him double the fee, the driver didn't mind at all.

This at least bought him some time. They would look for him at the office, his car still there, no other sign of him leaving. Blythe glanced at his watch, willing away the two hours that it would take to get home, knowing he couldn't risk a call, not even a short one. He hoped his wife would be home when he got there.

As the taxi pulled up just after five, Blythe paid the man as promised.

"No record, okay," Blythe pressed, the driver nodding, far from the first time he'd pulled such a stunt. Blythe didn't even wait for the car to move away, turning and racing up his driveway and in through the front door. His wife came out from the kitchen at the sound of his arrival, a dishcloth in her hands.

"What's wrong?" she asked, seeing his expression, taking in the earlier time that he was home.

"We need to go immediately," he said, taking the stairs up to his office. "Grab whatever you can carry and meet me in the garage in five minutes." He hoped they had that long. She didn't bother to ask him why, Blythe upstairs by then, vanishing into their bedroom and continuing into his study beyond. She dropped the cloth on the kitchen worktop, ignoring her urge to straighten it out, and picked up her bag. She filled a shopping bag with a few items from the kitchen, with no understanding of how long they would be away. Blythe's actions had suggested these questions were secondary.

She heard him bounding back down the stairs. She moved towards the door that led into the garage, an area they used mostly for storage. Blythe kept his car out in the front near to the charging point.

He followed her into the garage seconds later, locking the door behind him.

"You're starting to scare me," she said, as he pulled the covers off an old petrol vehicle he'd purchased many years ago, a classic vehicle that rarely got an outing. This only increased her sense of dread.

"We aren't safe here." If that was his attempt at reassuring her, he'd failed. He opened the passenger door for her, letting her get in before easing it closed, laying the blankets that had covered the vehicle to one side then getting in behind the wheel himself. He put the key into the ignition, the engine roaring to life. He pressed the button to open the garage door, light pouring into the space as soon as the door rose. Blythe checked his rearview mirror, pleading there to be nobody behind them, no men in front of the house blocking their escape. As the door opened fully, the coast seemed clear. He put the car into reverse, the engine revving as he played with the pedals, the car backing out of the garage with some speed.

"Where's your other car?" she asked, as he swung the petrol car around into the spot where his work vehicle should have been standing. Blythe closed the garage as he changed gear from reverse into first.

"I left it there," he said. "Got a taxi here. It will buy us some time."

"From whom?"

Blythe pressed another button, the gates to their house swinging open towards them, the road beyond clear.

"They know," he said.

"Who does? Who knows?" but his eyes gave her the answer. She swore as they raced away, the gates beginning to close automatically behind them.

"What happened?" she asked as they reached the first corner, the engine vibrating much more than a modern car did, the ride more bumpy, more old school than she thought it would be. She'd never been in a petrol car before, this very much Blythe's hobby, the man a collector, albeit only a few cars down the years. This was the only one he still owned, by far the most stunning vehicle, iconic too. She'd had no issues with him keeping it, though she'd not seen him take it out in months.

"The Commander had someone planted in my team. I discovered it the other day, got rid of him today," he said, before filling her in completely on his actions that afternoon.

"It doesn't mean they suspected anything," she said, believing his response perhaps to have been a little over dramatic.

"I know exactly what it meant," he said, well aware of such tactics. He'd used them many times himself in the past.

"And you've confirmed it all to them now anyway," she said, somewhat annoyed.

"I had no choice. If I stayed, they would have arrested me," he said, his face showing there was no need for her to argue. He knew more about that aspect of things than she did. She was happy that they hadn't detained him.

"So where are we going?" but before he could answer, he told her to get down. She sank down in her seat, Blythe doing his best to look the other way as he slowed down. A convoy of military vehicles raced past them coming from the opposite direction, and as he watched them in his rear mirror, they turned onto the road from which he had just come. They were heading to his house, he was certain.

He sped off, turning as often as possible, desperate to increase the distance from the area. The car he was driving did not exist on the System. Nobody knew he owned it. How long that remained true would determine their chances of getting away.

"You can get up now," Blythe said, his wife raising her head again. "They've gone."

She looked at him without speaking for the time being. Buildings raced past them, the road soon opening up onto a faster route, Blythe taking it and heading west. Anywhere would do, his wife catching Blythe regularly checking his rearview mirror, his hands tight on the wheel, the tank full and a can or two in the boot, but aside from that, they would be out of fuel. Petrol stations had long since stopped selling fossil fuel products.

25

It had been three days since Celebration Day and Herb had not ventured away anywhere. He woke at home that morning, as he'd done every day since getting his Gold-Collar. There was the smell of smoke in the air. It wasn't of anything burning, nothing to alarm him. The smell was definitely outside when he opened the windows, perhaps kids messing around that night in the alley behind his house, or the fading embers of a neighbour's bonfire. Not that it was really that time of year.

Herb admired his Gold-Collar again, experiencing a mixture of pride and dread. He hated what it meant. He'd not spent even one unit of the million that had arrived the same day he had visited the Colosseum. He didn't much feel like doing anything with it.

Three days into retirement and he already missed his old job.

Herb stayed in his pyjamas for now, his new shirt and new identity left in his bedroom, the man deeming it safe to ignore the rules inside his own home. He switched on the kettle, turning on the television. He kept to his usual routine, decades in the making, even if he had allowed himself an extra half hour in bed since leaving work for the last time.

From inside the kitchen, the steam issuing from the freshly made pot of tea––on a weekday usually there was only time for one cup but now he could allow himself time for several––he pulled the window blind up. At that angle, the sun was barely apparent in the distance above his back garden fence, he could now see the source of the smoke he'd woken to, evidence that the same kids might still be there. Smoke rose gently into the air in the alleyway.

Herb ran upstairs, dressing quickly, donning his new Gold-Collared shirt and pulling a jumper over it. The collar would remain clear, as had to be the case. He pulled on thick socks before going downstairs and finding an old pair of shoes, then headed to the back door, broomstick in hand, though he didn't expect any trouble. A good fright would be all these kids needed, him on one side of the fence, them on the other. They wouldn't know who he was, and he didn't want them finding out either.

Only, as he approached, with the telltale hum of an engine gently ticking over, Herb soon reassessed his options. The source of the smoke was far from children messing around. There was a petrol engine car tucked into the small alleyway behind his garden, the engine presumably running to keep the heating on. Something a man of his era was old enough to know about. Herb peered through a hole in the fence, catching a sight of the bodywork. He couldn't see the person behind the wheel, though he knew there was someone there, probably sleeping given the position of their head.

The keys to the gate which led from his garden into the alleyway hung in the kitchen. Herb had little use for the gate and hadn't gone through it in years. He thought about leaving them to it, whoever they were, though perhaps they had got lost? Perhaps they were wounded? It was no place for a car, anyway, and someone else might soon see the smoke and go looking.

Herb strode back across the garden and in through his back door, grabbing the single key that hung by itself from the peg in the kitchen and returned to the rear of his garden, this time continuing to the gate. He put the key into the lock and while a little stiff, it soon opened, the door swinging somewhat creakily in on him. Herb grabbed his broomstick again, not sure what he was doing, but not prepared to venture out empty-handed.

The car was a classic, that much was clear, something he'd seen in books but never up close. It seemed in remarkable condition too, which would mean it must have been worth a lot.

Herb hesitated at that thought—perhaps it was stolen, the thief there behind the wheel where they had slept for the night while on the run? He clutched the broom handle a little tighter and as he peered in through the window, the man woke, startled.

Herb nearly fell over backwards, the driver's door opening fast, as Blythe stepped out, a pained expression on his face.

Blythe looked Herb over, his eyes soon falling onto the man's Gold-Collar. Likewise, Herb couldn't avoid noticing the Red-Collar in front of him and someone who looked vaguely familiar, though Herb didn't know why.

"What are you doing here?" Herb asked, meaning both in that immediate vicinity—the alleyway—and that part of the city. Red-Collars rarely ventured into those parts.

"Are you alone?" Blythe asked, his accent matching his collar. This was no car thief, no chancer who'd come across something and stolen it. Herb nodded, only then noticing movement from a woman in the passenger seat. She had evidently woken with the sudden actions of both men.

"I'm no danger to you," Blythe said, reaching low into the car and having a word with his wife, who slowly got out, coming around the back of the vehicle to avoid Herb and then stood next to what would soon be clear was her husband. Blythe switched off the engine, his wife shivering.

"You've been there all night?" Herb asked, nodding at the car, though the answer to his question was clear.

"It was late when we found this spot," Blythe said, enough on the subject. They'd evidently been discovered. The fact it was by a man in a Gold-Collar and not a Black one meant everything to them at that moment. "Do you live here?"

Herb thought his emergence from a gate in the fence would be plain enough that this was the case.

"I do," he said, after several seconds of silence.

"Can we come into the warmth, at least? My wife is pregnant."

Herb looked towards the woman, younger than the man, if he really was her husband, and younger by some years too. He noticed the bump showing on her stomach. She looked frozen.

"Follow me," Herb said, pushing aside his own concerns. He'd never spoken with a Red-Collar, and here he was now leading two of them into his home. He locked the gate behind them, promising them the car would be safe. They waited for him to walk into the house before continuing a few paces behind, the backdoor still open as Herb had left it. He reboiled the kettle without even asking if they wanted anything to drink.

"There's tea in the pot if you fancy that," he said, mostly to the woman.

"I'm Blythe and this is my wife, Kassia," Blythe said, looking for recognition in the old man's eyes at the mention of their names.

"I'm Herbert. Herbert Bradley," he said, holding out his hand to Blythe as he mulled over the visitor's name, something registering after a while. "Blythe?" he quizzed. "That rings a bell," and Kassia looked at her husband a little alarmed. "What are you doing in these parts then, if you don't mind me asking? It's usually kids messing around back there, from time to time. I half expected to frighten another bunch just now, in fact, until I found your car."

"Things became a little difficult for me at work. We needed to take some time away, found ourselves in your street in the dead of night, and we had to get some sleep. That alley seemed the perfect spot," Blythe said, seemingly selective with his words, a skill Herb knew well, surrounded by young people all his professional life, aware of when they weren't telling him the whole story.

"No-one will spot you here, unless they go searching for you," Herb said. "Anyway, before we talk more, I think Kassia should have something warm to drink."

"A tea would be lovely," she said, her voice as well groomed as that of her husband. Herb, a teacher himself, had never felt so uncouth. He pulled two mugs from the cupboard, pouring the first cup, as the kettle came to a boil.

"I'll have a coffee, if that's okay," Blythe said, a hand going out to stop the second cup from being poured.

"I thought your lot only drank tea at this time of day," Herb laughed, reaching for some coffee. Instant granules would have to do. He'd never gone in for those fancy machines and, his new wealth aside, wasn't planning on changing that now.

"My lot? Oh, you mean Red-Collars. Believe me, we drink everything," Blythe smiled, his wife giving him a somewhat reproachful look as if he'd somehow spoken out of turn.

Coffee made, and a cup of tea poured for himself, Herb directed them both into his small lounge, the three sitting down before anything further was said, and this by Herb, doing his best at playing host.

"I guess you'll be needing something to eat?" he asked, "Especially since you are pregnant."

"We'll manage with the hot drinks for now, but thank you," Kassia smiled, a fine-looking woman if ever he'd seen one. Herb couldn't help notice the shabby nature of his home, his ageing furnishings, the sofas a decade past their best. He didn't entertain often, and never anyone who would have cared one jot.

They sipped their drinks in silence for a moment, the house peaceful.

"You live alone, I take it?" Blythe asked, the hands of a clock the only other audible noise from the rest of the house.

"I do," Herb confirmed. Recognition lit up his face at that moment. He'd worked out where he knew his visitor from, though as quickly as that realisation had come, it was followed closely by instant concern. "You're Blythe Harrell, the next Supreme Commander."

Blythe nodded slowly.

Herb swore, then apologised, then swore again. Kassia just laughed.

"We must get you writing more of our speeches with language like that," she joked.

"I'm sorry, Ma'am, and with you carrying a child too," Herb said, as if scolding himself for his manners.

"I doubt the little bugger can hear us yet," she said, mimicking him, and it drew a smile from the older man.

"So what are you both doing here, if you don't mind me asking?" They were a long way from their usual haunts. Prospective Supreme Commanders didn't need to go out canvassing, that much was clear.

"We're on the run, actually," Blythe said, feeling he had the measure of the man in front of him. A Gold-Collar still living at home, with no sign of extravagant spending. Blythe felt comfortable, recognising someone not acting like his peers usually did.

Herb looked them both in the face, from one to the other and then back to Blythe again, no hint of a smile from either visitor.

"I see," he said, finally. "Can I ask why?"

26

Vivian had avoided every appointment sent through from the hospital, the couple travelling with their baby son, she'd told friends. Even fellow mums, women whom she had met during the antenatal classes had called her out of the blue, leaving messages on her voicemail, wondering when she would join them at the sessions.

The System hated it when mothers went awol.

The one person Vivian could not track was the scientist behind the research; she was still without a name. She could not get any more information on her, and when she'd called the lab––the number redirected––the person answering the call had given the couple a corporate sounding answer.

That stopped them calling again, concerned that there was now too much Council control. They didn't want to put themselves on their radar.

Charlie was healing from the operation, though his plaster remained in place, and from what Vivian could see, there were still some weeks to go. Family had stopped asking when they would learn the date for the child. They'd soon come to believe it was bad news.

Social etiquette said that once a couple went silent over such a thing, you stopped asking.

There was only one other person Vivian could think of reaching out to, a man whom she had turned to for help in the first place, and someone who she would soon need to contact anyway to arrange the last part of the procedure. She was sure that he could find out the name of the scientist spearheading the research that would save the life of their baby. Devon might even tell them where to find her.

Vivian called, getting through to Devon immediately. He was surprisingly hands-on though she knew he could trust her. They both had a lot at stake in this, and she had paid him handsomely for these services. She guessed it was the least he could do. They scheduled a slot two days from then. She promised that she would be there.

ON THE DAY of the appointment, Stuart said goodbye to his wife. Vivian took their son with her as she walked the block and entered the same door that she had done a few weeks before. Devon was waiting for her in the main reception area, talking to the woman behind the desk.

"Mrs Bryant, if you'll come this way," he smiled, Vivian following him to the same office where she'd signed half of her inheritance away, though seeing her beautiful son as he looked up at her from the sling, his eyes blue and bright, she would have paid twice that.

Devon shut the door behind her and they took the same seats that they had done the last time they had met together.

"I take it everything is going according to plan?" he asked.

"It is, and though I want to arrange the last procedure while I'm here today, it isn't the only reason I came to see you."

"Go on," he said, putting the pen back onto the desk and closing his notebook.

"I can't find the name of the scientist behind my son's cure," she said, stroking the blond hair which had thickened considerably in

the last three weeks, though still the plaster stuck out, the boy past
the newborn phase.

"You want me to find her?"

"I think you'll have the access, yes," she said.

"Tell me what you have, I'll see what I can get."

She wrote the name of the disease, and what else she
remembered.

"Look, why don't you speak with the clinic and arrange a date for
the last procedure, then come back here."

Vivian remembered the way, holding her son in her arms as she
walked, getting to the reception desk in the clinic a moment later.

"My name is Vivian Bryant," she said, the lady smiling from
behind the desk.

"I'm aware of who you are, Mrs Bryant. Shall we find a slot to get
Charlie dated then?"

Vivian smiled. "I think he will heal within three weeks, on schedule, but I'm not sure."

"Would you like to see a nurse before we plan anything and get
their opinion?"

"That would be wonderful," Vivian replied, delighted that it
wasn't resting on her decision alone. The quicker they got Charlie
dated, the quicker life could return to normal and they could resume
their usual routine.

"I'll call through now," the receptionist said, speaking into the
handset for a little while, Vivian stepping back, allowing the woman
space. She took in the waiting area, trees in pots which had to be fake.
They were showing blossom, which couldn't have been visible yet.

Two minutes later a nurse had appeared, different from the one
she'd seen before but wearing the same welcoming manner.

"Please, come this way," she invited Vivian, who followed her a
little way down the corridor and into a side room. The nurse shut the
door, allowing them to be alone. "If you'll sit Charlie on your lap, I'll
look at the spot and assess how long he needs."

Vivian pulled her son loose of the sling, the boy kicking a little,
though soon she had him on her lap.

"It's not been easy these last few weeks," Vivian said, the nurse stepping closer, stroking Charlie's head before, ever so gently, starting to pull back the protective plaster. Vivian hadn't dared check beyond a few centimetres, desperate for it to heal but not wanting to hinder the process. It still seemed rather red, a scab around all four sides of the wound.

"This is progressing very well," the nurse confirmed, Vivian surprised by that but happy given what she'd said.

"That's a relief."

The nurse replaced the plaster with a fresh one, giving no sign that someone had tampered with it.

"I would keep a hat on him until you come back here," the nurse encouraged. "It'll cover the plaster up, enabling you to get out more."

She'd not thought of that.

"You said it's been difficult?" the nurse asked, writing a few brief words onto the computer, Vivian waiting for the nurse to finish before answering her.

"We've done our best to avoid every social gathering, though we are riding our luck."

The nurse gave a knowing grin. Vivian could tell she was far from the first mother to come in complaining about that.

"We can't rush the last procedure as the skin needs time to heal. That said, I think we've gained a week. You could bring him back in two weeks and we can complete everything."

"And the scabs?"

"They'll heal soon enough, perhaps even by then. They won't affect the dating, we'll be able to work around that area. In two months, nobody will be able to tell any difference," she confirmed, which was exactly why Vivian had paid them so handsomely.

"That's wonderful news," Vivian said, openly relieved. Even one week less of having to travel and dodge calls would be something they would welcome with open arms.

"You can now go back and arrange a slot with reception. Any problems, and you can call us. But we'll see you both back again soon," the nurse said, standing up and opening the door for Vivian, who thanked the woman and retraced her steps back to reception.

"Anything in two weeks works for us," Vivian said, the receptionist looking up, waiting for the confirmation. She tapped away on the computer, giving a date in exactly fourteen days, Vivian confirming she would be there. They could last another two weeks, then their nightmare would be over, and they would finally show off their son to their relatives and friends.

Vivian knocked on the door to Devon's office, mostly as a courtesy, though he ushered her in once she showed her face.

"Come, come," he encouraged. "I have some good news for you."

She took a seat, Devon printing off something from the computer, the printer jumping to life instantly. He stood, which seemed a slow process, his enormous frame not as nimble as it had once been, and he lumbered over to collect the printout.

"Her name is Katherine Vann," Devon confirmed. He handed Vivian the printout, the woman's face, personal phone number and work address displayed on the information he now handed her.

"This is the woman leading the research?"

"Yes. And I know why you've not been able to reach out to her. This last week, the World Council stepped in and massively funded Vann's research project. They've put their full support behind this cure, albeit a few weeks too late for your son, but you've done the right thing by him."

She was struggling to take in the news.

"What does that mean?"

He'd come across such funding input once or twice before, though he deliberately funded his own lab privately. He wouldn't allow the System to know his client base, nor the full extent of his operations.

"Means they are moving it into the final phase. They expect to have a confirmed within-life cure for this disease within months."

Vivian left with the information she'd been desperate to have, but also with the knowledge that her son's treatment was not only in the pipeline, but was mainstream and with a major announcement for the breakthrough possibly only a little way down the road.

27

Vivian sat in her car, Charlie away for a long walk in the forest with his dad. They'd done a lot of walking in the last few weeks. When not lost in the wilderness they'd taken a canal boat for a week. Anything to get them out of routine, to take them away from a world that demanded contact––a health check here for baby, a support group there, a registration event and yet more for baby. *Baby baby baby.*

She knew now why this happened, and why the System demanded it, the peer pressure––they called it the mother-support, mums looking out for other mums––was so intense, the messaging constant. They wanted sight of every child, wanted to watch them, making sure each set of parents was playing by the rules.

Vivian didn't know if her own actions that month had put her on their radar or not. Thankfully, she'd not built any particularly close relationships, not moving in only one circle. She'd been able to tell the various groups that the times worked better for the sleeping patterns to be part of it somewhere else. They all thought she was doing the classes, just not with them.

Vivian hoped none of these acquaintances would ever think to mention her name to the authorities. Why would they?

Still, being on the run constantly when life had no routine, when a new baby demanded so much, was difficult. They were still trying to work out how to be parents.

Vivian sat in the relative cold of the car, already having been there for thirty minutes. She'd come alone to this appointment because she didn't need her son as a shield to give her an excuse to get in. She was at the lab to meet Kate, the researcher who would offer a full life for their little boy.

It was still early, Vivian watching through the semi-misty windows from the edge of the car park. She'd seen very few people arrive so far, though the usual working day might not start for another forty minutes. Vivian had seen no mention of the World Council on the signage, something that was deliberately highlighted on all other Council establishments. They meant it as a sign of quality, of approval. They meant Council run facilities to be the best you could get.

Yet here she was, waiting for a woman whose work no other Council lab anywhere was doing. She smiled at that thought, while knowing this scientist at this precise laboratory had now become a focal point for the Council. The Council's name might not yet be on the signage at the gates, but they were in the background. Vivian would be cautious.

Five minutes later, the first new arrival pulled into a space on the other side of the carpark. The two cars that had been there when she arrived, Vivian assumed, were for security personnel working the night-shift. Most places had done away with actual people working these roles. Machines and sensors could adequately cope, though they lacked the personal touch. Perhaps that was the point?

The additional vehicle had a single occupant, a female. Vivian sat up a little straighter as she peered forward, her own car now somewhat conspicuously parked by itself, a long way from the others. She couldn't move now, though she regretted her actions, but she'd not wanted to get any closer, not wanted to park alongside either of the cars which she assumed belonged to the security personnel. To have them come out, knock on her window, asking her what she was doing there.

The side door of the car opened, a woman getting out seconds later. It was Kate, Vivian knew that immediately. A mixture of excitement at this realisation coupled with crippling fear hit her. She didn't know what to do next, Vivian frozen in her seat.

Kate glanced over at the car in the distance, the only unfamiliar vehicle there. Nobody usually beat her into the lab on a regular day. She spotted someone still sitting in the car and looked away soon enough. She sped up as she approached the building, suspecting a stranger being there so early as clearly Council surveillance. Her brother's world from the previous night pressed in all the more. She was becoming increasingly paranoid herself. Just having him staying in her house had caused that, and he'd been there all of one night.

Kate walked past the front desk, the man glancing her way, but she said nothing. All the usual security personnel, men who knew people's names, who would make polite greetings, had gone. All gone since the involvement of the System, replaced by personality-lacking shells of muscle, who sat there, glaring and scowling at those they spotted, but did little else. She would avoid asking the man about the new arrival in the carpark. He would know who it was, he and the Council were in this together.

Vivian watched the scientist disappear into the building and out of sight. She didn't want to leave it much longer, the early appearance of this woman giving Vivian a little more time to make the call. She wanted to catch Kate alone if possible, the conversation easier to have without too many extra pairs of listening ears.

Suddenly she didn't really know what to say. Was she there to thank the woman? Was it more than that? She knew it was more than that. She wanted to make sure Kate knew how vital the research was, how important it was to finish and publish the cure. Her Charlie needed this treatment. Vivian was doing this for her son, for the future of her little boy, so he could live long beyond her own years, happy and content.

Vivian forced herself out of the car, determined to get across the carpark before anybody else arrived for work. A light had gone on up on the third floor, evidently Kate and her working space. Vivian pulled her coat tight around her, the air fresh, her body cold from sitting in the unheated vehicle for some time, and walked purposefully towards the front door which she'd just seen open. No need for a security keycard or anything. She soon caught the eye of the man behind the desk who watched her enter the front door and stood as she closed the gap to his desk.

"Yes?" he barked, unhappy to have the interruption in whatever he had been doing.

"I have an appointment," Vivian said.

The guard looked at his watch. "We're not even open, it's too early. There's nobody here."

"I'm meeting Katherine Vann," Vivian said, ignoring the voice in her head telling her to run away from there as fast as her legs could take her. "They have sent me to help her research. I'm carrying a baby with the genetic condition she's researching," having thought through that line of reasoning in the car that morning. The guard seemed to acknowledge something in his thick-set eyes, his face red though the edge had been taken off the fierceness in his appearance now. He knew the name, knew it had been the woman who had just walked past him. Knew about the research.

"I'll call her now," he said, almost with a smile. Vivian stepped to one side, allowing the man to call in relative privacy, though she heard the occasional word. She heard him telling Kate that it related to the pre-birth list, something Kate must have mentioned, because Vivian had not heard him mention it. That confirmation seemed to settle things on the other end of the line, and the call ended. He motioned Vivian towards him.

"Name?" he asked, holding out a clipboard. They really did things the old-fashioned way there. She made up a name, taking the badge he handed her, and he told Vivian to go to the third floor in the lift and that Dr Vann would meet her there.

As the lift doors closed, Vivian doubted herself for a moment. What if there were others up on that floor, if the meeting was with more than just Kate? Soon the lift stopped, its ascent short, and the doors opened, the smiling and expectant face of Kate standing a few paces back. Vivian smiled at her, glad it was just the two of them with no signs of anybody else on that floor.

"This is in connection to the list I've asked about?" Kate quizzed, a little taken aback. She'd expected the person to be a Red-Collar, or at the least a Black-Collar. Vivian didn't fit the image at all, and if she were with child, it might be too early in the process to be any use, Vivian hardly showing any sign of being pregnant.

"Can we talk somewhere a little more private?" Vivian asked, the corridor in front of the lifts not what she'd had in mind.

"Sure," Kate said, all smiles, though she seemed edgy, perhaps even nervous.

Two minutes later they were sitting in a meeting room, the door shut behind them.

"Do you need any water or anything?" Kate asked.

"No, and I don't want to keep you long," Vivian said, which didn't seem to make sense right now to Kate, who'd been the one to request this information, she the one to decide how long this would take.

"You aren't from the Council, are you?" Kate asked, terrified that she'd walked into a trap.

Vivian let out a nervous laugh.

"My son Charlie was born a few weeks ago. He carries the condition that you are researching, and before he was born I heard something about your research. I didn't know you, didn't know where you were based, but I sent the hospital the medical files so they would take this all into consideration."

"You knew that a within-life cure might be possible?"

"Yes. I'd read everything I could on the disease, and you'd given me hope," Vivian said. "Hope for my son, hope that he would be free to live a long life."

Kate took in the sadness present in the woman's eyes. "But there wasn't good news, I take it?"

"They didn't seem to make anything of your research, didn't seem to take it into account with the dating."

There was silence for a while, the emotion plain to see in Vivian's face.

"How long did they give your son?"

Vivian shook her head. She wasn't about to say anything, wasn't about to give anything away, even if, in that room, she'd said plenty. She'd told this scientist, without words, that they had dealt her son a bad hand.

"He was born a matter of weeks ago. Less than a month and my son misses out, and now suddenly, everything is all go. You've been fast-tracked, fully funded, and even the Council are talking about a within-life cure." Vivian dropped a medical journal onto the table, something Kate had not seen yet, which stated that plainly. Some boast when they'd only just financed her. "What changed?"

Kate didn't know how to answer that, and didn't know the history of her visitor and their child, either. Perhaps there were other medical issues, other factors that weren't covered in her research there in that lab?

"I don't know what to tell you," Kate said. "I've said for a long time what I believe about this research," which Vivian knew to be true. These had been the articles that had given her hope in the first place, the basis of her appeal to the Council to have it all considered for her unborn child. She'd had to break the law to undo the damage, needed to hand over half her inheritance to get Charlie the treatment he deserved. Given a couple more months, that might all have been unnecessary.

"Something must have changed?" Vivian pressed.

Kate knew it had. It had all changed with that telephone call, with that downed aircraft and her own escape from certain death.

"There was a call," Kate said, determined not to give the details of where she was or what she was about to do. "From someone I'm sure is a Red-Collar."

"You've not met them?"

"Can't find them. Thought you might have been them when you arrived in that lift, if I'm honest," Kate smiled, the first sign in their conversation that any sense of connection might form, Kate's stiff exterior melting dramatically with that show of her human and vulnerable side.

"What did they say?"

"It was a man, and what he said didn't matter, but I know his own unborn child has this condition."

Vivian got it immediately. Her own life and that of Charlie had mattered little. Just another common White-Collar family, but this Red-Collar. Once he found out, he got things changed.

"So that's it, all it takes, is it? One of these people gets something that we've all been suffering with and suddenly everything changes for us all." Vivian seemed angered by that. Her eyes now opened to a world she'd not really known was there, but which had always existed, she realised. Kate recognised that look too, the two women gazing at each other in silence, both aware there was much more going on behind their puzzled expressions.

However, Kate also knew that hadn't been all it took. This caller had put much more on the line than just the welfare of his child.

They could hear the lift opening on their floor, the sign that others were now arriving. Kate looked around nervously.

"We should talk further," she said. Kate needed someone other than her brother to speak with and meeting a mother whose son would benefit from the research she had spent so many years working on seemed a natural outlet. "But we can't do that here."

"You're afraid of them?"

"I'm terrified," Kate confessed. Vivian thought of Devon, the man able to get her the name of Kate within minutes, an underworld kind of guy who seemed connected in all the right ways.

"Call me when you leave," Vivian said, passing Kate her number. "I might have someone who can help us both."

28

Kate had not told her brother about her encounter with Vivian for two days, the siblings continuing their unconventional house sharing for that week. Kate didn't mind the sofa, but couldn't sleep downstairs indefinitely. She knew he was still using drugs. Joe was often sound asleep when she left for work and out of the house when she got home.

When she caught him up on everything, he sat there listening to every word, glued to the story and not asking anything until Kate had come to the end of her narrative. She passed him the name and number for Devon Scott, a man whom Vivian had told her could help.

"You trust this guy?" Joe asked, taking the piece of paper, waving it in front of Kate as he spoke.

"I trust the woman who gave me the name, yes," Kate said. She'd spent a pleasant three hours with Vivian, even meeting Charlie when the father brought home their son. Vivian had confessed everything about what they'd done, how Devon was helping them, and their understanding of how things differed from what most people thought. Kate dismissed the nudge inside to tell Vivian all about her missed flight. Her brother had sworn her to secrecy. It wasn't safe to talk about it, not yet. He still talked in a way that suggested things could change.

Nothing changed, they all knew that, not now. Not in that era. People were prosperous, people had purpose. Life had value. Death wasn't to be feared anymore.

Yet Vivian had shown Kate something else. When confronted with it for real, when faced with the reality of holding your baby boy who'd only a few decades to live, doing your duty took on a new meaning. What duty was it for a mother to bury her own child? Who would ever say that was a fair world, the honourable thing to do?

She couldn't, not anymore.

Kate also knew now that things were not what they seemed. While she didn't share the extreme views of her brother, she knew he was right. Perhaps not about everything, but about the fundamentals. About the imbalance in the System, the separation of the classes. The world always stood divided between those who had and those who didn't. The Council intended their new era to bridge that gap. Recent events had opened Kate's eyes to the bitter reality. Nothing had changed. The rich still got richer, the poor more vulnerable.

"Well, what say we both do a little research of our own today?" he said, with a grin.

"You want me to speak to Devon?"

"I want us to speak to Devon, yes," Joe confirmed. Kate didn't feel so good about that. Her brother had a lot less time for people. He might endanger the whole setup.

"Vivian said he's a cautious man. I have a legitimate reason to see him," Kate said.

"Which is?"

"I need to find out who called me. I can link it to the research. If this Devon has access to the System records like Vivian told me he does, he'll be able to see my request for this information."

"And what am I supposed to do? Sit at home doing nothing," he said. She wished he did nothing when at home.

"You can come, but you wait in the car. Be my lookout."

He smiled at this. Knowing where the guy worked might come in useful later if he ever needed to pay Devon a call himself.

"Okay, I can do that," he said, standing up.

It took them an hour to get to the building: the area run down, though the facility itself seemed in good repair. Kate was happy to have brought her brother with her. Despite the Protocols, despite the crackdown on crime, there were always parts of the city that you avoided. This was one of them. She pondered whether contacting Devon was even worth the potential danger they were exposing themselves to. Joe assured her it was the right thing to do, his eyes alert as they pulled up outside, the carpark half full. They didn't move from the car for a minute, watching the surrounding area, a few people coming and going, two groups hanging around on various corners in the distance, though they seemed to allow the building in question a certain element of privacy.

"You wait here," Kate reminded her brother. "I'll be okay getting to the entrance," and she slammed the car door before he could protest, Joe locking it from the inside as he watched his sister navigate a path towards the address they had for Devon. She walked in through the front door without incident, vanishing from view as she did so.

As Kate entered the building, she wondered if she should have tried to call first, though that was all too late now. The decor was tasteful, expensive looking. The building had a comfortable feel, and as she walked up to the reception area, a warm smiled greeted her.

"How can I help you?" the woman asked.

"Someone gave me a name, told me I could find help here," Kate said.

"Okay, and who would you like to see today?"

"Devon Scott, please," Kate said.

There was a pause on the receptionist's face, the slight drop of the all-welcoming smile, perhaps the appearance of concern at who this visitor really was.

"Mr Scott is a very busy man," she commented. "Do you have an appointment, because I don't see one in the calendar?"

"I'm a walk in," Kate said. "My name is Katherine Vann." Vivian had found Kate because Devon had given her Kate's name and address. "I believe he'll be happy to see me." Kate looked up at the camera mounted on the wall which had moved from the front door onto her face in the last few seconds, a sure sign that they were aware of her. Perhaps it was Devon himself, sitting behind a screen, deciding if this latest visitor was trouble or a future client?

"Let me see if he has time for you," the receptionist said coyly, picking up the handset and lowering her voice as she spoke to her boss. It didn't take long for the confirmation to come through that he would see her. "He'll be out in a moment," the receptionist said, inviting her to take a seat, which she did. Anything to stop her fidgeting on the spot as she had been doing.

The sound of heavy footsteps coming along the corridor a minute later suggested Devon was approaching, and Kate rose to greet him as he came towards her, now around the corner, his face smiling, his huge hand stretched out for the greeting. She offered him hers, fearful he might crush every bone in her tiny fingers, but he seemed remarkably gentle for such an enormous man.

"It's a pleasure to meet you in person," Devon said, no hint at pretending he didn't know who she was, Kate appreciating that aspect immediately.

"You know who informed me about you, I take it," she said.

"A fine mother, that one," he said, speaking about Vivian. "She'll do anything for that boy of hers."

"She told me everything," Kate said, Devon with no doubt that she would have done.

"Tell me, Doctor Vann, are you as close to the breakthrough as Vivian hopes you are?" There were far more people than Vivian hoping that was the case, but Kate understood the context.

"I am," she smiled.

"Then I'm honoured to meet a real-life hero," he said. They entered his office now, the man closing the door behind them, inviting Kate to take a seat as he moved around behind his desk and slowly positioned his ample body into what looked like an unsuitable office chair, but it seemed to manage all right.

"So, what can I do for you?" he asked, formalities aside, getting down to business. He knew the scientist hadn't come to discuss his client.

"I need to find a name," she said.

"I see," Devon said, no moving from his laid-back position, listening to her words. "Go on."

"He's a Red-Collar," she said, taking in the Red on Devon's own shirt collar, as the man's eyebrow raised a fraction at what she had said.

"And what is this man to you?"

Her brother had drilled into Kate the absolute importance of not telling a soul about what had happened with the plane until they knew more, or unless there was no other choice. Kate remained button lipped for a while, chewing over how much to tell the man whom she had come to for help.

"He saved my life," she said, knowing she had to give Devon something, even if not the whole truth. There had to be an edge, more than just the basics, otherwise he wouldn't want to get involved.

"He saved your life?" Devon asked, sceptically.

"I thought my research was fruitless. I was at a low point. He helped me see otherwise," she said, weakly. Devon's eyebrows returned to normal and he made as if to move, as if this whole meeting were a waste of time. He didn't do thank-you reunions.

"Look," he started, Kate now panicking, knowing she had to give him more.

"I was going to jump," she said, this causing that one eyebrow to rise, the turn in the flow of conversation dramatic enough to cause him to sit back in his chair once again. "I had got to the point when I thought nobody would ever listen. I don't know how he found me, but as I stood on the top of that building, the ground so far away I couldn't even see the people below, my phone rang. It rang at that precise moment and a man's voice came through as clear as day."

"And what did he say?" Devon asked, drawn in fully to the story Kate was piecing together rapidly.

"Told me not to jump."

"He could see you?" Devon asked, stunned by the thought.

"That I don't know. I assume yes, he could. I didn't know what to say. He then told me my research was vital, and that I was close."

"What did you do then?"

"I stepped back from the ledge," she said, which was obvious, given the fact they were speaking about it now. "The next thing I notice is that funding pours into the research laboratory where I work. The Council has earmarked my research."

"You believe this is the doing of the same man?" Devon asked, giving the impression that despite the fascinating story, he was coming back to his earlier conclusion, that this didn't require his involvement.

"I believe it is more than that," she said, pleased to have caused his features to change so suddenly again at those words, determined now to deliver a compelling finale that would draw Devon in completely and offer her his support. "I believe this mystery man has a personal interest in my research. I believe that the man is expecting a child with the same condition."

"He's looking to help his own child?" Devon asked, a little sceptical that this would be the only conclusion, though if the caller was a Red, it wouldn't surprise him if that was the case.

"I believe so, yes, and this might hold the key to my breakthrough," she said, going out on a limb, but she knew nobody outside her lab would know anything about what kind of research they were working on. "Since the funding came through, I've had access to records I didn't have before, because my laboratory isn't Council *controlled*," she said, using a word her brother would use, the official terms being *Council Supported*. She knew Devon's medical facility next door was independent.

He smiled at that.

"I put a request through for a list of all known current cases, which they gave me right away," she said. "But the latest break-through requires us knowing who's also tested positive pre-birth." Devon knew these tests were yet to roll out for most people, and if they knew such a condition, the parents would probably abort. Yet this mystery caller had an interest, and if he was a Red-Collar, might have had the test done. It slotted together in his mind as Kate hoped it would.

"You think this man's name will appear on that list," he said.

"I do. And that's the thing. I've been told they sent me the list, so I know one exists. The person I spoke to at the Council confirmed he had sent it. He could see that it had gone, but something blocked it. It wouldn't leave their server. I've never had it."

Devon raised both eyebrows at this, aware of the mechanics needed to override something of that nature.

"You're sure they sent it?"

"Positive. The technician seemed genuinely confused, said he would follow it up. I heard nothing, naturally."

"And you need this list?"

"A list or a pre-birth example, it doesn't matter. It's vital that I have this for the final piece of my research. Finding a living foetus with the condition is rare. I believe this man who called me knows just such a case and without your help, I might not become the hero you think I am," she said, laying it on as thick as she could without going overboard.

He smiled, his eyebrows seemingly unwilling to drop back into their usual place just yet. An almost comical expression if she allowed herself to dwell on it, though Kate remained focused. She had Devon where she needed him to be, sure that he would come through for her now.

He picked up his pad at last, moving himself nearer the desk.

"It's a bit of a needle in a haystack, but I'll see what I can do. If he's stopped this report leaving the Council, I don't want to get involved with that aspect directly. He'll see my interest in the information. But I think I can trace him another way," he said, a game-plan forming in his mind. "Write your phone number here, please," passing her the pad, her name written at the top of a new page even though she'd not seen him touch it once since they'd been talking. "The number he called you on. Do you also remember when this was? It'll help me identify the incoming calls."

"There wasn't a number displayed," she said, writing the details, adding a rough time. The date didn't seem to register.

"I doubt there would have been, not someone being as cautious as he's evidently been. That suggests he's senior, with enough clearance to handle that side of things. All I'm looking for is the precise time of the incoming call and its duration. Once I've found that, I'll cross check with calls made by Red-Collar people, and I'll narrow it down until I have one known location. From there I should be able to identify who he is."

"You can do all that?"

He nodded.

Kate realised they had discussed nothing like payment for this service. She didn't have much.

"And about your fee?" she asked.

He waved her away. "You probably couldn't afford me," he said with a smile. "Look, seeing as Vivian gave you my name, and seeing as you're a real-life hero, I'll do this one for free."

"I cannot thank you enough," Kate beamed, genuinely grateful.

"It's my pleasure. I'll call you later with a name," and Kate walked towards the door. "One more thing," Devon said, Kate turning. "Say hello to that brother of yours when you next see him, won't you," giving her a knowing look.

29

K ate answered the call that night after dinner.

"I have a name for you," Devon said, both Kate and Joe listening to the call. Joe had denied any knowledge of who this Devon was and wondered how he knew Kate had a brother. He decided Devon must have seen them arrive in the carpark, must have had had people watching them. These people would have reported to Devon that she'd not come alone. It wouldn't have taken them long to know who he was too. Kate wasn't so sure it was that simple, but left it at that. Devon had the information for them.

"That was fast," Kate said.

"Take me off loudspeaker and I'll give you the name, Kate," Devon said.

"It's only me," Kate confirmed.

"That's funny," Devon said, his device hacking into her camera, the faces of both Kate and Joe very clear in the lens. "I could swear that was your brother Joseph looking at me over your left shoulder."

Kate picked up the handset, putting it to her ear.

"That's illegal," she said, something covered in an earlier protocol and made as serious as any other crime, the punishment severe.

"It would surprise you where people leave their phones, the

things they get up to," he laughed. "I don't trust your brother, Katherine," going formal on her once again. "He's mixing with the wrong crowd, and I fear he'll drag you into it."

"He won't," Kate said, determinedly.

"Grab a pen," Devon said. She confirmed a few seconds later that she had one. "Your mystery man is none other that Blythe Harrell," sure somebody of her standing would have come across the name before.

"*The* Blythe Harrell?" she asked, stunned.

He smiled at the confirmation that she knew him. "Without question. I knew it had to be somebody high in the System, but even I didn't expect it to be that high." Joe glanced at the name on the paper, but didn't seem to show any initial recognition of who the man was.

Devon didn't mention the fact that a note had appeared on the records that there was an all-channel alert out for Blythe at that moment, and that Blythe's current whereabouts were unknown.

"And you are certain?"

"As certain as anything," he confirmed.

"Well, thanks. I won't keep you any longer," she said, though Devon didn't quite seem in any mood to finish their conversation yet.

"One last thing, just for curiosity's sake," he said. "Which building had you been standing on at the time he saved your life?"

Kate reeled off the name of one of the tallest buildings around that had easy access to the top floor. She'd been to the cafe there once before and heard stories of people jumping from the unprotected viewing platform occasionally.

He thanked her and ended his call.

DEVON TURNED IMMEDIATELY to his computer. While Blythe had been smart in hiding his call so that nobody could directly tell it was him who'd called Kate that day, Devon had discovered where Blythe was at the time of the call. He was out of town, in the middle of nowhere, in a spot where nobody would notice him.

He was nowhere near the city, nowhere near the building Kate had mentioned when questioned. There was no way he could have known that Kate was about to jump. No way he would have known to intervene.

Kate was lying to him.

Devon sat back in his chair, pondering everything for a few minutes. Blythe had made contact, a call that had been for personal reasons as much as anything else. That much was true. The funding that had followed could only have been his doing, though Devon had no way of checking, not without another serious look.

Yet the story about Kate being about to jump was the one thing that didn't add up. She wasn't the type, the System with plenty on the record about Joe, the brother Kate kept visiting, desperate to talk him out of taking his own life, knowing the damage it would do to all the surviving relatives.

Kate was not suicidal.

Devon went down another chain of thought, his mind going over the details again. She'd been good with the details, hiding her actual account and the made-up story in half truths. The call had happened.

Devon came back to the line that Kate had said to him. *Blythe had saved her life.* He took in the call's time, which checked out, as did the date. He looked at the date. He knew those numbers, his heart now racing, everything inside screaming *no* while the more he typed, the more he dreaded finding out the truth.

Devon pulled up his building's security camera records from the previous day. He noted down the number of Kate's car as it sat in the carpark there, Joe unaware of the cameras as he waited there popping another pill.

Devon typed the registration number into another program, this System controlled, which showed the precise location of any form of transport for any period. It didn't take him long to see Kate's car drive to the airport on the day in question, where it waited for two hours then drove back home. It would repeat the journey to the airport the following morning, this time parked up for several days.

The call from Blythe had happened during those two hours of

that first trip. Blythe had been outside the city and far from the airport. Kate in a low-rise terminal building, packed with security. Not a place to jump from, nowhere offering access to the roof.

He already knew the truth before he checked one last thing, comparing the manifest for the flight in question. Kate's name was on it, though she never boarded. She had checked in, was in the airport, but never took the flight.

Blythe had called her. He'd warned her.

Devon swore.

———

TWENTY MINUTES AFTER THE CALL, Kate sat on the sofa still reeling from the shock, Joe across from her, finishing reading up all there was on Blythe.

He now knew who the man was.

"This is big," Joe said, placing the device back onto the table. She'd heard him whisper that repeatedly over the last ten minutes.

"You think?" Kate said, sarcastically. She didn't know about her brother, but she sure needed a drink.

"You're telling me that the future Supreme Commander has a child with an incurable disease?"

"That's just the point. No, he doesn't. I'll have published my research before their baby is born."

"What if you don't?"

She had not thought about that. It hardly mattered. Both knew she would. This was what she'd worked so hard for, the end near, the culmination of all that effort now within touching distance. She'd always wanted to make an impact in life. This was her one way of doing it.

"Joe, it's not only his child who needs this," she reminded her brother.

"Fine," he said, as if that had been an ethical option, anyway. "He gave you the man's number too?" Joe checked. He'd seen something else written.

"Yes, right here."

"Let me call," Joe said, reaching out for the piece of paper.

"What would you say?" she asked. She knew she couldn't call, not now. Not now that she knew who he was, not without some Dutch courage inside.

"I'll say we know what he did."

"Joe, I don't want this to become about blackmail," Kate warned.

"I won't say it like that," he shot back, as if he'd already thought this all through.

"What if the call won't even connect?" she asked, Joe grabbing his phone, dialling the number before Kate could say anything.

"It's ringing," he said, this enough to silence his sister for the moment. Soon she too could hear the tone, very much connected, very much still ringing. After twelve rings, it cut off, no answer. Joe picked up his device again, opening a website he knew about and entering the number into the search box. He passed the device across to his sister.

"What's this?" she asked, the area a better part of the city, an expensive area.

"It's where he lives," he confirmed, though Kate had come to that conclusion soon enough herself. "How long do you think it would take to get there?"

"We aren't driving to this man's house, Joe," Kate said.

"No, we aren't," he agreed with a smile. "I'll go alone, have a look around, see what I can find."

Thirty minutes later, they'd settled their differences on the subject, Joe with the keys in his hands, Kate waving him off from the window. As the car disappeared down the street, she turned and headed straight to the kitchen, the whisky supplies low, but getting hit hard for the next couple of hours. That much she knew.

JOE OVERRODE the controls on the route planner in the car two streets from Blythe's residence, parking up the vehicle and walking the rest of the way. It was dark, though he couldn't miss the obvious presence of military personnel all over the house in question. Joe carried on his march, on the other side of the street, hood up, as he passed the high gates. There were two military vehicles parked on the street, another behind the gates on the driveway. If they were meant to be an invisible presence, they weren't doing a very good job.

Did Blythe know that the siblings now knew his identity, was that an issue? A random phone call was one thing, this latest development something else entirely.

Joe decided against calling Kate. She might well be asleep already, it was gone eleven and the journey back at least another hour. Instead, he dialled the number for a friend.

"Where are you?" Joe asked. This man was part of the gang finding their way to them.

"Close," the other man said. Joe gave him his current location.

"Get everyone to meet me here," Joe said. He would need to get the car back to Kate for work the following morning, but would be back before his gang had arrived.

"I'll let you know," the man replied.

"Be careful, the place is swarming with Black-Collars."

"We'll see you in a day or two," came the confirmation, the call ending soon after. Joe smiled. They were close. That would give him a few more options. The area he was now in put distance between the gang and his sister, two worlds that wouldn't naturally mix. There wasn't space at hers for anyone else, anyway.

He hit home on the dashboard once he was in the car. It wouldn't help to be spotted in the area, and he'd doubled back via another road to reach the vehicle. Seconds later the car was moving away, taking him to his sister, his mind thinking over what he had just seen.

30

Herb stirred in his high-backed armchair, having fallen into a late morning sleep. For a moment he'd not remembered where he was, something that came with age, though soon enough his thoughts came back to him. The extra pairs of shoes by his back door helped, as did the mugs that still sat on his living room table.

He listened quietly; the visitors had gone up to his spare room to rest. He'd been sitting in his chair for some time, evidently dropping off himself. He checked the clock, lunchtime not far away.

Herb stood, stretching out the aches that went with falling asleep in an awkward position, and went through to the kitchen where he boiled the kettle. He soon heard a movement upstairs, the telltale sound of the bathroom door being closed.

There was so much he wanted to discuss with them both, their conversation so far interesting, even while he noticed Kassia needed a proper rest, and that Blythe would benefit from some shut eye himself. That had been over three hours ago.

Herb left the kettle to boil, walking to the back door and taking down the key to his garage, situated at the end of his garden, mostly storing the empty boxes for items long since past the time he would ever need to return them. He didn't have a car himself, didn't really need one. He'd always been able to walk to school.

Herb went down the path, ignoring the gate he'd opted for that morning, and turning to the little-used side-door to the garage. Once opened, he switched on the light. There were boxes every-where, most of which were empty save for some packing materials. There was one for the fridge, the television, the computer, several kitchen items, most of which he'd thrown away a decade before, and a dozen others, some of which he didn't even remember owning.

Thirty minutes later, a neat pile of flattened cardboard lay at the end of the garage, a small mountain of polystyrene packaging beside it. Herb glanced back out of the door, catching both his visitors standing in the kitchen. Blythe spotted Herb emerging from the garage, the older man waving and coming back towards the house almost immediately.

"I've been thinking about that car of yours," Herb said, a little breathless as he walked inside, closing the door behind him. "You'd better pop it in the garage. There's plenty of space, and it'll save anyone asking awkward questions."

"Thank you," Blythe said, nothing more to add on the subject. He'd woken up wondering what to do about the car himself.

"Did you get some rest?" Herb asked, addressing Kassia mostly. She smiled at Herb, flashing him her immaculate pearly white teeth that went with the overall package.

"It was very comfortable, thank you again," she said.

"I don't have visitors as much as I thought I would have," he said and added. "That bed's probably only had about six night's sleep on it," which explained the comfort somewhat.

Blythe stood. "I'll use the garage then, if that's okay with you."

"Right you are," Herb said and despite Blythe saying he could manage, insisted on following him out and guiding him into the garage. They walked back across the small garden five minutes later, Kassia watching them both from the window. They were still talking as they rejoined her in the kitchen, Blythe telling Herb how long he'd had the car and the two shared a conversation about his collection down the years.

"Do you intend to buy an expensive car this year?" Kassia asked, Blythe looking at his wife as if that was an insensitive thing to ask, Kassia not picking up the signs from her husband regarding Herb's feelings about all that.

Herb spotted the difference between husband and wife, and didn't want either feeling alarmed.

"It's okay, Blythe, it's natural for her to ask. She didn't mean any ill by it, I know," and he turned to Kassia with a smile. "And to answer your question, Ma'am, it's not really my thing. Not sure I'll change anything, really."

"But you must want to do something, surely?" she asked, Blythe going wide-eyed at that, Herb waving the shock away.

"That's the thing, I'm not sure what to think anymore," he said, the first hint that there was more going on inside the man than they'd fully grasped.

Perhaps they weren't so different after all?

They talked openly for an hour, Herb opening up about what he now felt, the fact he'd been a teacher for so many years and reinforcing to all those young people over the decades the right thing, their duty. He'd been a bastion for the Council, guiding his students on, encouraging them in what they already knew and sending them into the world as responsible adults. He spoke with pride about how many of these kids had done great things. He'd produced the most Red-Collars in the school, something he had always felt proud about, a genuine achievement, he said.

He then moved onto more rocky ground, sharing how as his own Celebration Day arrived, and though he thought he would be ready, he wasn't. He nearly broke down in tears as he confessed he now didn't know if he believed it anymore. He would have traded all he had for some more time, even if that required work. He missed the students, missed his colleagues. Missed the routine and thrill of working in the school.

He didn't want to die, didn't feel ready. There was life in him. So many others his age got to live another decade. He wasn't old, wasn't unwell, and while he wasn't as agile as he was in his youth, he was good.

"It's not that I think those who want to take the money and live it up are wrong," he said, through tears, "but that's just not me. I like my life. It's simple, functional. I don't know anybody who has retired."

Herb had never married, had no kids, worked with people younger than him and taught people who weren't even adults.

"Herb, we aren't here to judge you one bit," Blythe said, tenderly. He let Herb compose himself, Blythe now sharing his own awakening. He shared what he'd seen, shared how he knew there was this disparity between the various groups. Red-Collars were always in a different league, he admitted. Money stayed in families, passed from generation to generation. The game became how to keep it all, to not lose any. He shared everything, bringing it right back to the present, saying how he'd discovered about the plane crashes enabling those who were rich to save face against illness. Blythe admitted innocent people got caught up in that, admitted to his shame that he'd known about the flights for a while. He said that there was pressure from on high––he specifically mentioned the Supreme Commander here––to allow the collateral damage, as too many powerful people had too much to lose if there wasn't this option.

"The System is rotten to the core," Blythe admitted, his wife shocked at the extent of what he'd shared, Herb spotting she had not known everything that had just been said.

"It appears we have more common ground than we realise," Herb said, his eyes on Blythe, who nodded slowly in understanding. "We are both disillusioned by the world that we've surrounded ourselves in for our entire lives. What interests me most is what we now do about it."

He went silent, allowing the words to settle in for a time.

"We fled because they found out what I had done when I warned that scientist," Blythe said.

"You did the right thing in saving her."

"It was a selfish thing, too," Blythe said, looking at his wife, the carrier of their child, and his eyes were moist.

"It was the only thing a loving couple could do," Herb said, seeing them both, the challenge clear.

Silence held them tight for a while.

"That might well be the case, but it's wrecked my chances of becoming the next leader," Blythe said, doing his best to make light of the situation. But there was pain there, too. Herb had known for years that the man in front of him was being groomed for the role, pulled into office a decade earlier, twenty years younger than anyone else of his rank and always the front runner. The handover of power had already been talked about publicly for several months.

"Someone still needs to take over. The Supreme Commander cannot continue forever," Kassia said.

"My chances have gone," Blythe admitted. "And for what? I mean, what was I thinking?"

Kassia said nothing. There would have been other ways to stop Kate taking that flight besides telling her directly. Perhaps she would have become equally suspicious? Perhaps she needed to know. Perhaps they all did? Kassia had never known poverty, known nothing but privilege, born into wealth, marrying into wealth and power and, until recent events, destined to become the Supreme Lady, the belle of any ball the world over. What Blythe had shown her in recent days had opened even her eyes. Why should their baby in the womb have every chance, just because of their connections, more than other children?

"You raise an interesting question, Blythe," Herb said, the teacher in him coming alive once more, as he mused over the moral complications of changing such a System, broken as it was, rotten as had just been explained to him, yet praised by those it exploited, worshipped by those it abused.

"Which is?" Blythe asked.

"How do you change something that people like? Take my collar, for example," he said, flicking the Gold for good measure. "People work their entire lives for this dream. You break the System and you take this away from people. You'll have a riot, millions of people demanding you undo your changes! People expecting this year of luxury, this year of freedom, this money lavished upon them or their surviving relatives."

"Even when they know it's working against them?" Blythe asked.

"The System has brainwashed people for generations," Herb countered. "I've seen it firsthand, was bloody part of it myself."

"But it didn't work on you," Kassia pointed out.

"I had a moment. Like you both did, when you intervened with that scientist. You went against the System, went against the way they meant it to be. Proved it wasn't random, wasn't any accident. My moment was my retirement. It was getting to that day and realising, for the first time, that I didn't believe in it. That despite all I thought I believed, I wasn't ready. It wasn't *right*."

Right and wrong had gone out in the earlier protocols, as they all knew. Yet there they were, debating just that.

"Then what is the answer?" Blythe asked, slight desperation in his voice. He'd risked everything, but for what? A life on the run? Their unborn baby still needed this treatment, and if they took her for that, then the System would have them. "Is war or revolution the answer?"

"Perhaps," Herb said, though the last wars had been before he could walk. These were the things of history books now, society way beyond that. Only the military had weapons, the underground supply all but destroyed.

"It wouldn't even be a close fight, the military have all the firepower."

"And your two sons, would they fight?"

Blythe had shared with Herb about his two adult boys being in the military.

"I don't know what they would do. They might even be under arrest because of me," Blythe said, a move he'd made against others in similar situations. He hated to think of his own sons under armed guard while the authorities hunted for him and his wife.

"They don't have the numbers," Herb said.

"It doesn't matter. One soldier with a fully loaded weapon could down a thousand people and still have time to change cartridges," Blythe said, well aware of the capabilities of the military. "And you're forgetting the masses who would oppose any change. That would be those enjoying their Jubilee Year, plus the millions within five or ten years of it themselves."

"Could somebody not dissuade them?"

"That would be a hard sell, for starters," Blythe said. "Free health-care, a guaranteed job for life, money to retire and live the best year of their life, all coupled with the mindset drummed into us all from the age of six that dying at the right time is the honourable and noble and right thing to do. The System controls everything, don't forget. If they crumble, the entire financial model crumbles. Forget money in your last year, nobody would have anything to live on. The world would be brought to its knees."

"But it would be a much fairer world," Herb said.

"Would it? Where would the funding come from, where would the treatment? What if people couldn't afford it in certain cities? Do only some get the help they need while we leave others to die? There has always been a wealthy elite who've taken what they want from the people, and while we let you believe that wasn't the case anymore, we've just been much smarter at hiding it from you."

"Then what is the solution?" Herb asked, perplexed that they'd reached such a seemingly insurmountable situation.

31

K ate hurried out of the door, even earlier than usual, the phone call from her boss that morning not the start to the day she had planned. He'd demanded she come into work immediately, though he didn't give the reason why.

Kate sat back in her seat as her car drove her in, the passing fields that gave way to buildings as they raced past her window lost to her, Kate's mind racing for what had required the urgent summons.

The carpark was half full as she pulled in at eight, twenty minutes earlier than she usually got there and yet now one of the last to arrive.

Kate hurried across the carpark, a few colleagues milling around in the entranceway, Kate asking what they knew, which was very little. All seemed blurry eyed and wishing to be anywhere but there right then.

Five minutes later, the Director of the laboratory appeared in the foyer.

"Everybody, come through to the conference hall," he called, a glance towards Kate as he spoke, relieved to have spotted her, though he didn't smile.

They moved through saying nothing, filling the rows from the front, Kate taking a seat on the third row before being called forward by her boss.

"What's this about?" she whispered urgently, as the last of the staff slowly took their seats.

"They've pulled our funding," he said, no time to confirm anything more, telling Kate to stand to one side, as he addressed the rest of the room.

"I've called you all in first thing this morning because the Council is sending over someone at nine to explain our situation. Late last night I had a call. It wasn't a conversation, wasn't a warning, just a statement. They have pulled our funding completely," he said, the gasp that went around the room causing him to pause in his flow, though he soon raised a hand to suggest they let him continue. "Without this funding, it shuts us down. I'm sorry, most of you will have to go home today." Another loud gasp.

"I promise that we will sort this out." He glanced towards Kate, before continuing to face the shocked faces in front of him. "Nobody is to leave until after we've heard from the official. I doubt he will publicly give us an explanation," he warned. "Aside from the funding that we need to pay salaries, it pauses the research that we can do," again another glance towards Kate, this time with a pained look. "This is vital, lifesaving treatment, and a breakthrough I know we are all invested in." Half the room had only recently arrived at the laboratory, seconded in to help with the workload, some moving a long way to be there and therefore unable just to return to their previous employer.

AN HOUR LATER, the Red-Collar had addressed the room. He dismissed the meeting, saying he would speak to a few individuals. He turned directly to Kate, ignoring the Director who had stepped forward first.

"Can I have a word with you first, Ms Vann?"

Kate eyed her boss fearfully, though she nodded and followed the man to the room requested for these one-on-ones. He walked straight in, Kate closing the door behind her as she took the spare seat.

"Everything that follows this morning, everyone else I waste my time with is all for show, do you understand?" he announced, and she didn't understand any of it.

"Sorry?"

He smiled.

"It's called going through the motions. I'll speak to several of your colleagues, terrify your boss for a few minutes, but it's you I came to speak with, this one meeting my sole purpose. These five minutes together. This whole situation is because of you."

"This whole situation?" Kate asked, fearful now, alarmed for sure.

"The funding cut," he confirmed. "The moment we have Blythe Harrell in custody is the moment your research gets its funding returned." He smiled at the recognition Kate showed. She could not hide that she knew the name of their fugitive.

"I don't know where Blythe is," she confessed, the Red relieved she wasn't about to deny she even knew him. Everyone knew of Blythe, the poster boy of the Capitolium. Kate had heard her brother tell her Blythe was hiding at his home, under heavy guard. Joe had gone to stay somewhere nearby so he could gather with his friends and watch the house.

"Is that so?" he asked.

"I thought he was at home," she said.

"Yes, your drug-head of a brother would have told you that one, I guess, and I know he believes it."

"He's not at his home under guard?" Kate asked.

"Would I be here speaking to you now if that were the case, genius?" he smirked.

She understood.

"My brother is no threat to you," she said, concerned that they seemed to know where Joe was and that her brother was watching a building waiting for trouble.

"No, he isn't," the Red smiled, as if Joe were merely a fly on the window, something they could crush under their fist at any moment if they decided.

"If you touch him..." she started, her words cutting off for the fear coursing inside her veins.

"You'll do what?" he jeered. "We don't need him for you to fulfil your role for us here."

"I'm not doing this for you!"

He slapped her hard around the face at that, the shock of the impact matched by the redness of the handprint that would still show for the rest of their conversation.

"That's right, bitch, you need to learn your place," he sneered, his face inches from hers, his smile back. He reached up and touched the spot on her cheek that he had just hit. "One word of this to anybody and your brother jumps from the top of the Colosseum. He is rather mentally unstable, as we both know."

"You dare!" she snapped, her fight returning to her. "If you touch him, I'll destroy everything. The research, my papers. Nothing will ever come of it!"

"Do it!" he snapped, playing her at her own game. "See if I care."

She looked him in the eye for a full thirty-seconds, refusing to budge, refusing to blink. He smiled as he looked away first, catching a glance from the Director of the laboratory who had looked towards them through the small window in the door. The Red removed his hand from Kate's face, one last stroke on the sore spot with the back of his finger.

"You're a monster," she said, defiantly.

"You don't know the half of it. Deliver me Blythe Harrell and all this returns to normal. If you cannot deliver him, then the blood of everyone we've discussed is on your hands."

32

H e had only received the call thirty minutes before––hardly enough notice––and yet, as the convoy of three military vehicles and the sleek, black stretched vehicle of the Supreme Commander pulled into the parking area of Devon Scott's facility, not a single other vehicle was there.

No Red-Collar associated with Devon and his empire wanted to be anywhere near the place when the main man rolled up with his heavy security present.

Devon wore his usual smile and stood waiting at the main doors. The inner corridors which connected his building to the medical clinic had been closed, the wall now in place appearing permanent, the staff sent home for the day as a final precaution.

"Mr Commander!" Devon called, as if welcoming an old friend, the Supreme Commander stepping from his vehicle with little cere-mony as this was far from being an official visit. He glanced around the area, nobody there except for his security detachment and Devon. The Supreme Commander knew of this Red-Collar in front of him by reputation but had never had the misfortune of needing to speak to him.

He ignored Devon's outstretched hand as he walked on into the building, Devon turning with a smile––so this is how the Supreme Commander was going to play it––and followed him inside.

"Do your men want to follow?" Devon asked, the military remaining on the street.

"This will be just you and I," he replied. There was a frostiness there, something that didn't surprise Devon. Everything about the last half hour had suggested they had arranged this meeting in haste. Why did he need to see Devon so urgently?

"Please, let's go through to my office," Devon offered, his guest looking around the foyer with a mixture of surprise––which he didn't want to show––and distaste. He wanted Devon to see this but wasn't convincing enough. Devon smiled at that. He had spared no expense in making the building seem and feel like something you would find in the Capitolium itself, on the inside, at least. He couldn't do much about the surrounding area, but the land was cheap, those who worked the streets nearby even cheaper.

Devon waited for his guest to sit down before taking to his throne-like desk chair which his large frame more than filled. He would not bother to offer the Supreme Commander a drink. He didn't want to give him another opportunity to turn up his nose and refuse him.

"Let's be clear about one thing," the Supreme Commander said, as if laying out the opening argument in a business negotiation or a legal case. "I know exactly who you are and what you do here."

"Thank you for clearing that one up for me," Devon countered, sure that the boss-man didn't know everything his enterprise had their hands in, yet here he was anyway, which told Devon plenty.

The reddening face of the Supreme Commander at that response told Devon he was thoroughly going to enjoy the next few minutes, or however long this little sideshow was going to last.

"I'm surprised we let you join the elite," he sneered, Devon knowing full well that his guest meant him becoming a Red-Collar, the highest honour ascribed to anyone in the New World.

"I don't know," Devon said, his lips pursed, his head a little to one side as if he was playing with the man in front of him and enjoying it.

"With the number of high-ranking people within your circle who've come to me over the years insisting I help them, I'm surprised it took you as long as it did." Devon enjoyed the flash of malice that shot through the old man's eyes, though this was to be no physical confrontation. Devon had all the muscle in that department.

"Today isn't about me coming to you for help," he scoffed, though Devon would have begged to differ. Why else was the Supreme Commander here? "It's about us talking about the same common enemy and working out what we are going to do about him."

"We have a common enemy?" Devon asked, highly amused at the idea. "You and me?"

"Blythe Harrell," the Supreme Commander said, which was all he needed to say. Devon smiled, nodding in understanding.

"Your golden child, wasn't he?"

The Supreme Commander didn't answer that, knowing it to be nothing more that a cheap jibe by a cheap man.

"I need not tell you that this man threatens everything we have built, everything that keeps us above the rest."

"No, you didn't need to tell me that," Devon said. He'd been musing over Blythe himself all night, wondering where he'd vanished to, why there was no sign of him in all his usual spots. "So he has gone on the run, those stories are true?"

"He has."

"And he told a White-Collar about... about our *practices*," Devon said, not wanting to name the service his office did for the wealthy.

"He told her about your *Mercy Flights*, yes," the Supreme Commander said, pleased to have landed a blow of his own, the reaction on Devon's face enjoyable.

Devon swore.

"As you know, our entire way of life only continues because of our close control of the System. We only allow certain people to prosper, only allow certain people into our sacred group. We let them in once we know they've proved themselves and once they've shown that they offer us value. Like we did with you."

"I was also filthy rich," Devon spat, annoyance showing for the first time.

"Yes, you are, so very... *filthy,*" the Supreme Commander said, slowly, deliberately, no hint that he would ever conclude with the word *rich*. Devon represented nothing but a parasite, someone bleeding the System from the bottom, a necessary hardship, a small price to pay, but a cancer, not an organ. A bloodsucker.

Devon slammed his thick trunk of an arm heavily onto the wooden desk, unsettling his pot of pens. The man across from him didn't flinch, didn't show any sign of alarm, only smiled, pleased to have got under the big man's skin.

"I suggest you focus that aggression on Blythe," the Supreme Commander said, all too coolly. He was in easy control of the conversation now, Devon silently kicking himself for allowing his opponent the upper hand.

"You're asking me to do you a favour?" Devon said.

"No," came the instant response; he was in no way prepared to surrender his advantage. "I'm suggesting you see the strategic importance of us both working together to find this man and once we have, to bring him down."

Devon considered that for a moment.

"You want him dead?" he asked. Some come-down from mere weeks before, the Supreme Commander on every television screen endorsing his future successor. The same man now Public Enemy Number One.

"He's become too dangerous," the Supreme Commander said, Blythe's actions all he had to go on, though the fact Blythe had taken flight, gone off grid, merely backed that up. "I'll use all my influence and firepower to flush him out the conventional way. You, Mr Scott, need to use your underground networks to do what they do when looking for a rat that's gone to ground. You do whatever it takes to stop him, do you understand?"

"We can kill him?"

"He threatens everything you own," the Supreme Commander

confirmed, Devon's wealth connected to his dealings, actions that if exposed or if the System failed, would leave him with nothing.

"And there will be no retribution?" They had stamped murder out in the earlier protocols, the punishments severe, the criminals knowing it was impossible to get away with it, that killings had ceased.

"Not for Blythe. Not for anybody standing up for him, not for anyone protecting him. You have my word on that."

Devon smiled. That seemed a remit he could work with.

"I'll get right onto it," Devon agreed, his visiter now smiling and standing up, Devon doing the same. "And what reward do I get if I catch him?"

"Reward?" the old man quizzed. "The reward is we carry on as before, enjoying the trappings of life. You in your corner, me in mine, acting as if I know nothing about what you all do in this dump."

"I see," Devon said, following him to the door, letting his security team open it and guide their leader back to his car. Devon stood there, the two men's eyes fixed on each other as the cars pulled away, Devon standing resolutely in his doorway, the Supreme Commander in the backseat of his vehicle, their gaze only broken by the movement of the car out of the carpark.

33

Blythe sat in the kitchen the following morning, Herb yet to appear, though Blythe knew his host had risen early, the teapot still warm. Herb had probably gone to get dressed.

Blythe placed his device down on the sofa next to him, having used one of his many aliases to access the System—he'd been a ghost existing behind many guises for years—so they wouldn't know it was him. He didn't like what he had read, their actions solely designed to get to him. He had a call to make.

With movement on the upstairs landing, Blythe walked to the backdoor quickly, not wanting to be overheard, and needing to make the call immediately. He found the key to the backdoor and the one for the garage, and as silently as he could, opened the door and walked across to the garage.

Standing inside the small space, the light on, his classic car nestled tightly where he had left it, Blythe dialled the number he had for Kate, the same number that he had called once before. That call had set off this chain of events that had led him to that spot, far from home and with even fewer options.

"It's me," Blythe said, though he didn't know if she had discovered his identity. Given what he'd read about the laboratory that morning, it wouldn't surprise him if they'd told her about him.

"I know who you are," Kate said, almost in a whisper.

"You can speak freely, can you?"

"Yes," Kate said, though quietly.

"I saw the news about your lab," Blythe confirmed.

"They told me the funding only starts again once they have you in custody," Kate said, not sure why she was telling him this, but he had saved her life, even if that move had opened her eyes to another world, one that had now come down hard on her. Perhaps ignorance was bliss?

"I'll make sure you get the money," he promised.

"How?" Kate asked. "Last time I checked, they said you had vanished."

"Is it public news?" he asked. He'd not seen anything online about that yet, though expected it eventually.

"No," Kate said. "But I had a visitor to the lab, a nasty piece of work. Made it clear they want you."

The way she spoke didn't sit comfortably with Blythe. He read more into her words than he had time to ask about, though he had more pressing things for the moment.

"Are you wanting to turn me in?"

Kate paused. She'd thought about that. In the moments after that Red-Collar had told her Blythe was the reason for her loss of funding, she'd assumed that she would help. Then that man had hit her. It had taken a great deal of makeup to shield the finger marks that remained on her face so that her own brother wouldn't see them when she got home. She owed the System nothing.

"No," she confirmed. "That's the last thing I would do for the man who opened my eyes."

That seemed an interesting choice of wording, and not what he would have expected. Blythe had needed Kate alive, he still did, as he needed her to complete her research.

"I'm glad to hear that," he said, not wanting to be much longer.

Any incoming call to Kate's phone, especially from an unknown number, would be noticed.

"I'm scared," she said, close to tears now, unable to talk to her brother about any of it, as he would have gone berserk. She knew that wasn't the right approach, would change nothing. They would kill him if he acted rashly, she knew that. Any excuse and her brother would be dead.

Her emotion caught Blythe a little off guard.

"Are you in any direct danger?"

"I don't know," she said. "I don't think so, but that man who visited me..." and she broke down then, the emotion too strong. Blythe's mind raced. He couldn't give her his current address, that much was clear. While he doubted she was playing him—this was genuine emotion he was hearing here—there might be others watching her communications.

"I'll send you a location," Blythe said, knowing he had seconds left before he needed to end the call. "You get there, come alone, and I'll find you," he promised, ending the call. He typed her an encrypted message, naming an open park about two miles from them that Blythe knew about. He pressed send.

IT WAS THREE THAT AFTERNOON, the sun breaking through the clouds for the first time, as a man in jogging bottoms and grey hoodie moved along the pavements towards the park.

Blythe would swing by once, hidden behind the hood, seemingly just another average person going about his daily routine, a world that had continued to work despite his own life crashing to the floor in those last few days.

Blythe spotted Kate pull up five minutes later. He took cover behind a clump of trees, watching her for any sign of a tail—whether she knew she had one or otherwise. She seemed nervous, looking over her shoulder constantly. Not the actions of someone about to double-cross him.

Blythe stepped out from the trees as she approached, his sudden appearance initially startling her until she saw his face. They stopped a few metres apart from each other, as if under quarantine.

"Thank you for coming," Blythe said.

"I didn't know that I had a choice."

"Did you tell anybody?"

She shook her head. "I called my brother just now, let him know I'd left the house."

"Did you say where you were, what you were doing?" Blythe pressed.

"I said I was visiting my man of mystery," she confirmed. "I didn't say your name. Only he will know who I meant."

"He knows about me?"

"He's my brother," Kate said, as if that meant anything. Blythe was an only child. He didn't know what she meant. He knew his own sons were often the last to tell each other something, always competing, though their relationship had improved somewhat since they'd both become Black-Collars. Not that he saw them much now. Each was still racing to become the first of them to make it to Red. "You have nothing to worry about with him."

Blythe would have begged to differ, but left that thought unspoken.

They started walking, having attracted a few odd looks in the minute they'd been standing there, separated as they were. Blythe came alongside Kate as they circled the park, one eye constantly watching to see if they were being followed. He changed paths regularly, switching the angle, able to see a long way in all directions. It didn't appear that anybody posed a threat, though he didn't want to stay in the open for long. He pulled his hoodie back over his head, the look striking and so different from his usual power-broker image when he was being touted as the likely successor to the current Supreme Commander.

"Follow me at a distance," he said, "I've got a safe house where we can talk. We can't stay in the open," and he pulled away, jogging a little at a time, Kate keeping him within one hundred metres, though she closed the gap as he left the park. She followed him back to Herb's house, all the while convincing herself that she wasn't crazy for doing this. However, she couldn't see any way in which this would all sort itself out.

She refused to dwell on the thought that one call from her to the Red-Collar who had come to her office the previous day, informing him of where she was and who she was seeing, and it would all be over. She would get the funding, she would continue her research. They would save lives, her name going down in history.

But could she trust them, sure that they knew what she now understood? Sure that they didn't trust her. Also, what would happen to her brother? Despite it all, Blythe still felt like her best bet right now. He'd shown her more loyalty in that one call than the others had since funding her research. Being around Blythe didn't scare her, unlike those minutes with the man who had hit her.

She rubbed her cheek at that thought, the markings mostly gone, the pain too, though the memory would live on. She would never let that man back near her again, would refuse to be alone with him. She hoped she would never see him again. For that to happen, she needed Blythe. She needed a miracle, in an era that claimed to be the miracle. Claimed that miracles outside their own working didn't happen.

She had to believe they still did.

Soon she spotted Blythe approaching the front door of an average semi-detached house on a random street. The door opened, an older man standing there. Blythe waited, checking Kate had seen him, a woman also appearing in the doorway not long after. As Kate drew close, she recognised the woman as Kassia Harrell, Blythe's second wife. Kassia smiled as Kate drew near, her husband having called her from the front door when he arrived home, needing her to be present, needing her to reassure Kate that she could follow him in.

Kate entered the home without breaking her stride, Kassia closing the door quietly once she'd followed Blythe down the hallway.

Herb stood in the kitchen, an unlikely collection of strangers

around him now. Blythe made quick introductions, Herb already
filling the kettle.

THE CONVERSATION HAD BEEN LIVELY, Kate opening up about her treatment at the office, keen to share the details before her brother
showed up. She had taken a call from him, Joe telling her he was
leaving the house and coming to find her. She gave him the address,
knowing it was the safest place for him to be, only telling the others a
little afterward.

Blythe had not been happy.

"I'll be your lookout," Herb offered. "I can put my new collar to
good use." As a Gold-Collar, he would attract far less attention. These
people had the greatest freedom of all, aside from the highest
ranking Reds. Nobody would suspect a Gold, these people enjoying
what was the last year of their life, living the dream.

Herb's week had been far from that, though this had given him
purpose. He had nothing to lose by helping them, even if he didn't
know what it might achieve.

"We can't ask you to do that," Kassia said, Blythe putting a hand
on his wife's arm as she spoke.

"Thank you, Herb," Blythe countered. He'd seen this was something their host needed, something he wanted to do. It wasn't an
empty sentiment, something Herb might feel compelled to offer.
Blythe could do with all the help he could get right now. "I promise I
won't put you in any danger."

"More danger than I'm in with you all being here?" Herb asked.

Kate's phone buzzed at that moment.

"It's Joe, he's arrived," she said, addressing the others. Blythe
darted to the front window, scanning the street from behind the
curtains for any unwanted attention. He soon spotted the brother, Joe
looking as nervous as Kate had looked outside that park, though
carrying a little more arrogance than his sister. Blythe saw him pop
something into his mouth while he sat in the car, washing it down

with some water, before he got out, stretching as he stood on the pavement.

Kate opened the front door, Joe glancing around before crossing the road, jogging the last bit. They said nothing as he entered, Kate pressing the door firmly closed behind him.

"You were not followed?" Blythe asked, coming from the lounge, stepping in close to him in the hallway.

"No," Joe said, not liking the hostility, taking in the man in front of him, someone he'd been looking into intently for the last week. He'd stationed himself outside Blythe's home for two days already, all now futile, seeing as the man had never been hiding there. "Came straight from your house, in fact."

Blythe looked him in the eyes, turning to Kate and then to the others before addressing her.

"Did they say anything about knowing what your brother was doing?" he asked, his mind working quickly. Blythe knew how these people thought.

"Yes," she said, suddenly. "They knew he was watching your home," and at that, Blythe swore.

"We need to split immediately," Blythe said, going to grab his things, though he picked up a device he carried with him at all times. "Gather around," the three others––his wife not needing this, she'd already had it done to her––grouping together. Blythe opened his device, scanning them all.

"What's that?" Herb asked.

"It'll block your tracker," Blythe confirmed, something forbidden, something that could get them shot. "It'll mask who you are. You still give off a reading, so if stopped by anyone, they'll be able to identify you, but it will give another name."

"You'll make us invisible?" Joe asked, having heard talk of this, though he didn't know anyone who knew how to do it.

"Yes," Blythe said. "I'll do the same to your cars, too." His own car didn't need it. "We have only moments, we need to move." He gave them a landmark a good hundred miles from where they were.

"You know where that is?" he asked them all. They nodded.

"Good. Don't go the most direct way, but we meet there this evening at seven. If any of you think you're being followed, stay away. Am I understood?"

"We get you, captain," Joe said, his sarcastic smile menacing. Blythe didn't trust the man at all. The two siblings were as different from each other as could be possible in the same family.

"You take your car," Blythe ordered Joe, "and Herb, you take Kate's."

Kate looked at Blythe as if wondering what she would do.

"You'll come with us," Blythe confirmed. Having Kate with them would reduce any threat of Joe double-crossing them, not that Blythe would tell them that.

Minutes later they were hurrying out of the house, both the siblings' cars cleared of their trackers, Joe the first to leave, Herb soon following, though they went in different directions at the end of the street. Finally, the three who remained, tucked themselves into Blythe's classic car as he reversed out of the garage. He shut the garage door, and got back behind the wheel, his wife next to him, Kate in the back seat. He drove carefully down the tight alleyway before pulling onto the street.

It was only fifteen minutes later that military vehicles swarmed into the area, armed soldiers closing in on the target house, which was now empty of all its fugitives.

34

By nine they had their game-plan, the group having regathered, coming back together unobserved. They were unaware of how close the forces on their tail had been. Herb's name and details now joined the growing list of fugitives that the authorities were tracking.

It had been something Herb said that had given Blythe his ultimate idea.

He'd already concluded that time was not on their side. The longer they ran, the riskier it became. His tricks and hacks could only last so long. He knew the System would already have invested the full resources at the military's disposal and harvested their vast database. All focused on his capture. Once they had a sniff, they would move in fast. Blythe knew this only too well. The end would come quickly.

Therefore, according to Blythe, they had but one option: they had to go big and go early.

"What about the EBS?" Herb had said, the only one there old enough to remember when the *Emergency Broadcasting System* had last been tested. He'd once visited the studio of a local radio station with a group of his students. The studio showed them the codes, which were still active even if the days of needing such a service were long past. Only a high-ranking officer could use the codes, anyway.

Blythe could have kissed him, the idea coming immediately Herb asked the question.

"Here's what we'll do," Blythe began, detailing the stages involved, tasking each of them with their role in the operation, a mission that they could only pull off if they all did their bit. He warned them it might become dangerous.

"I'll take the first location," Joe said, ignoring the look of disbelief from his sister. "I'll gather my gang to that spot, get you the codes." Blythe nodded, Joe the perfect choice to head for a local radio station, in order to obtain the codes.

"Herb, I'll need you to go to location two," Blythe said. This was the location from where the EBS signal operated. Herb could see that coming. Blythe could hardly go himself, and Herb wasn't prepared to let either of the women go. "You need to enter the code into the computer there, tying the EBS into my device." That was something Blythe had mentioned a little earlier. "You'll get in with little fuss," the building being open to the public, even if not the room Herb would access. As a Gold-Collar, most would just smile and leave the hero to it.

"And you'll be ready?" Joe asked, car keys in hand, keen to get moving.

"I'll be ready," Blythe confirmed. "Good luck, everyone."

Joe turned, saying nothing more to any of them, even his sister. Kate already feared that she might not see him again, though in that moment, she'd never felt prouder of her younger brother. Joe already had his phone to his ear, coordinating with his gang to meet him at the local studio, they all likely to be there ahead of him. He promised to fill them in when he got there.

"I'll get going myself then," Herb said, Blythe handing him a phone, a spare one that he had, something that the System didn't know about. Joe would call Herb on it, giving him the code. Without the code, there was nothing Herb could do.

"Thank you," Blythe said.

"You just do what's in your blood, sir. Speak from the heart. I'm not sure how long they'll give you once we start," Herb urged. There had never been a worldwide announcement before, the System certain to do everything within its power to silence Blythe the first opportunity they got. Blythe would use every second he had, knowing their lives all now depended on it.

"Hopefully I'll make you proud," Blythe said, growing a deep appreciation for the man in the short time he'd had the honour of knowing him. Blythe hoped that he would see Herb again when it was all over. He knew the odds of them being able to change anything were slim, which meant it was likely they were all talking to one another for the last time.

The two women, standing alongside Blythe, watched as Herb also left.

"We wait now," Blythe said. Once they'd heard from Joe, he would have everything set up. All they needed to do for the time being was stay low, stay undercover, and pray.

———

THE ASSAULT on the studio was crude and rushed, Joe forcing his way past the reception area, the group of ten men with him downing the outnumbered security guards with base ball bats. Both guards, unconscious on the floor, were unarmed, the group racing forward, all the while knowing the alarm would already have been triggered.

Two of Joe's men barricaded the main doors, limiting their own escape, though also hindering what would surely soon be a full-scale military retaliation. They piled tables and chairs behind the door, the other men continuing to the upper floors, people who had been working there peacefully that morning already hiding behind desks. It was plain by their actions they knew their facility was now under siege.

Joe ignored these people, following the plan drawn up for him, two more men taking up a defensive position by blocking the stairway. It was possible the military response would merely be to drop troops onto the roof, have them abseil down the outside walls and in through the windows, smoke grenades and bullets flying against what was an unarmed raid. They knew it wouldn't be a fair fight.

On the top floor, Joe went straight into the room he was aiming for as four military trucks pulled up in front of the glass-walled entrance. Two dozen men emerged from the back of each vehicle, fanning out quickly, weapons raised.

Joe swore, his gang looking for cover. An explosion rocked the ground floor with shots heard moments after.

"Take cover!" Joe ordered, not moving himself. He had the codes in front of him, his phone out. "I'm in," he shouted into the handset, gunfire audible in the background of his call.

"Are the military there?" Herb asked, which seemed blindingly obvious, and concerned him greatly. He could hear more gunfire and shouts in the background.

"Write down these numbers," Joe shouted, reeling off the code. Once he'd repeated the numbers, Herb confirming he had them, Joe ended the call, shutting the door behind him, upending a metal filing cabinet that would at least hinder the opening of the door. He rang his sister Kate.

"I'm in," he said. "I've passed on the code."

"Fantastic!" Kate beamed, relaying the message to Blythe and Kassia, who were standing anxiously with her. "Now get out of there," though she soon heard the commotion in the background.

"That will not be so easy, sis," he said, resigned to the fact that he was not getting out of this one, as another explosion, this one much closer, rocked the building. The military seemed to show little regard for the damage they were causing.

Kate became desperate. "Don't you dare do this to me!" she screamed, Blythe coming closer, though Kassia held onto her husband, knowing he shouldn't interfere at that moment. This wasn't anything he could fix, they'd all known the danger. Blythe had to get things ready for the broadcast.

"We're unarmed," Joe said. "Massively outnumbered. They've come in like a sledgehammer. They aren't looking to take prisoners,

Kate." Joe had seen the fallen bodies of his friends. Soldiers were going room to room on each floor, sweeping the building expertly, the rooms holding the trapped civilians. Another gunshot sounded, another man no doubt dead.

"You're a good man, Joe," Kate said, resigned to the situation, wanting her last words with her brother to be kind ones.

"You destroy these bastards, promise me," he said, hearing kicking at the door. "Promise me!"

"I promise," Kate said, the sound of shouting coming through the phone now, the pounding of a battering ram against the door. Then the sound of splintering wood, the door pulverised and flying in on itself, the cabinet unmoved but the soldiers stepping over it. She could hear the voice of a soldier calling to the others that they'd found the last one. She heard the pleading of Joe as they dragged him out from underneath the desk.

She heard the single bullet that they put through his skull. She could hear the breath of a soldier as he picked up the handset from the deadman's hand, the call still connected. She heard his bitter words ringing in her ear. "You're next."

She ended the call, collapsing to the floor as Kassia held her, Kate inconsolable before summoning up her strength, focusing her mind. She had promised her brother that his death would not be in vain.

Blythe watched the two women, his throat tight, his hands trembling, as he set up his device, the camera that would soon address the entire world pointing his way. For the moment his mind felt blank, something he would have to change quickly.

HERB STOOD LOOKING up at the tall tower, not a broadcasting studio, but a station that held transmission devices which relayed communications into the network, and from there automatically around the world.

It wasn't the usual tourist haunt, but he strolled around as if he belonged, getting the smiles his collar now afforded him. Nobody would ask him what he was doing there, and nothing was off limits, anyway.

Herb got chatting to the lady on the front desk, the pair soon building a little rapport.

"I came here with a group of students many years ago," he lied to the woman. He spoke with relish as he told a story. "A fascinating day. The kids didn't think much of it, but they've never shared my passion for such buildings as this one. I appreciate the finer things," well aware that the building hosted no live shows as it might have done in the past, when radio still existed and where various stations each had a little room off the spiral staircase.

"I do too," she said.

"You don't mind if I have a brief walk around? For old time's sake, you know," Herb said, touching her hand for effect as he spoke.

"Be my guest," she said, all smiles. "A few more enthusiastic faces like yours each day, and this job wouldn't be half as boring as it is."

He took the stairs seconds later, smiling at her until he could see her no more, his phone sounding not long after. Herb checked no-one was around him as he answered. He had a pen and paper in his other hand.

Joe gave him the code.

Herb dropped the device back into his pocket, picking up his pace as he continued to climb. He had forgotten how many stairs there were. All they'd said was that he had to get to a room at the top of the tower.

Several hundred steps later, his heart pounding, his head somewhat light, Herb reached the top. The tower had significantly narrowed the higher up he'd climbed, so that the circular stairwell built into the external walls was rather tight by that point.

He entered the room, the door thankfully unlocked. He left the door open—he would hear if anybody came that way—and went over to the control desk. The screen came to life at his touch, and Herb reached for his phone again, calling Blythe. He answered it after one ring.

"I'm in place, talk me through it," Herb said, Blythe guiding him as he clicked on the screen, getting Herb to where he could enter the code. "It's asking for an authorisation code." This was not something Blythe had mentioned to him.

"Use this one," Blythe said, giving a code he'd never used himself, another of the emergency codes his rank carried.

"It worked," Herb confirmed, now looking at the screen he'd been expecting. "It wants the access code."

"Joe gave that to you, correct?" Blythe asked, their hopes resting on Herb's answer to this.

"Yes," he said. "Did he get away okay?"

Blythe's lack of answer was all that Herb needed to read the situation.

He focused on entering the code, double checking before he confirmed to Blythe it was in.

"Press enter, and then turn the dial on your right to *Outside Broadcast*," Blythe said. If an all-alert EBS message was ever going to be needed, it was highly likely that such a message might not come from a regular studio. The computer screen asked for a location code as Herb caught the sound of shouts coming from the stairwell below him, the sound of heavy boots coming up the metal steps.

"What's your location code," Herb asked, ignoring the approaching threat, not going to mention that to Blythe who needed to focus.

Blythe reeled off a number. All he had to do was start recording, and every screen on every device around the world would immediately relay his message.

Herb crept to the doorway, the sight of helmets coming up towards him something he would never forget.

"I'm in," Blythe confirmed, Herb shutting the heavy metal door, then locking it in place. He could not allow these men to stop the broadcast before it had started. "You get away from there now, okay. Once I'm started, they can't cut me off from the tower, so there's no need to stay any longer."

"It's a little late for escape plans," Herb confessed, Blythe sinking his head into his hands. "I'm secure. They won't get in easily. Best of luck," and Herb ended the call, not wanting to delay Blythe any longer.

Blythe didn't know what to say, his wife looking at him, seeing his reaction, but she said nothing to Kate. They could talk about it all later. She already feared what her husband knew.

Blythe stood in front of the camera, checking his smile in the blackness of his screen. But appearances were the last thing on his mind. He went over his opening words in his head. It was now or never. He pressed the button to go live.

35

T he global announcement took everybody by surprise. The System had never made such a move before. The face of Blythe Harrell appeared on tablets, televisions and advertising screens around the entire world.

The Supreme Commander stood there open-mouthed, though the move was not unexpected once the locations of Joe and Herb were factored into the equation.

"Good citizens of the world. My name is Blythe Harrell, your new leader," he announced, his opening words showing this was a coup, no questions there. The Supreme Commander scrambled all available personnel onto the streets at once.

"I've taken this unprecedented move today because, as one of the highest ranked people in the world, I've had an insight, had a life that few could dream about, that even fewer know about.

"We've been lying to you for decades," Blythe said, aware he had to paint himself in that light too. There was no escaping his past. "Red-Collars, myself included, have sold you a lie. The promise of freedom, the promise of choice. We promote the message we are all born equal, that nobility and royalty and fame are no longer important, are no longer of any value. Yet those with wealth have always had wealth, and as Red-Collars, we protect our own.

"We make rules while not following them ourselves, and I, for my sins, was party to that. I knew about it, turned a blind eye, even perhaps used it to my advantage."

He paused, dwelling on a word he'd used seconds before, something of an old word, a word the System no longer recognised, a word taught in school as belonging to a bygone age, an uninformed people.

"Sin, it's a funny word," he confessed. "We say there is no sin because there is no wrong, there is no right. There are only choices."

He shook his head.

"But that isn't true, as deep down, whether we are prepared to admit it or not, we know there is right and wrong, good and evil.

"The New World Council is rotten to the core, evil to the very top. Your Supreme Commander—a man who mentored me, who gave me his hand of blessing as his successor—now wants me dead. At this precise moment he is trying to find me, to stop me talking to you, to stop me telling you this truth.

"Truth, that's another word we do not teach any more. Another word that the Council has buried in their lies, so it leaves us with nothing. Only their message, *their* truth.

"They control you by fear. The fear of not behaving, the fear of losing out on your life, on your fortune. Without fear, as the Supreme Commander reminded me personally only this month, we cannot control you. We cannot blind you to the reality that you are prisoners to your surroundings.

"I will lead us all into a better future, a more equal future, and an equality for all, not just the wealthy folk, of which I have been one my entire life.

"I've met some incredible people, the best of these only recently. Hardworking and loyal people, those fighting for a cause bigger than themselves. People like the vast majority of you watching this. Honest White-Collar folk.

"I now need you to rise. Rise in voice, rise in protest, rise as one. We cannot overthrow this rotten System by force. The Red leaders, these traitors to the truth, traitors to real freedom, they control the military as they control so many things.

"I appeal to the Black-Collars, troops with whom I've spent much time over the years. There are good men and women amongst you, my two sons included. I ask you to show compassion today, to consider your actions and consider from whom you take orders. Will you dare to open fire on unarmed people, on men, woman and children who feel called onto the streets with my words and feel stirred to respond?

"Show restraint, show mercy, show peace."

He took a sip of water, allowing those few words to hang on the airwaves for a moment longer.

"Without a firm promise from me, I understand, without a clear vision for the world as it should be, there will be no change, no action, no calling to account of those in authority. They promise you so much, and we live in a world very different from decades ago. We live in a time of medical breakthrough, and yet six killers exist that still have no cure.

"Mark my words—one of these will have a cure, and this within months. And I know this because it was the trigger for my awakening, the event that sparked all this, the spark that will set the world on fire. Not a literal fire, I suggest, though if a burning down of everything is what we need then I say let it burn! Let them burn! But the spark I talk about now is the light of reason, that moment when I saw the error of my ways, the unfairness that surrounds so many.

"My dear wife is carrying a baby in her womb. This child has one of the six diseases that I mentioned. These incurable ailments are a plague to our breakthroughs, a reminder that while we tell you we control our own destiny, we are no more in control than before, not really. Not that you hardworking folk listening to me now ever had much control on your destiny. It was superficial. You comprise the vast majority of human life on this planet. Yet control has only ever been for the elite, those select few, not in their position of power by their own brilliance of mind or creative genius, but by wealth. No other reason. Wealth and perhaps status, family lineage. Money laid down for them by generations which have gone before, born into wealth and carrying that through to the generation that follows them. Red-Collars now will always produce the Red-Collars of the future. The System isn't open and fair, but self-serving and prejudiced. We let you believe you can all become whatever you want to be, but the truth is far from that. For most of you, where you were born, the accent you use, the wealth of your parents, not to mention the medical history within your family. These are the things that limit you, that separate you.

"Standing to my right, a little off-camera and being comforted by my dear wife, is a woman with a brilliant mind. An actual hero who would have been ushered into our sacred club of Red-Collared bigots had it not been for her brother. I got to know him and saw the bravery in his eyes. Yet a man whom this very System I represented deemed trouble. So much trouble that they could not consider his brilliant scientist sister for promotion. Couldn't allow her into the club, for the things she might learn, the lies she might discover.

"I'm honoured to know Katherine Vann, and her brother Joseph. Katherine is the scientist leading the research into the cure of one of the Six. Something that until this week, she had complete funding for, the results of which should guarantee a within-life cure of the first of these six final killers.

"Yet, stopping at nothing, the Supreme Commander cut that funding, physically threatening this brilliant mind—holding the lives of your children and their children at ransom at the same time— until they had caught me. Can you grasp that desperation? But it is worse even than this, the rottenness of the System.

"When we discovered our expected daughter had one of the six diseases, we had various options available to us but I saw a desperate woman who had a baby with the same condition and she had no such choices. And why? Just because she was a White-Collar. She knew a cure was within reach but because the lab was not Council-run and she was a White-Collar, no-one listened and her baby was given just four decades, less than his mother had left. In this age of medical breakthroughs no mother should ever know that they will have to bury their child.

"This research never had a chance, save for my daughter catching this deadly but soon-to-be curable disease.

"And I was selfish to start, I will admit this. My position allowed me to get involved, to jump the queues, to make sure we had the thing we needed and wanted.

"The big mystery of all, and something that keeps the majority in poverty and under control, is why is it only the White-Collars who get sick before their time? There are many things you do not know, too many things for me to cover in the minutes I have left, because I cannot be long, I know they are hunting me and if they catch me, so help me God.

"But one thing the System has always told you is that the elite are better because they live longer. They think of themselves as purer, better blood, better genes. You never see or hear of someone in the elite catching any of the curable but life altering diseases, do you? Why? Because we hide it. All cancers and tumors and diseases that would impact their way of life, limit the lifespan of their descendants and otherwise tarnish the family name and wealth, are hidden. They happen. Red-Collars are just as likely to get ill as the rest of you, but it will shock you to discover how we control it, how we keep it quiet.

"My world crashed into yours the morning that I realised this life-saving Doctor, whose research would not only cure the disease inside my unborn child, but do away with the stigma of it altogether, was getting onto a certain aeroplane on a certain morning."

Blythe hung his head in shame for a moment, taking another sip of water from his glass, the world holding a collective breath, as forces continued to move into position on the streets of the Capitolium.

"It was a flight I knew about because it coincided with the convenient way that those of the elite who are dying deal with their illnesses in secret. These flights, which are destined to crash, are crudely called *mercy flights*, which makes a mockery of those others who have innocently booked seats on the flight, as there always are.

"I knew this plane would crash, as did over two hundred of the passengers, all of whom were Red-Collars, and all of whom were dying. The innocent people who die on these flights—people like Katherine, who happen to buy a ticket—are deemed collateral damage. Their families are compensated, as we know, but that sits as no real recompense when we understand that there was planning behind these crashes, not error. Not a technological failing, nor pilot error. Design. Purpose. Reason.

"And it has to stop. Immediately." He paused again now, his thoughts of Herb. He'd yet to hear confirmation that Herb had escaped.

"A retired school teacher who I've only just had the pleasure of meeting, reminded me recently that any change will not be easy, even with the truth. Even knowing the one-sided nature of this world, there will be millions of you watching me now still wanting to accept what is coming to you. Men and women who have worked all their lives, the promise of this Jubilee Year perhaps a year or three away. You'll hear my words and feel threatened, because this is the carrot that has been before you for so long. This is the reason that you've struggled on, working every day, watching your parents do the noble thing, raising your children to do the same and looking forward to the day when you too received your payment, when you too are handed your Gold-Collar and you finally could do all the things we've promised you that you need to do. All the things that you couldn't afford to do in life, because there wasn't the time or opportunity.

"They kept it that way. All the while they lived in luxury, never needing to work, never needing to retire, living to the age of eighty without a care in the world, surrounded by every modern gadget that money can buy.

"All you had to look forward to was working until that last year, a year that this teacher friend of mine doesn't believe in anymore. And rightly so. He was only in his sixties, loved what he did and with all that we know now about medical care, could have gone on for years.

"And this is my promise! I can't break the System and expect you all to help me. You have too much to lose. So I will make sure now that you have more to gain. I will sign the new Protocol at the very moment I'm sworn into power, a ruling that will give the same retirement age for all, allow many years to spend that retirement, not just one.

"Why should you work to fifty-nine and then die at sixty? I will set a standard retirement age of sixty, perhaps longer if people like my teacher friend want it. But you will all have ten or twenty years to enjoy it. I'll make sure the million units remain, perhaps even look to increase it. I'll do away with the monopoly that is the Celebration Day, where the Red-Collar, System-controlled sellers do their best to claw back every unit that they can.

"I will break up the Red-Collar elite creating a fairer system for all. An alternative system, one that doesn't steal and cheat, one that doesn't turn a blind eye to injustice, one that looks to do the right thing for all in every situation, regardless of circumstance or background.

"This new protocol, the twenty-seventh when it comes into effect, will also apply to all those now in their Jubilee Year. You'll be allowed time, something that will enable you to see your grandchildren grow up, while you enjoy what will be the best years of your life.

"We cured old age a long time ago. They buried the details of this in that twenty-sixth version, lost in the amendments. With our medical system, nearly everybody will live an active life well into their late seventies. All the elite have already done so for decades, aside from those taking those flights.

"So I urge you all, for a better world, to rise. Rise now and take on this course of action. Storm the buildings and offices of those who would look to control you. Take back your own future and allow me to deliver this brighter future. A fairer future, for all.

"Rise now and go! Stand in the face of your oppressor and do not back down! Mobilise now before it is too late, and stand alongside each other, a vast army, risen from the ashes of life, drawn from the four winds, the downtrodden, the lowly, the desperate. Yet one people, one voice, one fist!

"Rise now and storm the streets!

"Rise now and take back control!

"Rise, my people, and lead us all to victory!" and with that Blythe finished, his arms raised to the camera, his face appearing for a few more seconds on the screen, until he cut the recording, his wife running to him, embracing him, words failing her but tears running down her cheeks. Blythe caught sight of Kate, who nodded in silent approval.

And slowly, from outside, they heard the voices. Heard the shouts of people taking to the streets, the first wave of people gathering, not knowing what to do but awakened to the moment, and presented with a glorious new future.

36

The news filled the screens for days, masses of people, some crowds as large as a million in the biggest cities, moving as one. Offices and houses were stormed, there were some cases of violence, but the majority just a passing over of power to those people now loyal to Blythe. People he had put into place, meaning the infrastructure didn't collapse, that cities didn't shut down. People filmed Reds having their collars ripped away from them, some beaten, others spat upon, most just shamed for the lives they had lived.

The marches continued, working up to the Capitolium itself, the centre of the New World, a world now in turmoil. Troops had circled the city, looking outwards, with orders to open fire the moment the crowd came too close.

Blythe Harrell, the instigator of it all, was in the crowds but higher up and to one side from where he could see what was going on. He pleaded for calm, the crowd coming ever closer, the terrified faces of the soldiers in front of them, soldiers vastly outnumbered even if they had the firepower. They all knew their bullets weren't enough, this wasn't a battle they could win. It wasn't a battle they wanted.

The soldiers were all dressed in identical armour, each one indistinguishable from the man or woman beside them. As Blythe watched, two soldiers stepped forward three paces from the solid line that had formed.

Blythe held his breath, fearful that this would become a bloodbath, a massacre that would serve nobody. His mouth opened as the two soldiers lowered their weapons, taking off their helmets, smiling to the crowd and to Blythe specifically, before they turned around, facing their colleagues, facing the Capitolium beyond.

Blythe smiled at the sight of his two sons. Their defiance against direct orders was serious, save for the fact he hoped things were about to change.

Several soldiers looked puzzled, shocked by their actions, though before long, others stepped forward, mirroring what these two men had just done. Soon the entire line had copied, the actions spreading around the whole city like a virus, until all those who had circled the centre of power to protect it now faced it, weapons down, protection gone.

Blythe moved forward, those around him in the crowd reaching out, touching his arms and back, cheering him. A roar went up, Blythe walking up to his two sons, who parted, allowing him to step through the ring that had formed.

Blythe walked forward, taking tentative steps at first. The knowledge that the entire ring of soldiers was moving forward towards the Capitolium, helped. Soon the vast millions behind pressed on too, the very central buildings now surrounded.

High in his office, the Supreme Commander, who had seen Blythe's emergence, summoned the small group of Black-Collars who still seemed loyal to him.

"Take the shot!" he ordered, pointing to Blythe. "Kill him before he comes any closer. Do it!"

The soldier picked up his weapon. He'd never disobeyed an order, and even now, with all the odds against him, he thought about doing his duty.

Blythe was leading a coup, and his Supreme Commander, the man he was there to protect, had given him an order.

He hesitated.

"Shoot him!" came the scream again from over his shoulder, the crowd now very close to the front entrance.

Blythe could see the unit of soldiers on the roof, the Supreme Commander behind them. He watched his mentor push the soldier aside, taking the weapon from him, his ageing arms shaking as he raised it, his eye pressed against the scope.

Blythe stopped walking, his two sons glancing up at where their father was looking as they too stopped. They both stepped in front of their father, very much a human shield.

"No!" Blythe called, but they ignored him.

For a while there was no movement, the crowd now aware of the standoff, the word passing quickly as they closed in and stopped walking, ten metres behind the line of soldiers. The unit on the roof lowered their weapons and the soldier whose weapon the Supreme Commander had taken stood open-mouthed as his boss refused to lower his gun, despite there being no clear shot. Despite two young men stepping in front of the man, he still aimed.

Then he fired, the shot catching the shoulder of Blythe's older son, the body armour stopping any serious damage, but enough to knock him to the ground. Another two soldiers stepped forward to fill the gap left by their fallen comrade, as another shot rang out, this one missing altogether.

The soldier on the roof, standing next to his boss as he fired his weapon into an unarmed crowd, had seen enough. He pulled the weapon from the old man's grip, and back-handed him to the floor.

Down below, a cheer went up, as those at the front surged forward as one, Blythe following them, his sons by his side. They raced into the building, the security guards standing down to let them through, and climbed the stairs towards the roof.

Blythe was the one to emerge first, the Supreme Commander still on the floor, the unit of soldiers edgy but with their weapons down.

An equal number of soldiers joined Blythe, led by his two sons, who stood either side of their father and just behind him.

"It's over," Blythe said, three paces back from the man who had just tried to kill him, and the one whom he would soon succeed. Blythe held out a hand, offering to help the old man back to his feet, which he did slowly.

His boss said nothing as he stood, his hand still tight around Blythe's, showing surprising strength for a man of his age.

"You'll never change things," he snarled.

"I'm not like you," Blythe countered, his hand now freed. Down below the crowds craned their necks, only those a little further back able to see the handover of power high above, the bodies pressed to the building, though no more had entered.

Blythe looked down at them all, too far away to see their faces, but knowing they were now looking to him.

"Are you going to kill me in front of them all?" the Supreme Commander asked, defiance in his voice to the last.

"No," Blythe countered, a look of surprise, perhaps disappointment clear on the old man's face.

"Well then, I really didn't know you, did I," he said, taking one step forward, as if to leave the roof, resigned to his fate, before he lunged, with everything left within him. He caught Blythe, gripping him hard and forcing their bodies to the edge, toppling them both over the side, the momentum and gravity now threatening to finish them both.

The crowd gasped at the sight, as one body fell from the roof, the other clinging to the ledge. They parted as the figure fell, turning twice in the air as a circle cleared, the concrete meeting the human flesh with sickening reverberations, a stunned silence ensuing on the ground. The call of *Dad!* came from high above.

Blythe clung on for dear life, his sons racing forward, fearing the worst and yet seeing their father hanging there, fingers going white. They grabbed hold of him by the shoulders, others soon pulling them all back to safety.

Down below, the bloodied body of their Supreme Commander lay in a tangled mess.

THE SETTING COULDN'T HAVE BEEN MORE different, though only two days had passed. The crowds had come, though most of the world watched from home, as Blythe Harrell was sworn into his new role, with only modest pomp and ceremony. Standing next to him on his left was his wife, and beyond her, Kate. On his right were his two sons, the elder with a sling on his bruised arm.

Blythe didn't want to speak for long. The world had heard enough of him for that week, but he knew he needed to say something. He'd insisted upon his family being on stage with him, which had never happened before at one of these events. He wanted Kate there too; she would feature in his inauguration speech as she had in his one before. This time they would get to see her.

"I have today drafted the twenty-seventh protocol," he said, smiling to the watching world, "that will forever change the System. We will counter-check it and write it into law soon after." He allowed a moment for the round of applause that followed.

"Standing amongst my family is also the new Head of Medical Research, Doctor Katherine Vann. As well as being allowed to continue her groundbreaking research for which she has become so famous, I have tasked her with the honour of leading the battle to find cures for these other five diseases that have, so far, continued to baffle us. I am confident that with her passion and ability, and her keen sense of duty, she will inspire a generation of scientists, who will one day, perhaps in her own lifetime, eliminate the threats that these killers pose."

An even bigger ripple of applause followed, Blythe himself holding up his hands and clapping along with everyone, glancing at Kate and then his wife.

"Our baby girl will be born into a world very different from the one we all knew, I promise you. And because of Katherine's research, she will live a full life along with all of you.

"Yet this change hasn't come without cost," Blythe said, another glance to Kate, who could only look at her feet now. "Brave souls gave their all for this cause, in what remains the most bloodless revolution perhaps known in all modern human history. But blood has been spilled."

The Supreme Commander had been buried in his family plot though with no official ceremony.

"Doctor Vann's brother was among that small group of people for whom the shedding of blood was unavoidable. Each of those eleven brave souls will receive official recognition, and the Collective will fully compensate their surviving relatives," he said.

The Collective, chaired by Blythe, was the new name for the World Council. The System was done away with. They all needed a fresh start.

"And there were many other nameless heroes too," Blythe continued, "people whose stories will come out, I'm sure, in the weeks and months to come, as we move on from here, as we rebuild what was damaged, restore what was broken down. I have removed the rank of Red-Collar from our options," they would ratify the wording in the new protocol. "Gone are the elite, from where I too have come. Gone will be the injustice, which will take time to see happen. Everyone who stood in power and control within in the old order who is not prepared to work with us in a more lowly capacity, has been arrested." He wouldn't mention the bloody battle needed to dethrone Devon Scott and his empire. Devon had gone down fighting, defiant to the end. His men soon surrendered when they realised that he was dead.

"I thank you once again," he said, stepping from the lectern, a smile to the people, a kiss offered to his wife. The party moved away from the stage, the global coverage ending there. Blythe smiled at a man at the front of the crowd and left his wife and sons to go and speak to him. Blythe walked up to the man, there by special invitation.

"It's great to see you again, Herb," Blythe said, embracing him, the two holding each other for a time. The advancing soldiers had tried to get to Herb when he was locked in the tower but the metal was too thick. When the people eventually took to the streets and the cameras showed the size of the crowds, those in the tower had fled, Herb freeing himself only hours later, when the threat had gone. He'd not seen Blythe since, though the new leader had been thrilled to hear of his survival. He'd insisted Herb join them all that day.

"You did a fine job, sir," Herb said.

"Speaking of jobs," Blythe smiled. "I hear a rumour of a certain school that would love to have their teacher back, if he's up for the task." Blythe didn't need to say any more. The smile that enveloped Herb's face took years off him. His eyes wet with joy, he bear-hugged Blythe once more, Kate and Kassia coming over to them both at that moment, embraces all round. Blythe introduced Herb to his two sons.

"I would like you at the signing tomorrow, Herb," Blythe added. "You've taught these protocols for decades. It would be my honour to have you witness this groundbreaking one for the Collective."

"It'll be my delight," was all he could say. They moved away, taking time to speak with several reporters and others they had invited. Finally Blythe had a little time with Kate.

"Do you have all you need?" he asked. She had moved with her entire laboratory to the major hospital in the centre of the city.

"And some," she smiled.

"Good." The future life of their little girl couldn't have been in safer hands. "We're naming our daughter Katherine," he smiled, leaving it at that. Kate watched the couple leave. She would see her mother soon, the pair needing to plan a funeral. She knew her mum would be okay. They both would. Joe had died a hero.

Kate watched an aeroplane high in the sky, flying off somewhere. She smiled at the fear, realising that she never had to be afraid again. Her brother had taught her that. She wouldn't cry, not here. She would go home and pour two glasses of whisky. The second glass would sit under his picture, perhaps not forever, but until she'd been able to lay him to rest properly.

She would be okay. She had her research to continue, lives to save, a better, brighter future to help build for all, and she was determined to play her part.

Blythe helped his wife into the waiting vehicle. He gave one last glance towards the crowds, smiling as he joined his wife in the back of the car, the look of satisfaction in a man who knew everything was about to change for the better. They were silent as the vehicle pulled away. The crowd parted to allow their new leader through.

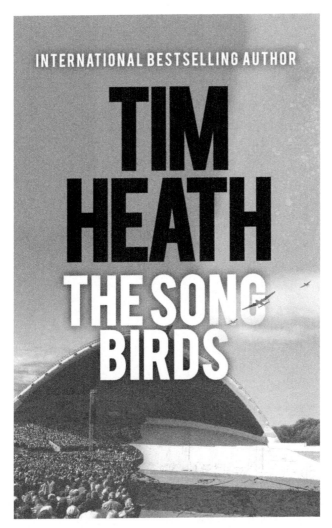

INTERNATIONAL BESTSELLING AUTHOR

TIM HEATH

THE SONG BIRDS

Four Random Strangers. Many Broken Lives. One Callous Act. "A gripping modern thriller with the twist of one hundred years of history." Johanna, a Finnish scientist living in Tallinn, is so career-driven that it's left her alone and single. Arto, an older man, travels to Estonia to experience his first Song Festival, his life in tatters, his prejudices ever present. Anna, a young Estonian, has no experience of her homeland's dark legacy and oppression but carries these feelings, passed down to her from her grandmother. And Kalju, a man who feels life has passed him by...

READER MAP
#TIMSREADERMAP

I've finally started a map where I drop a pin into every city and country that my readers tell me they are! And I would LOVE you to join in as well.

All you need to do (and do it before diving into my next book, go on) is use the hashtag **#TimsReaderMap** and when I spot it, I'll add a pin to the map!

The map page on my website is **http://www.timheathbooks.com/ reader-map** so you can check it out to see your little (or vast) home location represented! If you use *Instagram* or *Facebook*, why not snap a nice photo of the book too? If I've not yet spotted your post, you can nudge me.

For this book, you can also use the following hashtags to let the world (and me) know what you thought about the book! And a review on Amazon is *ALWAYS* welcome.

#The26thProtocol
#TimHeathAuthor

WEEKLY SPECIAL OFFER ALERT!
BECOME A SUPER-FAN!

I'm going to be doing a lot of special promotions with my books from now on. In fact, if you got this one in a sale (even if you didn't), you'll want to know when the others go on sale too. Plus, I'll be releasing a few special books free to those on this list.

So sign up to my mailing list today. I'll email you whenever there's a special offer (free or usually something like 0.99), plus let you know when I've got a brand new release––and did I mention throwing free books at you too?

After all, you're my fans––if you're on the list, who better to be the first to get my free books than you?

I will never spam you or pass your email address onto a third party. All I'll look to offer you is high value content. So, are you in?

VIP Readers' Group
http://www.timheathbooks.com/books/super-fans

ACKNOWLEDGMENTS

Want to support me as an author? Check out my **Patreon** *page—patreon.com/timheath*

Please also take a moment to leave a review on Amazon.

It's been fun to dip my toes into the wonder that is dystopian thrillers. I hope you liked it. I've been excited by my team, who've so enjoyed reading this book and helping me shape it. It forced questions, thoughts... perhaps you have some too, wondering why some things happened, why others didn't? I like that there are things to think about when you finish a book.

Wouldn't this make a great movie one day too?

As always, I have people who, without their help, this book would not have been what it was.

Thank you, Elizabeth, for once again editing the second draft, the first person (other than myself) to read the book. Your glowing endorsement (you might have already seen it on the back cover) gave me great confidence that this little book that sprung from me during a crazy first month of lockdown, might be another winner! I truly hope it is.

Thank you to my ART members, with shout outs to Fraser Drummond and Zan-Mari, who are forever helpful and brilliantly insightful. Thanks Mike for also spotting something during the last round of edits.

Thanks also to my wife, who loved this one and devoured it over the holiday ready for the final round of editing. The last lines are in the book because you knew the story needed to finish with Blythe, not Kate.

And thank you, my reader, for whom this book was created. Please let me know what you think. Please review, post photos, share with your reader friends. You have no idea how much that all helps me.

And wait until you see what is coming next...

THE NOVELS BY TIM HEATH

Novels:

Cherry Picking

The Last Prophet

The Tablet

The Shadow Man

The Prey (The Hunt #1)

The Pride (The Hunt #2)

The Poison (The Hunt #3)

The Machine (The Hunt #4)

The Menace (The Hunt #5)

The Meltdown (The Hunt #6)

The Song Birds

The Acting President (The Hunt #7)

The Black Dolphin (The Hunt #8)

The Last Tsar (The Hunt #9)

The 26th Protocol

Short Story Collection:

Those Geese, They Lied; He's Dead

OTHER STAND-ALONE NOVELS

"Fantastic read!! Longer than most books I've read lately, but worth every minute. Intriguing, interesting plot." Nigel Gamble is a man with everything––including a dark past. He took his name from his early business successes, but in reality, none of it was based on risk—only certain success...

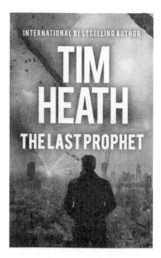

"I wish I could write a review as well as the author wrote this book to do it justice. Another magnificent literature masterpiece from Tim Heath." John awakes to find himself in a hospital bed with no memory of how he got there. Then the visions start. Destruction and death. A last chance. The only one who can save millions of people. He is no hero. Could he do what was being asked of him?

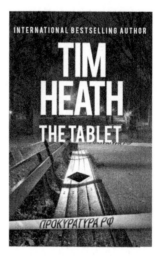

"Don't miss out on this fast-paced espionage thriller!!!" William Hackett finds himself in a system he doesn't understand. He's accused of a crime and the Russians want blood. His. Somehow this peaceful father killed a man in cold blood. A man about to launch a groundbreaking piece of technology. As political tensions rise, they will dance to a tune with the most sinister of crescendos.

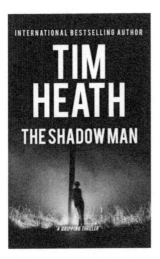

TIM HEATH

THE SHADOW MAN

A GRIPPING THRILLER

"Fast, gripping and a real page-turner—I couldn't put it down!" On the day the Chinese announce the opening of a state-of-the-art nuclear power station—decades in the making—three British spies disappear. Coincidence, or retribution?

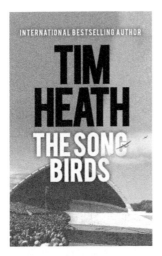

TIM HEATH

THE SONG BIRDS

Four Random Strangers. Many Broken Lives. One Callous Act. Johanna, a Finnish scientist living in Tallinn, is so career-driven that it's left her alone and single. Arto, an older man, travels to Estonia to experience his first Song Festival, his life in tatters, his prejudices ever present. Anna, a young Estonian, has no experience of her homeland's dark legacy and oppression but carries these feelings, passed down to her from her grandmother. And Kalju, a man who feels life has passed him by...

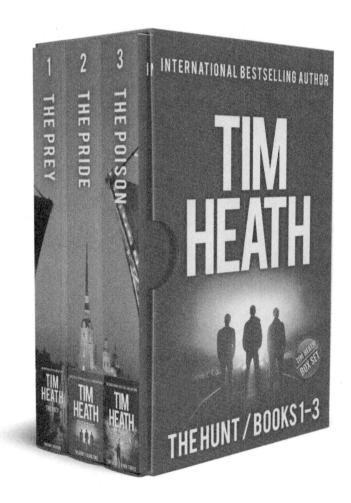

The Hunt Series (Books 1-3) - The Prey, The Pride, The Poison

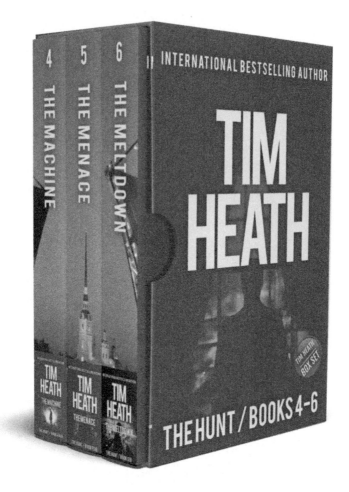

The Hunt Series (Books 4-6) - The Machine, The Menace, The Meltdown

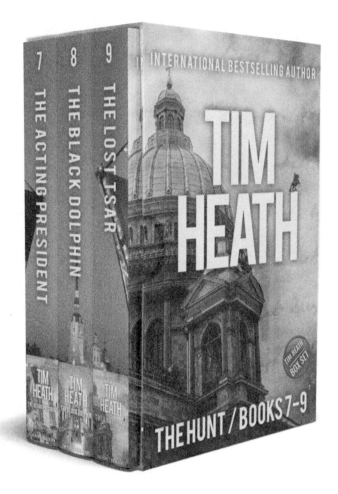

The Hunt Series (Books 7-9) - The Acting President, The Black Dolphin, The Lost Tsar

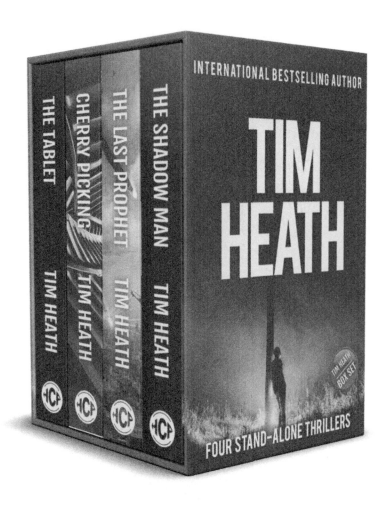

Tim Heath Thriller Collection—Four Stand-Alone Novels - The Tablet, Cherry Picking, The Last Prophet, The Shadow Man

ABOUT THE AUTHOR

Tim has been married to his wife Rachel since 2001, and they have two daughters. He lives in Tallinn, Estonia, having moved there with his family in 2012 from St Petersburg, Russia, which they moved to in 2008. He is originally from Kent in England and lived for eight years in Cheshire, before moving abroad. As well as writing the novels that are already published (plus the one or two that are always in the process of being finished) Tim enjoys being outdoors, exploring Estonia, cooking and spending time with his family.

For more information:
www.timheathbooks.com
tim@timheathbooks.com

- patreon.com/timheath
- instagram.com/timheathauthor
- facebook.com/TimHeathAuthor
- amazon.com/author/timheath
- bookbub.com/authors/tim-heath
- goodreads.com/TimHeath
- youtube.com/TimHeath
- linkedin.com/in/tim-heath-83144077
- twitter.com/TimHeathBooks

Printed in Great Britain
by Amazon

70027577R00169